Caroline Hemingway

RISING

THE DESTINY CHRONICLES BOOK 3

CARROWAY

This is a work of fiction. All names, characters, locations and incidents are products of the author's imagination and any resemblance to actual people, places or events is purely coincidental or fictionalized.

ISBN 978-0-9942028-2-6

Published in Australia in 2016 by Carroway

"Even the darkest night will end and the sun will rise."
-   Victor Hugo

I am so grateful for those who have believed in me, encouraged me and cheered me on. I have discovered that the sun indeed always rises – more beautifully and miraculously than the day before.

As always, this book is first and foremost dedicated to:

MY WONDERFUL HUSBAND HAMILTON AND OUR CHILDREN - you are my greatest fans, you champion me to write better. You make it all possible for me – I love you more than rainbows.

And second:

To the ONE who gave me this love of writing and the ability to use it. May I always cherish it and use it to transport others to a magical place.

Last but not least:

To every moment that taught me how beautiful life really is, that allowed me to explore new beliefs and find new dreams – I am truly grateful.

NAME PRONUNCIATION GUIDE

In order of appearance:

Aislinn	ASH - lin
Daemon	DAY – min
Phoenix	FEE - nix
Legion	LEE – jin
Struan	STREW-en
Balfour	BELL – for
Ceinlys	CAN – lis
Kaldakinn	KEL-da-kin
Sveinsson	SVEN - sen
Siobhan	SHI – vonn
Catriona	Ca - TRINA
Leif	LAYF
Ziah	Z (long i)-uh
Aedan	AY- dan
Cillian	KILL-yan

PROLOGUE

SHERBROOKE - SPRING 1648

SHE HID amongst the trees, watching and waiting – patience was part of the game and those who could not sit quietly or wait for the perfect moment missed out on the spoils or got themselves killed. Not her. She had taught herself how to wait – deathly still for the opportunity to take what she wanted. She crouched low in the wooded undergrowth, listening with her head half- cocked and smiled. She could hear someone coming. She pulled out her bow and arrow and readied it to take the shot.

The horse walked with a casual gait, the young rider looking weary and a little saddle sore. He seemed distracted and she chuckled. First lesson – never let your mind wander when travelling through the woods as anything could happen at any time. She waited for him to get a little closer.

A little more, almost there, she thought keeping her bow steady, straining to be let loose.

There was an art to archery – a skill she had mastered through sheer hard work and determination. One had to relax, to become one with the weapon and wait for the perfect moment to release the deadly arrow. Any tension in her body would be directed through the beautifully curved bow affecting the accuracy of her shot.

Now!

She released the arrow and it whistled through the air, silently yet powerfully, heading straight for its target. It met it perfectly, no errors just as she expected. She heard his gasp of surprise as he was unseated from his ride. She clapped her hands in delight – she loved it when she caught strangers off-guard by shooting the rope, thereby releasing the swinging log. He lay winded on the ground, trying to catch his breath, unsure of what had just happened.

She stood astride him, looking down, her bow aimed at his face.

He was surprised to see a slip of a girl behind the bow. She could not be more than twenty years old. She was beautiful with piercing eyes, not quite blue but more like wolf grey. Her long hair was wavy and almost black as coal.

'What do you want?' he asked breathlessly. 'I have no money or anything of value other than my horse.' He felt alarmed at this sudden attack, but he had to admit he was intrigued with this forest nymph.

'You think I am robbing you?' she asked incredulously. 'Nothing of the kind – I am not a thief. In fact I am doing you a favour if you must know.'

'How does knocking me off my horse and almost killing me count as a favour?' he asked sarcastically, his courage returning faster than his dignity.

'Don't be such a baby. If I had wanted you dead we would not be having this conversation. I aimed for the rope, not your heart. My arrow never misses.'

'Well it's a coward who hides in trees and shoots arrows at unsuspecting people.'

She flushed, angry at his impertinence.

'You forget I am still holding this arrow pointed at you and that is precisely why I have done you a favour. My attack has taught you never to be unsuspecting as you call it. Now, when you travel, you will be alert, ready for the unexpected. You're lucky it was me that knocked you off your horse and not someone with more sinister motives.'

'Well, thank you for not only humiliating me but also giving me a headache. I am eternally grateful. If however, you had come at me with a sword we would not be in this position, rather I fancy it would be you lying flat on your back amongst the leaves.'

'Oh I can assure you, I am equally adept at using a sword.'

'Why aren't I surprised?' he muttered sarcastically.

She put out her hand to pull him up. He looked at her scornfully, getting himself to his feet with a grunt of pain. His horse waited patiently and he hobbled over to it, pulling himself back into the saddle.

'Well, it's been fun,' he said. 'Am I free to leave now or do you have any other surprises in store?'

She eyed him out, noticing for the first time his striking emerald green eyes and thick dark hair. It was not every day she got to dismount a handsome young man. Usually it was old men travelling to and from Sherbrooke to trade at market. Today had been a pleasant surprise.

She bowed deeply and waved him on his way. 'Certainly sir, have a safe journey now.'

He laughed at her audacity. She was feisty, whoever she was. He kicked his heels into the side of his horse and cantered off leaving her smiling as she replaced the arrow back in the quiver. She loved her daily adventures in these woods. Today had certainly been better than most.

CHAPTER 1

THE PAST RETURNS

AISLINN stood at the woodstove cooking their dinner. Drew would be home soon and she wanted the meal ready for his arrival. He worked long hard hours at the practice so they both valued the time they spent together in the evening. Once the children were in bed it was their time to relax and talk about the day. Isabel was a young woman now and came and went like a free spirit. It worried Aislinn at times how her eldest daughter was so carefree and reckless. She certainly was not the young lady Aislinn imagined her little girl growing up to be. Still, her parents had allowed her to follow her dream of being a midwife and she would not try to mould her own daughter into something she did not want to be. They also had two other children, Jaimie who was seventeen and Logan who was fourteen. After Jaimie's birth, Aislinn had complications and could never bear another child as a result. They had been devastated at the time, wanting a bigger family. She remembered growing up with many siblings and loved it and Drew always wanted more children as he remembered how isolated and lonely his own childhood was. They never mentioned his twin, Daemon anymore – it was too painful and a part of their history they would rather forget. Logan had been a godsend to them – his own mother had left him at their surgery door in a basket when he was born. They tried tracking her down to no avail – the woman simply vanished and did not want to be found. As there was no family to take the little babe in, Drew and Aislinn opened their hearts and their home to the little boy. Now he was truly one of the family and they loved him dearly. He had been the inspiration for the Heart and Home Shelter they founded. They had converted the old cowshed on their property into a home that could house orphans. Maggie, a wonderful older lady cared for the children who came through its doors. Old Doctor Williams, Drew's father, took it upon himself to oversee all the medical issues that faced them with the children. The home never had more than eight to ten children at a time, but at least there were facilities for children who found themselves without parents.

The door burst open and Logan bounded into the kitchen.

'Slow down young man before you knock things flying,' she cautioned.

'Sorry Mama,' he apologised giving her a kiss on the cheek before stealing a scone and running out the door again.

'I saw that,' she yelled after him smiling at the joy he had brought them.

He was quite different to her other two children looks wise. They had not kept his adoption a secret from him – they believed in telling him the truth about who he was and where he came from and especially how much they loved him. Jaimie had thick, dark wavy hair like Isabel, whereas Logan had fair straight hair and green eyes.

Drew came in behind her and smiled. She was deep in thought he could tell. He tiptoed up and encircled her waist with his strong arms, nestling his face in her neck and breathing her sweet scent in. Even after all these years she still smelled of lavender and honeysuckle. He loved her as much as he had the day he married her – in fact he loved her more if that were possible. They had a good life together and three beautiful children. He felt grateful for all the blessings they had.

'You're home,' she murmured wriggling herself around to face him. His face was still handsome and his violet eyes deep. He was just starting to grey at the temples and somehow it made him look more distinguished. He pulled her close kissing her deeply, the passion of their relationship as strong as it was when they first met.

'Now that was nice,' he murmured as she pulled free to rescue her stew cooking on the stove.

A knock at the door made them both look questioningly at one another. Usually after-hours calls meant only one of two things – either someone was in labour or there was a medical emergency.

'Not tonight,' Aislinn groaned. She was really hoping that they could have a quiet night in together as a family.

Drew opened the door surprised to see a young man standing on the threshold. He did not recognize him as a Sherbrookian.

'Yes, can I help you?' he asked.

'Are you Doctor Drew Williams?'

'I am. Do you have a medical emergency?'

'No,' the young man smiled. 'I am Phoenix, Legion and Gwendolyn's son. I've come to Sherbrooke to notify you of my father's death. He died a few days ago as a result of a hunting accident. My father told me how you helped our family years ago and I thought that you should know of his passing.'

'Come in' Drew said to the young man. 'I am truly sorry to hear of his death.'

'Yes, it came as a shock to us all. I will miss him terribly. My mother has not been well since her brother died many years ago – she will not talk about him but she has never forgotten what happened to him. They never found his murderer and she has become rather bitter and angry as a result. It was my father who raised me.'

Aislinn and Drew glanced at one another. So Gwen had not told her son about their involvement in Daemon's death or that Drew was his twin brother.

Was the past coming back to haunt them?

Surely fate would not be so cruel.

'You must be tired after such a long journey,' Aislinn said, compassion for the young man overruling her fear. 'Stay and have dinner with us and if you need a bed we can offer you Logan's bed. It's not much but you are welcome to stay.'

'Thank you, I will gladly stay for dinner, but as for the bed I have already organised a room at the inn.'

Phoenix sat at the table and Drew poured him some wine. The sun shone through the windows in orange rays as it readied itself for bed. The soft light was beautiful on the whitewashed walls of their cottage. Aislinn loved this time of day. The boys would be home soon and who knew when Isabel would make her presence known. Aislinn assumed she had been with her brother again. Isabel doted on Struan and spent endless hours with him. He did not help, encouraging her to be carefree and a little wild at times.

'I guess I have both of you to thank for being here,' Phoenix said.

'What do you mean?' Aislinn asked.

'My father told me many times how you saved me when I was born. He said that your quick thinking and skill saved not only me but my mother too. The truth is that I could have sent a messenger to tell you of my father's death, but I wanted to meet you both. I also wanted to get away from my mother at this time. I do not know how to comfort her – she feels like a stranger to me.'

He looked ashamed and Aislinn patted his shoulder in understanding.

'I'm sorry your mother was not there for you growing up, but I do know she loves you – I saw how she looked at you when you were born – you were the light of her life.'

Before Phoenix could answer the door burst open and Isabel flew through it looking excited and flushed.

'Can you children never enter the house like normal people,' Aislinn complained.

'Mama, I've had the best day ever,' she blurted out excited.

It took a few seconds to comprehend they were not alone and that a stranger was sitting at their table. She looked across the room and her eyes grew wide, startled and surprised.

'Isabel, this is Phoenix. He has come from Griswold to inform us of his father's death. We are old friends with his parents and we have not seen him since he was born.'

Isabel said nothing – she just stared at the young man, her cheeks turning crimson.

'Say something young lady,' Drew growled. 'Have you lost your manners?'

'Perhaps she lost her tongue when she ambushed me in the forest,' Phoenix suggested.

'You did what?' Aislinn groaned. 'Isabel we have told you time and again to stop harassing people in the forest. You promised us you would end this nonsense.'

'I don't hurt anyone – it's just a little sport,' she defended. 'Besides how else am I supposed to practise my archery and fighting skills?'

'On a target, Isabel, like other people do,' Drew said. 'Apologise right now to Phoenix and this will be the last time we have this discussion about your antics in the forest. You will not be allowed to see your uncle Struan if you continue this behaviour.'

'I'm sorry,' she said to Phoenix. Her gritted teeth and painful expression were not lost on the young man and he smiled seeing her discomfort and anger at being treated like a child in front of him.

'Phoenix has had a tragedy in his family Isabel, and your timing for this is not only poor but also very insensitive. You cannot behave this way. I am tired of getting complaints from the local villagers who are too afraid to travel through the forest because our daughter is terrorising them. Promise me it won't happen again.'

'I promise,' she said.

'She's got her fingers crossed behind her back,' Logan said. No one had seen him come in with all the drama and he was enjoying catching his sister out.

'Logan,' she glared at him daggers in her eyes.

'If you go back on this there will be consequences young lady,' Drew warned. 'Do you understand me, Isabel?'

'Yes Papa.'

The family ate dinner and reminisced over the time they spent at Griswold castle when Phoenix was born.

Aislinn said nothing about her history with Legion. Clearly Phoenix doted on his father and it appeared he had turned out to be a wonderful father and a changed man. Everyone deserved a second chance. Aislinn felt a little guilty that Gwendolyn had lost her way after Daemon's death. That was her fault – she had done that to her and yet there was nothing she could do to change it – the past was the past.

Phoenix had grown into a lovely young man. It was amazing really and gave Aislinn and Drew so much hope for the young children at Heart and Home. As long as there was love given from at least one person a child could grow up secure and happy. Aislinn hoped that Gwen would snap out of her isolation now that Legion was gone. Surely she would realize she needed her son more than ever now. The young man seemed grounded and spoke lovingly of his father.

'My father was far from perfect. He told me all about his past and how he used to manipulate and hurt people. He wanted me to know that power is not the greatest thing to gain, but that love and respect and kindness far outweigh it.'

'Sounds like he did a good job then,' Drew said. 'That will stand you in good stead when you are the Lord of Griswold.'

'Yes, after his wake I will be rightfully set in as the next Lord of Griswold. Would you come to my ceremony? I would be most honoured to have you there and I know it would have pleased my father. Perhaps it would be good for my mother too, seeing old friends.'

This was the moment they had been dreading. They would have to tell Phoenix some of their history otherwise he would think they were rejecting him.

'I'm not sure that would be a good idea under the circumstances,' Aislinn said. 'You see Phoenix, Drew is actually your uncle Daemon's twin brother. They were separated at birth and they were identical. Seeing him may only open old wounds for your mother and cause greater pain.'

The young man looked shocked at this information. He was just a baby when Daemon died.

'I had no idea,' he said. 'Mother never mentioned it.' Then his face lit up. 'Maybe that's exactly what she needs – a shock to her system – a way to finally face reality. Lord knows pretending the last twenty odd years has not helped. Maybe this will be the thing that jolts her back to reality.'

'I don't know Phoenix, we don't want to make things worse,' Drew said caution in his voice.

'Please say you will come – if not for her then for me. I would hate to be made the Lord of Griswold and have strangers fawning over me seeking favour. It would be nice to know that someone was there who knows my history and family. I doubt Mother could get any worse than she is and who knows, it may even help.'

His desperation tugged their hearts. They agreed to make the trip and pay their respects to Legion before seeing his son elected the new Lord. It seemed strange to Aislinn that they would be attending the wake of a man who had given her extreme pain in the years past – a man who nearly destroyed her family twenty- eight years previously. A lot had changed in that time.

⌘

Isabel stood her ground, sword in hand. The look of determination said it all – her brow was furrowed in concentration as she balanced herself. The metal blade swung at her and she ducked the blow ready for the next one that would come. She was agile and quick and she loved the adrenaline that coursed through her veins when she was fighting. Her mother and father did not understand it but she did not expect them to – they were in the business of saving lives not taking them. What they did not realise was that they were more similar than they thought. She too would save lives and protect people but it would not be through medicine but through her weapons and bravery. She had first felt the rush of adrenaline when she was just ten years old. An older boy at school had tried to bully Jaimie and steal his lunch. She had caught him pushing her brother up against a wall. She asked him nicely to please let her brother go but he had laughed at her and told her to run along. That had made her very angry. Without thinking she had jumped onto his back and locked his head in a stranglehold. She remembered how he grunted and wheezed trying to get air. Then he tried shaking her off his back but she would not let go. Finally she growled in his ear that if he ever bothered her brother again she would come back and hurt him. Before letting him go she bit him hard on his shoulder. He whelped in pain and ran to tell the teacher who just happened to be her aunt Maddy. She had been in serious trouble and everyone had chastised her, even her parents. The only person who had secretly congratulated her was her uncle Struan.

'Well done Isabel,' he said. 'No one should ever be able to make you feel threatened. However if you really want to learn how to fight then you must do it properly. Biting isn't really the solution.'

So she had started spending time with Struan and he had taught her everything she knew – how to fight with a sword and shoot a bow. She had proved a quick learner.

'Have you had enough yet?' Struan asked seeing her distracted.

'Yes, I think so. I've been feeling frustrated ever since Papa found out that I ambushed Phoenix. Not being allowed to go out into the forest is driving me crazy but I promised Papa and so I had better at least lie low for a while.'

'You're wicked Isabel Williams,' he laughed. 'I hear you're all going to Griswold for the young man's ceremony. Is he handsome Issie?'

Struan always referred to her affectionately as Issie ever since she was a little girl.

'I haven't noticed,' she said defiantly and Struan smiled knowingly.

'I'm sure you haven't,' he said sarcastically ducking the sword that she swung at his head.

⌘

Aislinn packed for their trip to Griswold. Fortunately none of her pregnant ladies were due to give birth for a few moons and old Doctor Williams had promised to cover Drew's patients while they were away. Jaimie agreed to stay and care for the little farm and to help Maggie with supplies for Heart and Home. Mac and Imogene had also offered their help with the orphanage while they would be away, which made Aislinn feel less worried about leaving Jaime alone. Logan and Isabel would accompany them to Griswold. Isabel had complained bitterly but after her shenanigans in the forest, Drew was adamant she would travel with them and not be left to terrorise the locals while they were gone.

They met Phoenix at the Sherbrooke Inn. He smiled as he pulled himself into the saddle. He could not miss the scowl on Isabel's face. Clearly she was not happy to be making this trip. Even when she was angry she was beautiful. She certainly was intriguing with a mind of her own. They made their way out of town with Drew and Aislinn leading the way. They had made this trip many times before. Phoenix rode next to Isabel who pretended he did not exist. He could not resist teasing her.

'I must say I feel completely relieved to have you with us on this trip. Who else would protect us from danger or ensure we don't become distracted on our journey?'

'Very funny,' she retorted.

'Why are you so hostile to me Isabel?'

'You really have to ask?' she replied surprised. 'Thanks to you I am forbidden from practising my skills in the forest now.'

'Well I'm sorry that you got into trouble, but using actual people to practise on is a bit cruel and heartless don't you think?'

'I don't hurt anyone.'

'That's true Isabel, but you do humiliate people and that can be more hurtful than a physical injury.'

She had not thought of it that way and was surprised that he was so concerned for others feelings.

'I'm sorry if I humiliated you,' she capitulated. 'That was not my intention.'

'Apology accepted, and truthfully you are the prettiest adversary I've ever come face to face with.'

He did not miss the corner of her mouth turning up in a little smile although she tried to hide it. For now they had a truce.

CHAPTER 2

THE REUNION

GRISWOLD 1648

GWENDOLYN sat staring out of the window. She felt angry deep inside. Phoenix had deserted her at this difficult time in her life. She felt betrayed by him – he had run off to the woman who had caused her all this pain the last two decades. She resented him for that.

Why hadn't he sent a messenger to Aislinn and Drew?

Deep down she knew the answer. He did not want to be alone with her – she was a virtual stranger to her own son. Aislinn had stolen her joy and made her a bitter woman. As a result she had shut out her husband and her son – it was ironic really. She always feared being alone thinking Legion was cold and cruel, but in the end she had become the very thing she despised in him the most when they were first married. She also felt angry with herself. She had wasted twenty- four years being bitter with no closure. She had wanted to turn Aislinn's confession over to the authorities and to see her thrown into jail for the rest of her life but something had stopped her. It was fear that Aislinn would tell the courts that her brother was a monster, a rapist. She did not believe that, but what if others did? Then she would not only get away with her crime but Daemon's name and memory would forever be sullied. Instead she had allowed Legion to convince her to burn the letter and to let it go. She had never forgiven him for choosing Aislinn and Drew over her family. They had stolen her family and she had let them. She hoped it was not too late to get to know her son. She wished she could tell Legion she was sorry but she would never get the chance now. He lay in the bottom of the castle, his body being prepared for his wake. It had happened so suddenly and she felt partly responsible for his death. If she hadn't been so cold and unavailable he would not have spent hours of time out hunting with Phoenix. She recalled the day it happened. She heard the men shouting in the courtyard and she knew instantly that something was wrong. Looking out her window she saw Phoenix lifting his father's body gently down from his horse. Her son looked stricken. The dark red stain across Legion's stomach said it all. He had been gored by a wild boar. Phoenix had yelled for help and some guards had carried their Master's body in to the physician but it was too late. There was nothing they could do for him. No magic would ever bring him back.

She knew she was in trouble when she could not weep. Her emotions had been so controlled by hatred that all sense of feeling had shrivelled up within her. For the first time in years she felt something else – not pain and the constant anger that lived with her but fear at what she had become. She wondered why everyone she ever loved was taken from her. Did the Great One despise her so much that he was punishing her? She remembered the Elders words all those years ago – that there would be a reckoning if Legion did not give them money to build their sanctuary. They were cursed – they had to be. It was just after their visit that everything started to go wrong. Legion had laughed off their threats but now she wondered if there was truth in them. Her fear extended to her son – what if he was taken from her? She would die if that were to happen. He must be protected at all costs.

As she mulled over the events she heard horses in the courtyard.

Phoenix was back at the castle.

She could hear the well-wishes of the men as he dismounted his horse. The last time she looked out her chamber window she saw her husband's body returning from the hunt. This time as she looked out she caught her breath. It was Daemon standing in the courtyard. She felt like an icy bucket of water had been poured over her. Then she saw Aislinn Williams and realized it was Drew she was looking at. She had forgotten how alike they were – identical really. She felt a fresh stab of longing for her dead brother and sadness threatened to well up. She pushed it down - she had to think of Legion and Phoenix now.

What are they doing here? Who is that pretty young girl with them? Her thoughts tumbled, her mind in shock.

Phoenix seemed overly attentive to her. She felt a wave of jealousy hit her and she almost wept with relief. Jealousy was an emotion – she felt something other than numbness.

⌘

'Welcome to Griswold,' Phoenix said.

It was vastly different to the way Aislinn remembered it. Twenty-four years ago it looked ominous, a mausoleum with its dark stone walls and bleak grounds. It had looked like the prison it was. Now it seemed far less threatening and almost homely. The stonework looked clean and there were even gardens in different parts of the castle.

'This is not how I remember it,' she said. 'It's rather pretty now.'

'Yes, my father thought that planting gardens might help Mother with her sadness and give her something beautiful to look at. I think we have enjoyed them more than she. It certainly has changed the castle and made it less harsh looking. The clean stonework is a result of the upcoming ceremony – the servants have scrubbed every corner and it has come up quite well don't you think?'

Aislinn could see the enchanted look in Isabel's eyes. She had never been in a castle before and she stared wide-eyed at everything around her.

'It's magnificent,' she breathed.

Logan nodded in agreement – he was equally enamoured with the grandeur of it all.

'Come, let me show you to your rooms.' Phoenix ushered them in through the large gilded doors.

Aislinn prayed she would not find herself in the south tower again and was extremely relieved when they were escorted to the west wing. They were given two adjoining rooms – one for Isabel and Logan and the other for her and Drew. They were beautifully decorated with ornate fabrics and furniture.

'I hope this will be comfortable enough for you while you are our guests,' Phoenix said.

'This is more than adequate thank you,' Aislinn replied.

Isabel ran and jumped on the bed, rubbing the soft velvet throw against her cheek.

'I could get used to this,' she sighed.

Phoenix smiled. 'I'll let you settle in after our long journey. I will have tea sent up for you and we will have dinner at eight.'

'Thank you Phoenix,' Drew responded. 'That will be much appreciated.

⌘

Dinner was a sumptuous affair with roast pheasant on the menu. They all enjoyed the meal but felt sad that Gwendolyn did not join them. As they were having their sweet treats she made an entrance. Aislinn stood, unsure how she would react to seeing them. She came over and smiled warmly at them both.

'Aislinn, Drew, it is good to see you both again.'

'Hello Gwendolyn, we are so glad to see you although we wish the circumstances were different. Our heartfelt condolences about Legion – we were very sad to hear of his accident.'

'Thank you, it's been a difficult time, but I am so glad you have come. I certainly never expected you to travel all this way, but since you have you are more than welcome.'

Aislinn could not read the expression in her eyes. Was she really glad to see them or was she just trying to be cordial? Her smile seemed genuine but her eyes were cold and hard.

'Phoenix was very convincing in getting us to attend his ceremony and we thought we would like to pay our last respects to Legion,' Drew added sensing Aislinn's tension.

'That is very kind of you both. Who have you brought with you?' she asked looking at Isabel and Logan.

'This is our eldest daughter Isabel and her youngest brother Logan. Our elder son, Jaimie, stayed to look after the orphanage we run.'

'Still doing good deeds I see,' she smiled.

Was there a hint of sarcasm in her words?

Although the conversation flowed they could tell it was strained and awkward. Gwen was trying really hard to make them feel welcome with her words, but her heart was not in it.

'The wake will be tomorrow – we have been waiting for Phoenix to return to lay his father to rest. Then we will wait three days before we officially declare him the next Lord of Griswold. I hope you are comfortable. If there is anything you need don't hesitate to ask Phoenix,' she added.

'Thank you Gwen.'

She left them to go back to her chambers. Seeing Drew reminded her so much of Daemon and it was almost unbearable. Harder than seeing Drew though was seeing Aislinn, smiling and happy; living her life as though nothing had happened. It stirred her anger afresh.

That woman should pay for what she did to Daemon.

She may have eased her conscience when she wrote her confession letter but it was far from over in Gwen's mind. She would have her revenge yet – she would take from Aislinn Williams the things that were most valuable to her. She would not rest till she saw her broken and crushed.

CHAPTER 3

THE WAKE

THE WAKE was well attended by the people of Griswold. Legion had changed so much and was well loved by his people – a vastly different man to the one who viciously attacked the Hamilton family and Ziah all those years ago. Aislinn smiled to herself as she looked around at the people who had come out to pay their respects to him. This was proof that one could change – the Dark Lord had become someone different, someone who cared about others. Nothing was ever set in stone – it was not fate or a sovereign god that made them who they were – rather it was one's own choices that determined the path one walked in this life and Legion had been living proof of darkness and hatred choosing to walk a better path. Aislinn could not help but admire the man she had once feared so greatly.

Gwendolyn sat rigid throughout the ceremony, her expression cold and harsh. Phoenix openly wept for a father he clearly doted on and loved deeply. The contrast between mother and son was blatantly obvious. Aislinn's heart ached when she thought how Phoenix had grown up without his mother's love and touch. She could not imagine abandoning her own children – her life would be incomplete without them. Still, it was credit to Legion for raising such a lovely young man.

Once the wake was over they all attended a tea in the Great Hall.

'Aislinn,' a familiar voice called. She spun around delight on her face.

'Regent,' she squealed and flung her arms around the large, ebony skinned man who grinned, his white teeth filling his face. 'What on earth are you doing here?'

'I should ask you the same thing. I have accompanied the Great One to the wake. He really wanted to be here. He never stopped loving Legion, even when he was at his worst. I guess that's why he is the Great One. I don't know how he does it.'

'Quite simple really,' the Great One said coming up behind them. 'Love doesn't require effort – you either love or you don't and I choose to love no matter who the person may be. No-one ever disappoints me because I don't base my affections on performance. I love because I want to, because I choose to.'

'Great One,' Aislinn said hugging the old man affectionately. 'It is so good to see you.'

'You surprise me Aislinn,' the old man said. 'More than that, I admire you for returning here after all you have been through.'

'We came for Phoenix – he is the one who asked us to come. Besides, Legion did an admirable thing raising him so well.'

'Ah yes,' Regent interjected. 'I forget that you and Drew saved him during childbirth.'

They chatted and caught up on all the news of Lionsgate. It was wonderful seeing her old friends again and a pleasant surprise. She felt comfortable and safe for the first time since she had arrived.

The Great One eventually excused himself to go and talk to Gwendolyn. Logan and Isabel also tore themselves away to go and raid the food table. They had never seen such an array of fine foods and they were making the most of it. Aislinn watched as Phoenix approached her daughter and began to converse with her. She smiled, watching her daughter's body language. Isabel may pretend that she found the young man annoying and a nuisance but her response told a completely different story. It appeared her daughter was rather attracted to the young man and Aislinn could not blame her – he was handsome with his green eyes and pitch black hair.

'Aislinn,' she was stirred from her musing by the Great One; concern in his eyes and voice.

'Oh, you're back from speaking with Gwendolyn already.'

'Yes, there wasn't much to say I'm afraid. She is rather a closed book. I got the sense that she somehow blames me for Legion's death. I have no idea why but that is what I felt. I want to warn you Aislinn – something is not right with her. Be careful. I'm not sure whether she has forgiven you for Daemon's death and I fear she may be a volcano about to erupt with years of bitterness and hatred. Just make sure you are not in her path when she does.

Aislinn paled. She had assumed that when no-one came to arrest her for Daemon's death that Gwen had chosen to forgive her and believed her account of the events leading to his death.

What if she hasn't and is waiting for her pound of flesh?

⌘

'I'll feel much better when we can get away from here,' Aislinn said to Drew as they sat in their room in front of a roaring fire.

It had been an emotional day after the wake and everyone felt a little fragile. Phoenix had asked Drew if he could take Isabel and Logan for a ride in the afternoon to show them his lands and to get his mind away from the castle and his loss. They had agreed. It was good to have Logan chaperone them although Isabel hardly needed a chaperone – she could take care of herself more than adequately and if any man tried to force himself upon her he would surely find an arrow or sword protruding from his belly. They did not fear for her but rather anyone brave enough to tackle her boisterous, strong-willed personality.

'Are you concerned about Gwen?' Drew asked.

'I wasn't until the Great One warned me. He knows more about people than anyone – if he senses something is wrong then I trust him with my life.'

'Only three more days' sweetheart,' he said wrapping his arms around her and drawing her into his strong, hard chest. She always felt safe with Drew.

'As soon as Phoenix is made Lord of Griswold we will leave. We will say we need to get back to the orphanage which is true.'

'This place has changed so much and Legion has really made it quite beautiful with all the gardens, yet somehow it still feels cold and frightening to me. I guess my past memories have come back to haunt me and aren't so easy to shake off.'

'Don't load up feelings of guilt Aislinn – they will be a burden too big to carry and will crush you. You did what you had to do to survive – to protect yourself and our future family. You did the right thing,' he kissed her hair. 'I know I would have been lost without you if Daemon had had his way. You saved me.'

'I know I did – I didn't have a choice at the time and if it had to happen over I am sure I would do the same thing. It's just hard when I see the consequences of my actions affecting others. Gwen has had her life stolen from her as a result of my actions and Phoenix lost his mother.'

'Darling woman, that was not of your doing. Gwen chose to isolate herself – you cannot be responsible for people's choices even when bad things have happened in their lives. We all go through hardships at various times and we can never blame others for the way we choose to respond. Gwen made her choice – Phoenix lost his mother because she chose to shut him out.'

'I know,' she sighed, reason trying to win over her heart which felt heavy.

'That just shows me how beautiful your heart really is sweetheart. You have always thought more about others than yourself. It is a beautiful trait but don't let it suffocate you in guilt you should not feel.'

'I knew I made a good choice when I married you,' she smiled. 'Never a wiser word said.'

He kissed her and wrapped his arms around her protectively.

CHAPTER 4

SAVED

THE DAY of Phoenix's inauguration dawned bright and clear. It was as though nature had declared that something new was beginning – that the sadness of the previous days was gone and a fresh start was unfolding. The kitchens bustled with preparations for the feast that would follow the ceremony. Everyone rallied around doing their chores to ensure that everything ran smoothly. Phoenix stood in his father's chambers. He ran his hand over his beloved books and felt close to the man he loved so dearly.

'I wish you were here today father,' he whispered to the empty room. 'I miss you.'

He wiped away a tear and turned to leave for his own chamber. It was time to get ready for the ceremony. He walked down the echoing passage deep in thought. One other person occupied his thoughts besides his father. Isabel Williams consumed too many of his thoughts and now she was even appearing in his dreams. They had spent a delightful day riding a few days ago and even though her brother had been with them he felt as though it were only the two of them in the whole world. He realized he was developing feelings for her very quickly. She was a complete enigma to him. She was certainly a strong, independent young woman with a fierce streak in her and yet he had seen a soft, feminine side to her that made her appear almost vulnerable. He could not quite work her out and yet he believed she would be fiercely loyal and protective of anyone she chose to love. He had to admit he did not want her to leave when her parents returned to Sherbrooke. The thought of never seeing her again pained him.

He shook his head as if to clear away the spell she had woven on him.

'Time to focus and get this thing done,' he muttered as he pulled off his shirt and threw it in the corner of his room.

'Can I come in?' a voice boomed from the other side of his chamber door.

'Balfour.' Phoenix was delighted to see his friend at his door. 'Come in and help me with this cloak. It's ridiculously heavy and I'm not quite sure how to wear it.'

Balfour and Phoenix had been friends since they were eight years old. They had met when Phoenix had snuck out of the castle to go and catch fish. He had been forbidden by Legion to wander off alone as he was inclined to do. Even at a tender age he was adventurous and curious.

Phoenix could hear his father's words as if it were yesterday.

'It is unsafe for you to wander about alone Phoenix. You will one day be the next Lord of Griswold and there are many who would try to stop that from happening. You must take a chaperone with you when you go out of the castle. Promise me you will never go out alone.'

He had promised his father and he had kept his word until that fateful day. He could not find anyone to take with him as all the servants were busy. He had heard the stable boy talking about the big fish that got away and he could not resist trying to catch it. He had tried to convince him to accompany him but the young man had too many chores to complete.

He had ventured down to the river with his fishing pole alone. Once his line was in the water he sat on the mossy bank waiting for a bite. He had drifted off to sleep in the warm sunshine. When he woke it was getting dark and the cold earth seeped through his clothing. He had scrambled to his feet and pulled the fishing pole upright only to find that his line was caught in some tree branches hanging over the bubbling water. He had to get his line back or his father would know he had left without a chaperone. He pulled on the pole twisting it left and right hoping it would release its grip on the tree. It did not budge. So he laid his pole down on the bank and slowly inched his way along a gnarly tree branch hanging over the water. He carefully moved toward the line he could see tangled up in the branch. He had almost made it but the weight of his body on the old, decayed branch was too much. It gave way plunging him into the icy river water. He had managed to grab hold of a branch still attached to the bank but he knew then he was in serious trouble. The water was freezing and unless he could have pulled himself out he would have frozen to death or been swept away in the strong current. He had felt fear for the first time and a feeling of utter helplessness.

'Help,' he had screamed, praying his words wouldn't be carried away into the dusk air. He closed his eyes and clung to the branch. His hands had become numb and were losing sensation. He knew he could not hold on much longer. Suddenly two strong arms plucked him from the icy water and folded him in a warm shawl. He passed out. When he awoke he was in a warm cottage. His father stood over him – a look of sheer relief and anger etched across his brow.

'Don't ever put me through that again,' he growled before snatching his son up in a bear hug.

That was when he met Balfour.

'This young man heard you calling,' Legion told him. 'He ran and got his father to save you. Thanks to his quick thinking you are safe and will see another day.'

Ever since that day they had become firm friends and had been inseparable. His father had offered Balfour's father a position in the castle. He was entrusted with the care of all the horses and the stable hands as well as other livestock. He had been delighted with the position and accepted it gladly. Times had been hard and not every tenant on the land in Griswold was able to make ends meet when the elements did not favour them. This ensured that he would always have income and could care for his family. So he would work in the stables and Balfour was able to join Phoenix for his daily lessons. Legion had wanted the boy to have an opportunity at education – after all he had saved his son's life.

⌘

The inauguration went smoothly as Phoenix was set in as the next Lord of Griswold. Aislinn and Drew watched the young man, whose life they had saved as a baby, become a man with his own people to rule. They felt proud of who he had become. Balfour watched his best friend, who he had saved as a boy, become his Lord and he felt grateful to have such a good friend. Gwen watched her son, torn between pride and joy at the young man and sadness at their lost bond. Nothing had been able to save their relationship. Isabel watched fascinated with this young man. She could not help but admire all that he would rule over. It was a fairy-tale. She had tried to be indifferent to him, but it was hard when he looked at her with those deep green eyes and smiled at her. He was too good looking for his own good. She felt sad they would be leaving soon, even though she had complained bitterly at being brought here. She grudgingly admitted it had been an adventure.

The celebrations went on long into the night and the villagers enjoyed the feast thrown by their new Lord.

'Thank you for coming,' Phoenix said to Drew and Aislinn as they came to say goodnight.

'It was a good day Phoenix,' Drew said patting the young man on the back. 'Your father would have been so proud of you today.'

'Thank you. I hope I will be half the man he became,' Phoenix said.

'We will have to leave tomorrow I'm afraid,' Aislinn said. 'We really need to get back to the orphanage and our patients.'

'I understand, but please don't leave until after breakfast tomorrow. I have some things to discuss with you before you go.'

They agreed and retired to their chamber, leaving Logan and Isabel enjoying the feast.

'May I have a word with you?' Phoenix asked Isabel.

'Certainly Lord .... What do I call you?' she giggled.

'You don't have to call me Lord anything Isabel – Phoenix will do fine,' he laughed.

She followed him to his parlour where they sat and drank a glass of wine.

'Your parents are leaving tomorrow,' he stated waiting to see her reaction.

'Already,' she exclaimed. He smiled glad at her response. She did not want to leave either.

'I don't want you to go,' he said, so softly she wasn't sure she heard him correctly.

'Did you hear me?' he asked when she did not respond.

'Why do you want me to stay?' she asked her heart pounding in her chest.

'I want you to stay and train my archers and warriors,' he blurted out, not sure what else to say.

She felt disappointed.

Stupid Isabel, what did you think? That he wanted you to stay because he had feelings for you.

'Well I don't know,' she responded stiffly. 'I don't think my parents will be too keen on my staying here alone.'

'Leave that to me, I will talk to them. Please say you will stay if you have their permission. I need your expertise Isabel.'

'All right, I will stay if they give their consent.'

⌘

He could kick himself. Why hadn't he told her the real reason he wanted her to stay. The truth was that he was fearful she would laugh and reject him.

The mighty Lord of Griswold afraid of a slip of a girl.

It was ridiculous, yet she made him feel like a little boy again.

Get a grip Phoenix. You are a Lord, responsible for people not a gibbering idiot.

He was glad she had agreed to stay – now all he needed to do was to convince Aislinn and Drew that he needed her help – that would be the hard part.

He would need to think up a persuasive argument to win them over. He flopped down on his bed, exhausted after the day's events. It was not long before his eyes closed and he fell into a deep sleep his dreams filled with a girl with grey eyes and dark wavy hair.

⌘

'It's out of the question,' Drew said firmly.

They were congregated in Phoenix's parlour and his suggestion that Isabel remain on at Griswold both alarmed and terrified them. They had not anticipated this.

'Why can't I stay Papa?' Isabel demanded her eyes fierce and determined.

Phoenix threw her a cautionary glance urging her to remain quiet and let him deal with the situation.

'I can assure you Doctor Williams that no harm will come to Isabel while she is here. I give you my word.'

Aislinn felt sick. How did they explain their fears to this eager young man without telling him the full story and their fears of his mother taking out her anger and bitterness on their daughter? He misunderstood their concern as over-protective parenting when it was so much more than that. The truth was that they knew Isabel was a strong woman and could care for herself, thanks to Struan's training and instruction, but without knowing she was in danger she would be vulnerable and unsuspecting.

'We know you will do everything to protect her,' Drew said, 'but there is more to our concerns than you understand and we cannot say anymore. Isabel, you have to trust us when we say that we cannot leave you here,' he directed his attention to the defiant young woman who stood feet apart and hands on her hips.

'Phoenix, would you let me have some time alone with my parents?' she said.

He left the room, giving them time to work it out. He had hoped that they would be convinced of his need for her expertise.

Why are they so worried about letting her stay? They have a secret and it is the reason for their reluctance. Is it Mother?

He mulled over the possibilities. Nothing came to mind.

'Why can't I stay?' she demanded. 'I am a grown woman and can take care of myself. Your past experience in this castle is just that Mama – past! You can't put that on me now. Your parents let you follow your dreams, even at risk to yourself, yet you are trying to control and pamper me. I won't have it.'

'I know you feel that way Isabel, but there is real danger to you here – it is not my past experience that is scaring me.'

'You can't protect me from every little bit of danger Mama. I am an adult and I need to protect myself. I trust Phoenix to look out for me. Please let me do this, I'm begging you.'

The look of desperation in their daughter's eyes made their hearts ache. They knew they would lose her anyway if they forbade her. She would not forgive them. Aislinn nodded numbly at Drew.

'There is one condition however on your being allowed to stay,' Drew stated firmly.

'Oh thank you Papa,' she flung her arms around his neck and kissed him on the cheek.

'Don't be so hasty Isabel, you don't know what the condition is yet.'

'Anything, I will do anything,' she gushed her eyes sparkling in anticipation.

'Well this condition doesn't just depend on your agreement – it depends on someone else agreeing to it too.' She looked confused as did Aislinn.

'You may stay on condition that Struan is willing to come and stay at the castle while you are here. I am sure he will be able to help you with the training and in return we will feel happier knowing you have someone in your own family to watch your back. Of course he has to agree to these terms.'

'I agree,' she said, pleased at this idea. She adored her uncle Struan and he would be a great help training the men.

'That means you will have to travel back to Sherbrooke with us and when he is ready you can both return to Griswold together.'

Her face dropped but she realized that her father would not concede otherwise. She was willing to compromise to follow her dreams.

Living in a real castle, training and fighting with real warriors.

It was a dream come true.

'I accept,' she beamed.

CHAPTER 5

LOSS AND GAIN

STRUAN readily agreed to accompany Isabel back to Griswold. He remembered how awful it was in the South tower room when he and his siblings were prisoners, but he didn't have as many bad memories due to his fever and infection. He was spared a lot of the fear and torment which was a blessing in disguise. He could see how excited Issie was about the adventure and he had to admit he was rather thrilled to be able to share his skills with Phoenix's subjects.

Struan had never married, not because he did not want to, but because fate had played him a dirty hand. When he was twenty-eight he met a beautiful young woman called Ceinlys. She had deep chestnut hair and very fair skin. She was one of the most beautiful women Aislinn had ever seen and she had a personality to match. She was gentle and caring and loved people. Everyone loved her in return. Struan was completely smitten from the moment he saw her in Sherbrooke village. She was the daughter of the new Blacksmith and had only just moved to the village from the Highlands. He began to woo her and with his equally good looks they soon made a striking couple, she with her red hair and he with his raven head. The Hamilton family had been delighted when she had agreed to marry Struan. It was just one moon from their wedding when a freak accident left Struan heartbroken. Ceinlys was visiting her father at the forge to take him some food. It was a dark, cold, rainy day and she dashed through puddles and the miserable weather to get under cover and escape the elements. As she entered the forge a streak of lightning filled the sky followed almost instantly by a loud explosive thunder roll. The large stallion her father was busy shoeing startled at the sudden noise and reared up knocking her to the ground. She did not stand much chance as she was trampled by the terrified beast. Her father had rushed her to Drew and Aislinn, but they could not do much to help her. They made her as comfortable as possible while Struan held her in his arms and told her he loved her. Instead of marrying the woman he adored, he buried her before their life together could begin. It had taken its toll on him. He had never gotten over Ceinlys.

⌘

Gwen could not believe it. *How dare Phoenix invite the Williams girl to stay!*

She did not want anything to do with that family – they had caused her nothing but heartache. Not only would she have the daughter staying but her uncle would accompany her. It would be hard to be civil to them, but she would have to try if she did not want to further alienate her son. He would be furious if she treated his guests with disdain. She had noticed his growing affection for the girl and it worried her. She would have to make sure his affection did not develop any further.

⌘

Phoenix was delighted that Isabel was returning. He had a spring in his step that did not go unnoticed by Balfour.

'She must be something special,' he teased his friend.

'She is certainly a mystery,' Phoenix laughed. 'I think you will like her.'

'I'm looking forward to getting to know her. Now why did you call me here?' he asked his friend.

'I have a proposition for you. How would you like to be my personal advisor and right hand man? My father's advisors are old and set in their ways and I don't know or trust them as he did. I need someone who will always have my back and Griswold's interests at heart. Who better than the man who has saved me and been there for me as a loyal friend and confidant?'

'Won't your father's advisors be angry at losing their position?' Balfour asked concerned.

'I will offer them another role – one equally important – don't you worry about the logistics - just say yes.'

'It would be an honour to work with you and serve you,' Balfour smiled.

'Well you can start by making sure Isabel is safe while she is here – I promised her parents that I would protect her. For some reason they are fearful for her – I think there may be more history between them and my parents than I imagined. Just watch my mother. I get the impression she is not delighted at Isabel and Struan's imminent arrival.'

⌘

Phoenix was consumed with Isabel's stay and local matters surrounding his new kingdom. There were always day to day issues that needed to be resolved. What he did not know was that trouble was brewing far from Griswold, but it would travel like an avalanche and hit them with great force and power.

CHAPTER 6

THE NORTH

KALDAKINN

SUMMER was fast approaching which meant that the Northmen of Kaldakinn were readying themselves to raid before the icy winter months descended upon them. Their ships had been repaired throughout spring and their supplies made ready to sail to the southern regions. Their success in the raiding season was paramount to their survival in the long harsh months that would blanket them in icy snow and frozen lakes. Thorfinn Sveinsson checked the provisions once again. He was a large man with a muscular build. His long hair and beard were fair and he had a weathered face that had seen fifty-five years of battling the elements. He was the Earl of Kaldakinn and commanded respect from all those who lived in his village. He was a fierce warrior and never expected his men to do anything he would not do himself. He had seen many battles over the years and wore the scars on his face and body as testimony. For the last few years they had plundered other northern villages and taken food and treasures with them. This was the first year they were venturing further south to new lands they had heard tales about. Travelling south to raid was nothing new for Northmen– other clans had been doing it for centuries but their clan had never attempted it – mainly because Thorfinn's father had not been willing to take the risk as Earl. Instead they had waited for other clans to head south and attacked when their men were away. Now that his father Sveinn was gone and he was Earl, Thorfinn believed it was time to do as many other Northmen had done before – head south and explore what was out in the world. It was a risk, an adventure and Earl Thorfinn knew they risked much if they failed. Still they had no choice. They had plundered all their local tribes and the supplies and treasures were becoming sparser with each raid. Now they needed new raiding grounds to see them through the winter. They were a fierce people and they butchered anyone who stood against them in their battles. Thorfinn smiled and looked up at the heavens thanking the gods for a good and successful raiding season to come.

Northmen were spiritual people. They believed the gods would help them and guide them in all they did. Thorfinn was proud of his heritage and of his name. His people believed that with your name you inherited the character and traits of the person you were named after. He had been named after Thor, the god of thunder and the son of the great god Odin. He was strong and courageous and Thorfinn hoped he displayed some of his hero's traits. He was also named after his grandfather Finngard who was Earl two generations before him. He was an adventurous man who desired to travel away from the North and discover what was out in the world. Many had called him reckless and insane but he was a visionary. Unfortunately he had been pressured to remain within the borders of their country. Thorfinn thought of the old man now with fondness. He had listened to him talk of far off lands as a boy and he wondered if his grandfather was watching him from Valhalla and whether he would be proud of him for venturing beyond their borders.

'Is everything ready?' she asked watching him as he gazed out over the water.

He smiled at the woman he shared his life with. She was so different from the women who were born in the North. She had darker hair and eyes. It had taken a while for her to be accepted when she first came to Kaldakinn. The women found her a threat and her life was in danger, so he took her under his wing and before he knew what had hit him he had fallen in love with her. They had been together for thirty years and she was as much a Northman as he was now.

Siobhan was grateful for this giant of a man who was fierce in protecting his family and in battle, yet he was tender and compassionate when he believed in something. It was what made him a great Earl and why he was loved by their people. They knew he would rule fairly. She would have been dead had it not been for Thorfinn. She remembered how her village had been plundered by Northmen from Eyjasund and how she had been captured by the Earl as a prize for his son. Never had Northmen ever ventured so far south before and her village had been totally unprepared for the frightening savages that swooped down on them in mass fury. She had watched her husband being murdered at those savage's hands. She was terrified at what awaited her. She thought she would die. Earl Reynir's son Olaf was unkempt and vicious. He forced himself upon her daily and she refused to fight back as she had made that mistake only once. She had been rewarded with a severe beating and he had been even more brutal in his handling of her. She was terrified she would fall pregnant with his child – she had to escape before that happened. Her opportunity came when she was sent out to collect herbs in the hills with some of the other women. She waited till everyone was busy with their task, then she wandered away from the group. She had no idea where she would go or how she would survive but even dying out in the wilderness was better than a life as Olaf's slave. It was Thorfinn's raiding party that found her almost frozen to death in the hills. He had hoisted her up on his horse holding her close to his warm body and covering her with his fur pelt. She had fallen in and out of consciousness for days after she arrived at Kaldakinn and her body shivered with fever. Thorfinn had made sure she was cared for and that she pulled through. She later discovered that the seer had prophesied her coming.

'The south and north will unite by the fate of the gods, not in bloodshed or war, but through love; and their offspring will change history.'

He had not understood what the old prophet meant until he discovered Siobhan in the forest. He could tell that she was not from their Northern tribes. She looked different to their women and as she mumbled in delirium she spoke a strange dialect. He had stumbled upon the woman the gods had declared important and it was his task to see that the god's desires were fulfilled. Siobhan had been very wary of him at first – she believed she had escaped Olaf's evil clutches only to be captured by an equally evil Northman. Thorfinn proved patient with her fear and distrust. He took her into his home and cared for her without expecting anything in return. She found him an enigma and slowly she began to trust him and eventually to love him. There were mixed reactions from the people of Kaldakinn when he wed the stranger. Some had come to know Siobhan and love her but others believed that she would bring nothing but disaster on their tribe. It was only the seer's prophecy that made the men of Kaldakinn hold their tongues. One did not argue with the gods – what they decreed was what would be.

He pulled her close and kissed her on the forehead.

'Yes we are almost ready to sail.'

'Are you nervous?' she asked. She always felt a little apprehensive when he left to raid but this time it was magnified at the unknown territory they would sail into. There were always losses when the men went to raid- she had seen many women anxiously waiting when the ships sailed into their village only to find their men had been killed in battle. She prayed she would never experience that.

CHAPTER 7

LOVE BEGINS

GRISWOLD - LATE SPRING 1648

'DON'T tense your arm,' she said holding the soldier's elbow as he pulled the string on the bow backward.

She moved down the line of archers as they aimed at the targets correcting their posture and aim. Isabel and Struan had been at Griswold for over a moon and they had worked hard training the soldiers and readying them for the coming summer months. Although Griswold had never been attacked by men from the North, it had not escaped Legion's attention when he was ruler that these daring men were getting bolder each year and travelling further and further south. They had no choice but to increase their army and since many of the men called to fight were simple villagers and farmers they did not have the skills necessary to go into battle. Isabel and Struan were changing that. Balfour and Phoenix watched in admiration as the young woman instructed the men. She did not lack confidence or skill and berated the men when needed and praised them when they did well.

'She is a remarkable woman,' Balfour said to his friend. 'No wonder she has captivated you.'

Phoenix blushed, brushing off his friend's comment. 'You are imagining things. She is nothing but a friend.'

'Keep telling yourself that and someone else might sweep her off her feet. If you don't want to take a chance then perhaps I will court her.'

'Don't you dare,' Phoenix threatened.

His friend laughed –'I told you there were feelings there. Don't be afraid to take a risk Phoenix – fight for what you love and want.'

'Maybe I will,' the young Lord of Griswold said.

The training came to an end and Struan and Isabel joined them.

'They are coming along nicely,' Struan said. He was in charge of teaching swordsmanship.

'Yes, you have made some excellent progress. We will be well equipped come summer. Thank you both for all you have done. It's good for the men to feel empowered to protect their families.'

He hesitated a second before he continued, 'I was wondering if you would join me on a ride this afternoon Isabel?'

The young woman flushed, surprised at his invitation.

'That is, if your uncle will give permission,' he added quickly.

'Certainly Phoenix, I trust you with my niece. She is well able to take care of herself as you have experienced first-hand.'

Phoenix laughed remembering how he had been unseated by Isabel in the forest near Sherbrooke when they first met.

'That I have,' he said 'and I wouldn't be fool enough to make that mistake again.'

'Then I accept,' she said.

Later that afternoon Isabel and Phoenix rode across the rolling green hills of Griswold, her raven hair billowing out behind her as she galloped ahead. Even on an afternoon ride she was competitive and full of energy. She was like a wild horse fighting against containment, a free spirit who wanted to enjoy every moment and experience. That's what was so attractive about her. She was unlike any of the women he had met. There had been numerous maidens brought to court to meet him. His father had wanted him to have an opportunity to meet someone who would complement him. The truth was that he found all the women so dull and boring. Yes, they could all do beautiful needlepoint and sing or play an instrument; they were all refined and educated, but he wanted someone he could laugh with, someone with a streak of mystery and energy and none of the maidens at court had that. He did not think he would ever meet such a woman, that is, until he found himself on his back staring up into grey eyes, an arrow pointed at his face. Isabel was certainly unique. He kicked his horse harder urging the stallion to catch up to her as she raced away.

They stopped at a stream and watered their horses. Isabel kicked off her boots and lifted her skirts as she paddled in the icy water. Her child-like enthusiasm was contagious. She let out a squeal when he splashed her and the game was on. They splashed one another, each squealing and growling in turn.

'Do you give up?' he asked out of breath.

She lifted her soggy skirts in response and ran headlong at the unsuspecting Phoenix, knocking him backwards onto the grassy bank as she landed on top of him. She quickly straddled him pinning him down with her legs, a victorious smile curling the corners of her mouth. He could not help but notice the creamy skin of her revealed thighs as she pinned him down.

'Now what do you have to say for yourself?' she panted. 'This is the second time I have caught you off-guard.'

'I am ashamed, I must admit,'– he played along letting her think she had won. He relaxed ever so slightly and in that split moment she thought he had surrendered. She let her guard down and that was her downfall. The moment he felt her attention waiver he flipped her over onto her back pinning her down in the soft grass with his strong body.

'Now who has lost focus?' he smiled at her frustrated expression. 'The teacher becomes the student now,' he mocked and laughed at her furious face.

'Let me go.' she warned through clenched teeth.

'I think not, there should be some punishment for attacking the Lord of Griswold don't you think?'

'What do you mean?' she asked 'You can't punish me.'

'I think I can and I will have justice,' he smiled. Before she could retort he kissed her squarely on the mouth. She struggled as he held her squirming body.

No! His mind screamed at his body. He did not want her this way – he wanted her willingly and he felt ashamed of what he had done. He pulled away realizing their game had gone too far.

'I'm sorry Isabel,' he muttered releasing her. 'I shouldn't have done that.'

He shifted his weight so as to move away but she surprised him, pulling him back toward her kissing him sweetly on the mouth, passionate yet innocent at the same time.

His heart sang. *She did want him as much as he wanted her.*

'What now?' she asked as they pulled apart, each breathless and flushed.

'I wasn't punishing you when I kissed you,' he said. 'I have wanted to do that from the first infuriating moment I met you Isabel Williams. I know we have not known each other long but I also know that I don't need many moons to work out how I feel about you. I'm in love with you.'

She stared at him, her grey eyes dark with emotion. He had not expected to see her so vulnerable, so honest. He always believed her to be a woman in control of her feelings, but her eyes filled with tears at his declaration.

'Don't cry,' he whispered kissing her cheeks.

'I'm sorry,' she half laughed through her tears. 'I'm just so happy. I love you too,' she added as he kissed her again.

⌘

'I love her mother and I intend to make her my wife if Drew and Aislinn give me their blessing.'

He had known his mother would have reservations. He had sensed her dislike for Isabel from the moment she had first come to Griswold and he did not understand it. She had done nothing to make Gwendolyn loathe her so intensely. He was not going to back down – he loved her and he would have her as his wife – it was not his mother's decision.

'Phoenix, you cannot be serious. She is wild and uncouth. Your father would not approve and you know it. There is something you need to know. Before he died your father arranged a marriage between you and the daughter of the Lord of Ebondeen. He was going to introduce the two of you at the Summer Ball. It is all signed and sealed – if you go back on your father's wishes and word, you will not only ruin his integrity but also possibly cause war between our two kingdoms.'

'I don't believe you Mother. Father would never have arranged a marriage without consulting me first.'

'But he did. I have the papers to prove it. I will have them retrieved from the archives and brought to you. Until then, I at least ask you not to pursue this relationship with Isabel Williams or you will both get hurt by it.'

'Get me those papers,' he said angrily striding out of his mother's parlour.

CHAPTER 8

DECEIT

EBONDEEN

LORD Conall Macphaid had ruled Ebondeen for the last thirty-five years. He was wed in his early forties and only began fathering at the age of forty-six. Now he was nearly seventy and the old man had only one daughter. His wife had died during childbirth and Catriona was all he had. She looked so like her mother that sometimes Conall found it almost too hard to bear. Her honey gold hair hung down her back in silky waves and she had a smattering of freckles across her nose. She hated them but they actually added to her beauty. Green eyes and high cheekbones completed a very pretty picture.

Conall had a good relationship with the Lord of their neighbouring kingdom, Griswold. He and Legion had worked together to keep the Northmen at bay. He had been saddened to hear of Legion's untimely death. Still, he liked the young son who had taken over his father's rule. Phoenix was a well-rounded young man.

His musings were ended by a messenger at his door.

'Master, there is someone here wishing to speak with you. She says she is from Griswold.'

His curiosity was piqued. *A woman from Griswold – who could it be?*

'Send her in.'

He was surprised to see Gwendolyn when she pushed back the hood of her cloak. He had only ever seen her once when he visited Griswold to discuss matters with Legion. They had been standing in the gardens when he looked up and saw her watching them from the window. As soon as his eyes connected with hers she moved away, but not before Legion had noticed.

'Who is she?' he had asked.

'That is my wife Gwendolyn. She is a recluse as you know.' He could hear the sadness and loss in Legion's voice.

Conall knew what it was like to lose a wife but it must be hard losing a wife who was still alive and living in the castle walls. His heart had gone out to Legion.

'Lady Gwendolyn,' he said bowing his head respectfully.

'Lord Macphaid,' she returned the courtesy.

'What can I do for you?'

'I am here to see about fulfilling my dead husband's final request. Legion wished to talk to you about this matter but unfortunately his accident prevented him ever getting here.'

She pulled out a document and proceeded to hand it to him. It was a marriage agreement. He perused it carefully his brows rising as he read the document. It appeared that Legion wanted Phoenix to marry his daughter Catriona. He had all the terms drawn up and the paperwork was even signed by him at the bottom of the document.

'Well,' said Gwendolyn after a time. 'What do you think?'

'This comes as a surprise,' Conall responded. 'I had no idea Legion wanted to unite our kingdoms. How can I be sure that this is not a ruse to seize our kingdom? I want to know that whoever marries my daughter will treat her as an equal when it comes to ruling Ebondeen. This is her inheritance after all.'

'I understand your concern Lord Macphaid, but Legion was a man who thought about the future. He believed that we should not isolate ourselves but should strengthen ourselves in alliances. The Northmen will come one day and we need one another to protect our people. This marriage agreement promises our support and army in the event of an attack on Ebondeen. This will benefit both our kingdoms.'

Conall Macphaid was torn in two. He would have trusted Legion had the man been standing before him as he knew him as a man of honour, but this woman he did not know. What were her intentions really? On the other hand she was right. Every summer they prepared themselves for the arrival of the Northmen and so far they had been fortunate to escape their raiding. One day they would not be so lucky. He was not getting any younger either and Catriona would need someone to take care of her when he was gone. He thought of Phoenix and what an outstanding young man he had become. The truth was that he could not wish for a better young man to wed his only daughter. Catriona would not be averse to the idea either. She had talked non-stop about Phoenix when she had seen him with his father at a county fair they had all attended many years ago She had begged her father for an introduction but at just seventeen he had laughed it off as a teenage crush.

'I agree,' he said to Gwendolyn picking up the quill and dipping it in the ink to add his signature to the agreement. 'They will make a dashing couple and I trust Legion's judgement. If your son is anything like him, my daughter will have made a good match.'

'You have made me very happy being able to fulfil one of his final wishes,' Gwen gushed.

'Let's drink to our families becoming one,' he said pouring a rich red wine into two goblets.

'To our ongoing union,' she toasted as they clinked their goblets.

She breathed a sigh of relief. She had set her plan in motion – played all of them to get her way. She would do anything to keep Phoenix from marrying into the Williams family. She thought about what would happen if he found out that she had forged the document. Legion had no such plan to wed him to Catriona – he believed Phoenix should choose his own wife and marry for love – a vast difference to the beginning of their own union. That was why he was adamant the young man should love the woman he chose to spend his life with. She had enlisted the help of an old wizard who had worked with her father in Griswold to recreate Legion's signature by the use of magic. Then she had added his seal and dated the document to before his death. All she had to do was convince Conall that it was his last wish. Now she had his signature on the document she could present it to Phoenix as if the document always existed. He loved his father so much she knew he would be torn in two as to what to do. She would convince him to make his father proud and marry Catriona. Heaven forbid he ever find out what she'd done as he'd never forgive her and their relationship would never recover.

.

Chapter 9

Sons

Kaldakinn

SIOBHAN stood on the wooden dock watching as eight ships sailed for the south. The men sang and chanted as they rowed the boats out of the fjord toward the open sea. The women and children waved and silently prayed to the gods that this would not be the last time they saw their husbands. Summer raiding had begun and it would take them over a moon to get to the south. The women did not expect to see the men till autumn when they would hopefully return laden with treasures and supplies. In the meantime they would harvest their summer crops and care for the land together with the older men. They also had to prepare against attack from other northern clans looking for a vulnerable target. Thorfinn always planned well – he took strong fighting men with him when he raided but he also made sure to leave someone he trusted behind to protect the village. Leif Gunnarson was one of his closest friends and a strong warrior. He and some other men would ensure that Kaldakinn was safe while they raided. It gave the women peace of mind knowing they would be safe.

Siobhan turned away as the last ship sailed out of sight. She was not only anxious for Thorfinn but also her eldest son who was going on his first southern raid. She was more afraid for him than Thorfinn even though he had seen battle for many years. He had raided local villages with his father before but this was something completely new for them both. She felt uneasy. She knew he was fearless and strong, like his father, but a mother never stops worrying for her children.

Erik was twenty-seven years old and fiercely independent. He had been that way ever since he was born. He was a contradiction – fierce in battle and courageous too, but what was different about him was his deep sense of justice and his care for others. That was an unusual trait for a Northman – most were raised to be ruthless and survive the elements at all cost. Siobhan supposed Erik was unique because she had not been born and bred in the north and she had taught him to care about others and to think before he acted and spoke. As a result he had the best attributes of both his parents. Many young girls in the village had tried to woo him but he had not been swayed by their manipulations. He was determined to find his true love – of course the other young men mocked him and called him 'evnukk' which meant eunuch. Sexuality was important to the men of the north. One's strength and manliness was determined by one's sexual prowess and so virility was highly praised. Erik just smiled when they taunted him, just as he knew the women had a wager going as to who would be the first to seduce him. He was secure in himself to not let it affect him.

He was tall, over six feet, which he got from his father's side of the family and he was well-built as a result of years of cutting wood, helping to build ships and farming. His hair was not as fair as most of the other Northmen yet he was still blonde with hair down to his shoulders. He pulled it back in a plait and shaved the sides and back of his head as was the custom. He had a beard but preferred to keep it short and neat rather than long like the older men of the tribe. The most striking feature of his face were his eyes which were ice blue like many of the other Northmen – it was the one thing they did have in common. He had deep dimples when he smiled that made his face extremely attractive. Most of the men of Kaldakinn had tattoos on their arms and torsos and Erik was no exception, however he had chosen to only tattoo his right shoulder with elements of nature that he loved.

He sat on the ship gazing out at the open sea. The fjords were behind them now and the sails had been set to catch the gusty wind and set them on a course for the south. He hoped the gods would favour their journey by giving them good winds and calm seas. There was a sense of expectation and excitement among the men – they were finally going to see the south.

'What are you thinking?' Thorfinn asked as he sat down on the wooden deck beside his son.

'What an opportunity it is to see more of where mother has come from,' he replied.

'I too am looking forward to seeing new things. I have waited years for this day. My father would not risk leaving our lands to travel south but I cannot live that way anymore. It is about more than just raiding, Erik. I know the men are looking forward to the plunder, but for me it is more about discovering how others live and what we can learn from them. Knowledge is far more powerful than wealth. Without knowledge and wisdom one can only ever achieve so much.'

'Thank you father, for bringing me on this journey.'

'Learn as much as you can Erik, for one day you will be Earl of Kaldakinn.'

⌘

GRISWOLD

Another son was in conversation with his parent but it was not as amicable.

'I don't want to marry a complete stranger Mother.'

'Phoenix, I have provided you with the documents your father had drawn up as you requested. The least you could do is consider his last wishes. He knew what would be good for you and the future of Griswold. An alliance between Griswold and Ebondeen would protect our people from the Northmen and as Lord it is your responsibility to think of your people first and foremost. You don't have the luxury of making an enemy with our neighbour. Lord Macphaid is expecting you to honour the agreement he made with your father. You will humiliate Catriona if you refuse to wed her.'

'What about how I feel mother. Does that not count? I don't love her. I love Isabel.'

'Love is a luxury for dreamers Phoenix. You cannot have your head in the clouds – you are a ruler, now act like one. Your father gave up love to marry me because he knew it was the right choice for Griswold.'

It was a gross exaggeration of the truth but she would use any argument to sway him.

'What do you mean Mother? Father loved you even though you shut us both out.'

He was angry with her for insinuating his father did not care for her when he gave up everything for her. His words stung her.

'It's true – he learned to love me Phoenix, but he did not marry me out of love. He gave up his true love to marry me.'

'Who was she mother?'

'He was in love with Aislinn Williams.'

Phoenix looked shocked. He had never heard his father speak of Aislinn as though he cared for her. The only reference he made to her was in telling him how she and Drew had saved his life when he was born. Things were beginning to make sense.

No wonder Mother doesn't like Isabel. It's because of her mother.

'Why didn't he marry her?' he asked.

'In those days your father was at odds with the Great One and Aislinn would have weakened him,' she lied. 'He married me to gain the power of my father who was a formidable wizard in his time and to protect Griswold from the Great One's wrath. He did what was necessary to protect his kingdom and his people. Now it is your turn to put your feelings aside and do what is best for Griswold. Marry Catriona and secure your rulership.'

'I will agree to keeping the documents in place for now mother and to meeting Catriona, but I will not be rushed into a wedding.'

'I understand,' she said smiling slyly, 'but you do know that even in the arrangement of this marriage the terms of alliance still stand and we are to fulfil the terms set out in the documents as will Conall Macphaid should we need him.'

'I understand Mother,' he said resigned. He had no intention of marrying Catriona but would not tell his mother that right now. He needed time to think.

'I will organize the Summer Ball – what better time to introduce you to your future wife.'

CHAPTER 10

OBSTACLES

LIONSGATE

THE GREAT ONE shook his head in disbelief. He was watching Gwendolyn in his Mirror of Time and her deviousness and deception was disturbing. Her bitterness toward Aislinn had soured her and made her into an ugly person. She was determined to make her son pay for her pain. He had seen this too many times in people's lives. Revenge only brought more pain – it never brought closure and one had to sell one's soul to see it through. Once a person crossed that line they could never go back. When a vengeful act is committed, whether through word or deed, it can never be undone. Gwendolyn was selling her soul right now and she didn't know it. She was determined to create as many obstacles as she could to keep Phoenix and Isabel apart. It was time he paid her a visit. He owed that to Legion and to Phoenix.

⌘

SHERBROOKE

Aislinn and Drew had come to terms with Isabel's absence. The cottage was so quiet without her and even with two teenage boys in the home it seemed like some extra force of life and energy was missing. The only thing they did not miss was the local farmers complaining that she had ambushed them in the forest on the way to market. They had had word from both Isabel and Struan that things were going well at Griswold and their help was being well received. Aislinn sensed that Isabel was losing her heart to Phoenix by the way she glowingly spoke about him in her letters. The indifferent front she put on was gone and a softness and tenderness was coming through. Aislinn hoped that her heart would not be broken and that she would find the kind of love she and Drew had together. Still, their own romance had not been plain sailing and they had worked through many challenges and obstacles to be together. If true love was there then nothing would stand in its way.

Aislinn finished the letter she had written to her beautiful daughter. She rolled it up and tied a ribbon around it ready to be sent. Phoenix had been true to his word – he had made a Monwing available for them to send messages to and from Griswold and that had given them peace of mind.

'Can I come in?' a familiar deep voice asked.

'Regent,' Aislinn shrieked delighted to see him. It had been a while since he had come to Sherbrooke and it was so good to see her dark-skinned friend.

He wrapped her in a bear hug and swung her off her feet.

'You're crushing me,' she laughed as he set her on her feet. 'What brings you here?'

'I am on my way back to Lionsgate. We've just been to Cragshelm to help families who were affected by the flooding.'

Cragshelm was the neighbouring kingdom to Sherbrooke and Aislinn was familiar with the terrain as she and Drew had been called there on the odd occasion when their local doctor was unavailable. She was saddened to hear that they had been affected by flooding. She knew how devastating it was to lose one's home. She remembered how she felt as a young girl when her home was burned to the ground and she lost everything. The feeling of hopelessness and despair could be overwhelming.

'How is Isabel doing?' Regent asked.

He knew that Aislinn and Drew were concerned about her safety after the Great One warned them about Gwen's mental state.

'Everything seems to be going well and Phoenix has kept his word about looking out for her. She is in her element,'Aislinn laughed.

'That's good to hear. Do you know how much longer she and Struan will be there?'

'No we have no idea, but if I'm reading between the lines correctly I would say that Isabel has lost her heart to more than Griswold castle. It is a concern to us both as we worry about her safety. Don't get me wrong, we have no concerns about Phoenix – he is a wonderful young man but maybe it's time we told them the full story.'

'Perhaps that wouldn't be such a bad idea,' Regent said.

⌘

GRISWOLD

Isabel was furious. She looked at Phoenix and stood, hands on hips, eyes flashing and shook her head.

'You can't be serious,' she shouted at him. He looked apologetically at her and tried to diffuse her fury.

'Isabel, calm down,' he pleaded. 'I had no idea my father had arranged this marriage, I assure you.'

'It's the fact that you even allowed your mother to believe that you are considering it that has made me so angry Phoenix. Why didn't you stand up to her?'

'You don't understand – we don't have much of a relationship. It is not about standing up to my mother but more about respecting my father's wishes that I have not refused my mother. I love you Isabel and I have no intention of marrying Catriona, but this involves politics and I could start a war with the Lord of Ebondeen over this. I need to diffuse the situation carefully. Give me time and I will work this out – I promise you.'

He drew her into his arms and he could feel the stiffness in her body. She was not going to make this easy for him but he refused to let her go. He nuzzled her neck and could feel her resolve begin to weaken.

'I love you - don't ever doubt that,' he whispered.

'What are we going to do?' She sounded sad and forlorn – so very unlike the feisty young woman she was. He realized she was afraid that they would lose one another.

'We will find a way through this sweetheart – love will triumph and we will be together.'

He kissed her, tenderly at first, then with increasing urgency and passion. They were meant to be together – she was the one he was destined to spend his life with. Nothing would stop them. He would do everything he could to make sure it happened.

⌘

Gwendolyn felt smug – she had convinced Phoenix that Legion had planned this marriage and now preparations for the Summer Ball were well under way. The sooner Phoenix met Catriona the better. She could not have him getting more and more attached to Isabel. His devotion to his father would be her trump card but she would have to move quickly while his emotion and grief were still raw.

She made lists for the kitchen servants and wrote out invitations to the ball. Soon all would be set in motion. Phoenix may resent her now but he would thank her in the future when Griswold's future was secured by an alliance with Ebondeen. This would bring them together in the end – she was certain of it. He just needed to see that she had his best interest at heart. She smiled, it would all work out.

CHAPTER 11

ANTICIPATION

THE NORTHMEN had been at sea for four weeks. The elements had been good to them and they were making good progress. Just a few more days and they would hopefully land on the shores of the southern tribes. They did not know what to expect but already the temperatures were warmer as they headed south. Thorfinn had high expectations for the raids ahead. Their supplies were beginning to dwindle and they would need good winds to get them to the southern lands.

'Great Odin, we ask you for good winds to speed our journey,' he muttered up to the heavens.

He looked at his son, proud of the strong young man who arm wrestled one of the other young warriors. Erik would make a wonderful Earl one day. For now he would teach him as much as he could and they would take the world together.

⌘

Catriona could not contain her excitement. Her father had told her of the arrangement put in place for her to wed Phoenix. She recalled how attractive he was when she had seen him at the county fair years before. Now that he was a more mature young man she was certain he would be even more handsome than she remembered. She was looking forward to the Summer Ball where she would be introduced to him. Their invitation had arrived from Griswold castle and in a few days she would come face to face with the man she would wed. She got butterflies in her stomach just thinking of it. She opened her wardrobe and looked at the myriad of dresses.

Which one should I wear?

She had to look her best, to find something that would make her eyes sparkle. She wanted him to be captivated by her as she was when she first laid eyes on him.

⌘

Isabel felt nauseous. She held the Summer Ball invitation in her shaky hands. It was addressed to her and Struan. She read the words again and her heart ached. Gwen had made sure that the invitations clearly spelled out the reason for the upcoming ball.

Isabel Williams and Struan Hamilton

You are cordially invited to attend the Summer Ball held in the Ballroom at Griswold Castle on the eve of the fifteenth day of the mid- summer month. It is my pleasure to host this event in celebration of the upcoming intended marriage of my son Phoenix to Catriona, daughter of Lord Macphaid of Ebondeen.

Dress will be formal

Lady Gwendolyn

Isabel had sensed from the very first day that she met Gwendolyn that Gwen did not like her for some reason. She did not understand it as she had done nothing to antagonise the woman. Perhaps she did not like her because she was a threat to Phoenix's alignment with Ebondeen. Phoenix had promised her that he would find a solution and she dearly wanted to believe him, but this invitation was a slap in the face. She did not wish to attend the ball. How could she watch him pretending to be with another woman? They would have to dance together and Catriona would be on his arm all evening – she could not bear to go through the charade. She ripped up the invitation in anger, scattering the many fragments all over her room. Then she flopped down on her bed and yelled into her pillow as she punched it with her fists, sending down feathers fluttering into the air.

⌘

Phoenix was angry. *Damn his mother.* She had sent out invitations that obviously put him in a predicament. Everyone who received an invitation would know the ball was a celebration for his future nuptials to Catriona. She had manipulated him and his resentment grew. He knew that Isabel would have received one and that she would be devastated by it. She would not get the better of them – they would be together. He would play her little game at the Summer Ball but that would be the last time. He had a plan but not one that could be implemented a week before the ball. In the meantime he had to talk to Isabel and reassure her of his love.

⌘

SHERBROOKE

Aislinn kicked her horse in its side urging the beast on. She was tired as she had just attended a difficult birth. She had been called out during the night and it had taken many hours for the baby to make its entrance into the world. Now all she wanted was to get home, have a strong cup of tea and close her eyes. She was surprised to see two horses tethered outside the cottage. Drew would be at the practice and the boys would be at school. She dismounted and entered the white-washed cottage dripping with honeysuckle.

'Mama,' a voice greeted her.

'Isabel, what are you doing here?' she exclaimed in delight. She hugged her daughter and realized just how much she had missed her. It took just a few moments for Aislinn to become aware that her daughter was sobbing into her unruly hair.

'What's the matter darling?' she asked perplexed at her daughter's distress.

'I couldn't stay there any longer Mama. Gwen has arranged for Phoenix to marry the daughter of the Lord of Ebondeen and she hates me – I just don't know why. Phoenix has promised me that he loves me but he doesn't know how to go back on an arranged marriage without causing a war between Griswold and Ebondeen. It was best I leave and come home. I made it easier for him because I love him – I know he has to put Griswold first, but it hurts so much, Mama. How will I ever get over him?'

For the first time Aislinn noticed Struan in the corner of the room. He nodded at his sister and she gave him a grateful nod. He had brought her safely home.

'I'm so sorry Isabel, I truly am,' she said holding her daughter as she cried. 'Nothing I say will take away the pain, but time is a great healer of all things. Just take it one day at a time.'

⌘

Gwendolyn was delighted. She had hoped her invitation would upset Isabel so much that the young girl would leave. Her plan had worked. The young girl had packed her bags and she and her uncle had fled the castle immediately. Phoenix had been furious with her and refused to speak to her, but she knew that he would come around eventually. Catriona was a beautiful young woman and any man would be attracted to her. He would soon forget that young woman who had bewitched him. The Williams women were a nuisance when it came to casting spells on men that did not belong to them. Phoenix wanted to rush off after her but with the ball just days away he was unable to without offending Lord Macphaid and possibly causing a war.

Now it was time for the two young people to meet at the Ball that evening. The castle was abuzz with activity for the summer event. She smiled – it was all coming together so nicely. What Gwen did not know as she played matchmaker and hosted a ball was that eight ships sailed into the river mouth between the kingdoms of Ebondeen and Griswold.

CHAPTER 12

HONOUR

THE SUMMER BALL was a great success, at least in the eyes of Gwendolyn, Catriona and Lord Macphaid. Phoenix played the game, being chivalrous and polite to the young woman who fawned over him in a sickly sweet manner. She was beautiful in her apricot ball gown that shimmered and billowed as she moved - there was no denying that, but despite her beauty Phoenix had only one face in his mind when he danced with her. His heart ached for Isabel and he wondered how hurt and angry she must feel, especially since he had let her go and had not followed. He would rectify that as soon as he woke up in the morning. He made polite conversation to Lord Macphaid and acted the dutiful host. Finally he managed to pry himself away from Catriona when a young man asked her to dance.

'Are you all right?' Balfour asked sensing the strain his friend was under.

'I'm playing the game if that is what you mean,' Phoenix replied. 'I miss her.'

'Well as your advisor I feel it is my duty to remind you that you are the Lord of Griswold, not your mother. You should decide what is best for you and your people. I managed to do some digging regarding this arranged marriage. I knew your father almost as well as you did and I have never believed he would do this without consulting you first.'

'What did you find?'

'With a little monetary incentive I discovered that your mother had the document drawn up. She paid a wizard to replicate your father's signature. I don't know how she managed to get Lord Macphaid to believe it was Legion's dying wish but I have confirmation from a scribe at Ebondeen that she only brought the document to their castle a few weeks ago. That document was not signed and sealed before your father died.'

Phoenix felt sick.

How could she be so devious?

She had manipulated them all and his loathing for her was fuelled by Balfour's information. He would not forget her treachery.

'Thank you my friend – I will deal with this.'

'I told you I would always have your back. You are a brother to me Phoenix.'

The rest of the evening passed in a blur. Phoenix could not wait for the pretence to be over. He could barely look at his mother, such was his disgust. He was relieved when he could finally retire to his chamber, where he packed his saddlebag ready to leave at first light.

⌘

The Northmen made camp on the banks of the river while they strategized their raids. They had scouted the two kingdoms and decided that Ebondeen was less fortified and easier to breach than Griswold. It would not be long before their presence would be discovered, but as they were a fearless people intimidation was part of their tactics in scaring their enemies. – they wanted the inhabitants of Ebondeen to feel afraid as their attacks would then be easier. They had heard the many stories of southern tribes giving Northern clans many gifts and jewels just to be rid of them. They hoped their presence would frighten the Lord of Ebondeen into a similar circumstance. If they didn't have to fight to get their plunder it would be a huge advantage and many lives would be saved. The men were delighted to be ashore and they managed to kill a boar which they roasted over the red hot coals. They looked forward to fresh meat after weeks at sea.

⌘

SHERBROOKE

Isabel had been home a few days and each day she hoped her heart would feel a bit better – it did not happen. She found herself weeping at odd moments and she felt a sadness that threatened to engulf her. Her parents were worried about her, so much so that they even tried to encourage her to go into the forest to practice her archery skills.

'I never thought we would be giving her permission to go and ambush farmers,' Drew said, 'but what else can we do – she needs something to take her mind off him.'

'I'm worried too,' Aislinn said. 'It is not like her to be so sad.'

Isabel had no desire to go into the forest. Once she had loved the adventure of it but now it just reminded her of how she met Phoenix and it hurt too much. In desperation Aislinn and Drew sent her to the village with Maggie to buy supplies for Heart and Home. She had grumbled that she did not want to go but they had told her it was essential for her to keep busy and get out and about so she had begrudgingly gone with the older woman.

Aislinn was surprised to see Phoenix dismounting his horse when she went out to hang the washing.

'Phoenix, what brings you here?'

Was that disapproval in her voice he wondered?

'I am here to see Isabel, Mrs Williams.'

'Please, call me Aislinn. I don't know if that is a good idea. She is pretty heart broken by your upcoming marriage and we don't want to see her any more hurt than she already is. She needs time and space to get over you. Seeing you will just open those wounds again.'

'I understand how you feel but she needs to know that I have no intention of marrying Catriona. I love her and I want to be with her.'

'From what she says it sounds as though there is more at stake than just a marriage. Breaking the agreement could cause war between Griswold and Ebondeen. She doesn't want to put you in that position or endanger your life.'

'That would be true if the agreement were legitimate but it has come to my attention that my mother forged those documents and I intend to prove it. I have no intention of marrying Catriona. Please, I need to see her. I love her more than anything – she needs to know that.'

She could hear the desperation in his voice and it reminded her of Drew twenty-four years previously when he had begged her to give him another chance. She had listened to her heart then and it had given her the best years of her life. Phoenix reminded her of the man who had fought for her all those years ago. She was not surprised that Gwen had deceived her son. It gave her the answer she had been looking for – clearly Gwen still harboured a grudge over Daemon's death. She felt a stab of guilt that her mistake was haunting their children and that they would pay for it. Well she would not let her win this round.

'Then you had better come in,' she relented, waving him in and offering him a cup of tea while they waited for Isabel to return from Sherbrooke.

⌘

Isabel was shocked to see Phoenix sitting at the dining table with her mother when she returned from Sherbrooke with Maggie. She paled, unsure what to say or do. Eventually she spun on her heel and ran out. Phoenix looked at Aislinn forlorn and she waved him out after her.

'What are you waiting for? Go and tell her,' she urged. He did not need to be prompted twice.

He found her pacing up and down near the barn muttering to herself.

'Isabel,' he said softly. 'Can I talk to you please?'

'There's nothing you can say that will change my mind Phoenix. You have a responsibility as Lord of Griswold and you must do what your father thought best. You will have added strength when you have an alliance with Ebondeen. You know as well as I do that the Northmen will be coming soon – after all that is why you had me and Struan come to Griswold in the first place.'

'Would you just stop chattering and listen to me for one minute,' he growled, frustrated with her ramblings. 'I did not bring you to Griswold to strengthen my army, although you and Struan did a superb job. I asked you to stay because I love you and could not bear the thought of ever losing you Belle.' It was the first time he had called her that and her heart lurched at the term of endearment.

'Yes, but that was before things changed. You don't have the luxury of following your heart. You have to rule with your head Phoenix.'

'What happened to the free, adventurous Isabel – the girl who knocked me off my horse and challenged me in Sherbrooke Forest? You sound just like my mother now Isabel.' He shook his head at her logic.

Surely she could not really believe that!

'The marriage agreement is not valid,' he blurted out, 'but even if it was Belle, I would never marry Catriona because I am in love with you.'

'What do you mean it is not valid?'

He explained his mother's treachery to her and she looked shocked by his revelations.

'Why does she hate me so much Phoenix?'

'I don't know. but she did tell me that my father was once in love with your mother. Perhaps that has something to do with it. I don't care what my mother thinks Isabel, I want to be with you and she will not keep us apart. I love you.'

They spent the next few days talking about their future and how he would find evidence of the forged documents. Isabel had a spring in her step again and her old enthusiasm for life returned. Drew and Aislinn were relieved their old daughter was back.

⌘

Gwendolyn was annoyed that Phoenix had left the castle. She had no idea where he had gone and Balfour would not divulge any information other than to say that he had business to attend to in some of the villages. She had wanted to talk to him about his marriage to Catriona – to strike while the iron was hot but now she would have to wait. Lord Macphaid and Catriona had departed for Ebondeen the day after the ball and Catriona had been bitterly disappointed to discover that Phoenix had already left the castle.

'Duty calls my dear,' her father had made light of his absence but Gwen was seething at her son's inhospitable behaviour.

Now she paced up and down in her chamber wondering where he was. It had been almost a week since he had left abruptly and she had had no word from him.

'Enter,' she called when someone knocked at her door.

A messenger stood in the entrance. He was not anyone she recognized and she waved him in – maybe Phoenix had sent her word after all.

'What can I do for you?' she asked the flustered young man.

'I am seeking Lord Phoenix,' he said.

So it was not a message from him.

'My son is away at the moment, but you can pass the message on to me.'

The messenger handed over the scroll and she opened the document. The seal of Lord Macphaid did not escape her attention. She read it quickly and paled at what she read.

'How long ago did the Northmen arrive?' she asked.

'They have been camped along the river for eight days and each day they make their presence a little more obvious. Lord Macphaid believes it won't be long before they attempt to attack the castle at Ebondeen. Already they have raided some of the local villages and plundered the people. We need your armed forces to help us or Ebondeen is doomed.'

Gwendolyn realized that her marriage agreement had pledged their soldiers to supporting Ebondeen in a time of crisis. She had never expected it to be so soon. She had no idea how Phoenix would feel about this – he had hardly had time to come to terms with the arranged marriage never mind going to war with the Northmen on Ebondeen's behalf.

'Get me Balfour,' she instructed the servant who had ushered the messenger in. He scuttled off to find the Master's advisor.

This was not good news.

Where was Phoenix when he was needed?

She pondered on what to do. They had no choice but to send men to Ebondeen to give aid. If the Northmen attacked them then Griswold would be next. They would need Lord Macphaid's support when the time came. For the first time Gwendolyn felt glad that Isabel and Struan had spent months training their soldiers. At least their men would be prepared.

Balfour strode into the room looking annoyed at being summoned by Gwendolyn.

'What is it that you want Lady Gwendolyn?' he asked, his animosity not lost on her.

'We have a problem and I need you to get a message to Phoenix,' she barked at him. She quickly filled him in on what was happening. He looked grim.

'I will send word immediately,' he said striding out the door.

CHAPTER 13

DECISIONS

BALFOUR rode as hard as he could. He knew where Phoenix was, but he had no intention of telling Gwendolyn that he had gone to Sherbrooke to pursue Isabel. His horse snorted and strained under his weight as he urged the animal on. They could possibly be on the brink of a bloody war. Gwendolyn had put them in an awkward position with her forged marriage agreement. She was putting all their lives at risk. He cursed her actions, his words lost on the wind as he rode like the devil.

His journey took two days and he was weary as he had not taken much of a break other than to water and feed his horse. His relief was tangible when he finally headed into Sherbrooke, almost dismounting before his horse had come to a standstill. He rushed into the Inn and asked where the doctor's rooms were. The inn-keeper assumed he had a medical emergency and directed him immediately to Drew's practice.

Drew was surprised to see the young man, so hurried and obviously agitated. He realized that something was horribly wrong and this was confirmed as he listened to his story. He closed up the practice, mounted his horse and headed home with Balfour hot on his heels.

Phoenix was alarmed to see Balfour. The young men embraced and then Balfour told Phoenix the news of the Northmen's arrival on the river banks of Ebondeen. It was not what Phoenix wanted to hear.

⌘

Lord Macphaid was becoming more and more anxious each day the Northmen settled in Ebondeen. His villagers were becoming more and more afraid and many had lost their homes as well as livestock. Fortunately there had not been too many lives lost as yet but Conall knew it was just a matter of time before these savages raided the castle and many would die. He wished that Phoenix would arrive with reinforcements – time was running short. They could hear the Northmen who chanted war cries daily in the distance. Conall's spies had reported that they were scouting out the castle daily looking for weaknesses to breach the walls. People were becoming fearful of these warriors who seemed to lack fear. If Phoenix did not arrive soon they would be forced to negotiate with these savages. He did not want that to happen. If they gave in then what would stop them returning each summer for more plunder.

No, the only solution is to fight and for all the neighbouring kingdoms to unite in ousting the Northmen. Damn it Phoenix, where are you?

⌘

'What are you going to do?' Balfour asked his master and his friend. Four pairs of other eyes reflected the same question. They were eating dinner around the table and there was a measure of anxiety and tension. Struan had come over the minute he had heard Balfour's news.

'I don't see that there is any choice really,' the young lord said. 'Conall Macphaid will be expecting me to honour this farce of an agreement as he doesn't know what my mother has done. If I don't send men then I may have a war anyway. The other concern is that if we don't eradicate the Northmen then Griswold will be attacked next and I will need Macphaid's help then. We must get back to Griswold and rally troops.'

'I'm coming with you,' Struan said, his voice determined and daring anyone to contradict his decision.

'I'm going too,' Isabel said equally determined.

'No Isabel,' Phoenix said before either Drew or Aislinn could object. 'I cannot go into battle knowing that you could be in harm's way. You will be too much of a distraction for me if you are there.'

'That's ridiculous Phoenix and you know it,' she challenged. 'I was good enough to train your men with their bows and arrows and you know firsthand how good I am, and yet you think I am not good enough to fight a real battle. What about how I feel? I can't just sit here wondering whether you are safe.' She burst into tears and stormed out the door, leaving it rattling on its rusty hinges as she slammed it.

Phoenix looked stunned at her outburst. He looked at Aislinn and Drew hoping for some suggestions.

'I think you should go after her,' Drew said. 'You need to work this out between you before you leave otherwise your head and your heart will not be in the battle and that is not good for either one of you.'

Phoenix nodded and bolted out of the door to find the woman he loved so dearly. He found her down by the stream angrily throwing pebbles into the water that bubbled as though nothing in the world had changed.

She wiped at the tears that rolled down her cheeks. He placed both hands on her shoulders and pulled her back against himself. He felt her shudder as another sob escaped her.

'I'm afraid for you,' she whispered. 'I want to be there to have your back.'

'I love you for that darling,' he whispered into her neck as he kissed her. 'I have Balfour to watch my back – he has done it all these years quite successfully. I have to know you are safe. It is more dangerous for me to worry about you in battle. Please Isabel, I need you to do this for me. I love you.'

'I love you too,' she sobbed. 'It kills me to let you go alone but I will do as you ask. Just promise me you will be safe and that you will come back to me?'

'Nothing will stop me getting back to you, I promise.' He kissed her as though he would never let her go and she drew every breath and ounce of him into herself.

⌘

Balfour and Struan had left not long after to rally the troops at Griswold. They aimed to be at Ebondeen within a few days. They hoped they would not be too late. Phoenix had agreed to meet them at the border of Ebondeen and Griswold in Neverend Forest. They would use the cover of the forest to scout out the whereabouts of the Northmen before planning their attack. Phoenix hoped to send a message to Conall outlying their plans via one of his Monwings. No Northman would be able to intercept the flying creature whereas any messenger on horseback would be ambushed and killed. In the meantime Phoenix had a few things to attend to before he went into battle. He wanted every moment he could spend with Isabel before he left.

⌘

Gwendolyn fretted and raged – she had no idea where everyone was. Balfour had not yet returned and a messenger from Conall had sent a threatening message issuing an ultimatum that they honour the marriage agreement by sending reinforcements. She felt afraid for the first time in a long time. If only Daemon were here – he would know what to do and say to encourage her. The men in her life had let her down – Legion and Phoenix – they had both chosen Aislinn Williams over her and she resented them both for it. Now when she needed them most, neither of them were there for her.

CHAPTER 14

HEART AND SOUL

SHERBROOKE

'DO YOU Isabel take Phoenix to be your husband, to love him and honour him all the days of your lives?'

'I do.'

'Do you Phoenix take Isabel to be your wife, to love and cherish her as long as you both shall live?'

'I do.'

Mac smiled at the young couple standing before him. She wore the beautiful wedding gown the Great One had made for her mother and it fitted her like a glove. Mac was delighted to have the privilege of marrying his grand-daughter. When he had married Aislinn he had no idea he was marrying her to an imposter. He hoped this union would have a happier beginning. Isabel stood beside Phoenix her hair falling in raven cascades down her back and ivy entwined into a wreath upon her head. They had not had much time to organize the wedding. It had been as much a surprise to Isabel as it had to Aislinn and Drew.

'I want to marry her before I go and fight in Ebondeen. I want to know that she and I have a future,' Phoenix had said to Drew when he had asked for Isabel's hand in marriage. 'I love her more than anything and I promise you I will take good care of her.'

Drew had been impressed with the young man's passion and devotion to his daughter. She needed someone like Phoenix who could reign her in, who would tame her impulsiveness without stifling her and yet love her wildly at the same time.

'I give you my blessing if that is what Isabel wants,' he had said.

Isabel had been delighted and then tearful when Phoenix had got down on one knee beside the river and asked her to be his wife. He had placed his father's signet ring upon her middle finger since it was too big for her ring finger and promised her he would get her a real wedding ring after he was back from Ebondeen. She shushed him with a kiss and told him that as long as he loved her as much as he did she would need nothing else. They had called for Mac to marry them immediately as Phoenix would ride out the following day to Ebondeen. Now they stood side by side as man and wife and he gently lifted her off her feet and kissed her on her full lips.

'This is the beginning of a beautiful life together,' he whispered to her.

'I love you,' she whispered back.

There was no wedding reception or celebration as Phoenix only had a few hours till he left. Isabel rode with him to the inn at Sherbrooke. They shared a simple meal and then retired to his room. She looked at him, love in her eyes, hiding her anxiety and awkwardness at being with a man for the first time. She trusted him and she knew he would not hurt her.

'I wish we could stay in this moment forever,' he said drawing her into his arms.

'Let's just enjoy every moment of tonight,' she whispered.

He gently lifted her in his arms and carried her to the bed setting her down on the edge. Then he lifted her hair and breathed in her scent.

'I don't ever want to forget how lovely you smell,' he murmured. He slowly unlaced her dress and helped her to shed the heavy folds of fabric. He admired her athletic form in her sheer undergarments.

She truly does not know how beautiful she is.

'Isabel,' he groaned. She pulled him to her and they fell back onto the bed as he kissed her tenderly at first then more urgently as their passion ignited. They both knew the time they had together was limited and they did not want to waste a minute of it together. They came together in love with desperation and fear lurking just under the surface and even the fleeting moment of pain that Isabel felt as they became one was not enough to quell the hunger and passion they felt for one another. She did not want to separate herself from him as they lay entwined– she feared if she let him go that it would all just be a sweet dream and that she would wake to find him gone. One night was all they would have for now and she dreaded saying goodbye to him in the morning. They talked and made love throughout the night until they both fell into an exhausted sleep in the early hours of the morning.

He did not want to wake her when it was time to leave. She looked so peaceful and happy. He kissed her gently on the lips and left a note on the pillow next to her.

'See you soon my love,' he whispered as he left the room.

Isabel woke a few hours later. She sat bolt upright, panic engulfing her. The bed was empty beside her.

So it was a dream.

Then she noticed his ring on her finger and saw the note on the pillow. She snatched it up and opened it, reading the words inked onto the parchment.

Thank you my beautiful Belle for making me the happiest man in the world. I love you.

She held the note to her chest and whispered, 'Come back safely to me Phoenix, please.'

She did not want the dream to end there.

CHAPTER 15

THE PLAN

GWENDOLYN was relieved to hear that Balfour was back in the castle. She rushed out to the court to find him and was surprised to find Struan with him.

'Where is my son?' She demanded without as much as a greeting.

'Phoenix is not coming back here – he is meeting us at Ebondeen. We have come to rally some troops and we will leave in a few hours.'

Gwen was bitterly disappointed. She wanted to try and right a few things with Phoenix before he went to fight a battle. Now she would not have a chance to say half the things she wanted him to know. Despite her coldness she did love her son even though she had no idea how to show it.

'Please keep him safe,' she said to Balfour. He nodded his head then disappeared to gather their forces.

'Why are you here Struan?'

'I came back with Balfour to help fight against the Northmen.'

'So Balfour came to find Phoenix in Sherbrooke? Is that where my son is?'

Struan realized too late that Gwendolyn was fishing for answers and that she would put two and two together. He cursed himself silently. He would not satisfy her curiosity.

'I need to help Balfour,' he dismissed. 'Good to see you again.'

He left before she could corner him again.

Gwen felt her anger stir afresh. She had wanted to make right with Phoenix but he had clearly betrayed her again. He had run off to Isabel the moment the Summer Ball was over. He had chosen her once again over his kingdom and his family. That family was evil. They had to be removed from their lives. She would do anything to ensure that the Williams family never came to Griswold again.

⌘

Phoenix rode hard to the border of Ebondeen. He had not wanted to leave his new bride but he had a duty as a ruler to keep the people of Griswold safe. Neutralizing the Northmen was the only way to do that. He hoped they would not be too late. Despite the fact that he was riding into what could be a gruesome battle he felt insanely happy. He thought of Isabel and the night they had spent together. He could imagine her fragrance and the feel of her soft skin against his and he smiled. He was a lucky man and he loved her more than anything in this world. He could not wait to begin his life with her at his side.

⌘

Thorfinn could sense his men getting restless. For over ten days they had camped along the river banks of Ebondeen. They had carried out some local raids amongst the villages, but now the men wanted more than poor villagers' trinkets and livestock. They wanted to breach the castle at Ebondeen and get their hands on some real wealth. He could understand their impatience – he too wanted to see some progress. For days their scouts had circled the castle looking for a way to breach the walls. It seemed an impossible task. The huge wooden gate was heavy and archers manned the walls to deter any men from scaling it. The only place they could possibly enter the castle was through a drain at the back of the castle. It was a small opening about the size of an animal hole and it was covered with a metal grill. Thorfinn and Erik had discussed this option of gaining access to Ebondeen.

'No man will fit through there,' Erik had said worried.

'You're right about that son, but it is not a man we plan to put through there.'

'What do you mean?'

'The slaves we took from the last village raid will be the ones who will help us get into the castle.'

Their last raid had not only given them livestock to live off while they raided the kingdom of Ebondeen. They had taken women and some children as captives. The women provided their meals and the men took their pleasures from them, unwilling as they were. That was the one thing Erik hated about his Northern culture. He disliked using force to get what he wanted. He did not mind war or even raiding as it was necessary for their survival, but he could not stand to see a man force himself on a woman when she had no way to protect herself. The men had once again tried to manipulate him into taking one of the young girls they had captured but he had refused them yet again.

'They won't turn against their lord father,' Erik said convinced.

'Yes they will if they have the right motivation,' his father answered. 'Any man will do what he has to do in order to survive – these women and children will be no different. You will see.'

⌘

Isabel had returned home to her parents. It felt strange to be a married woman and yet nothing had changed in her life other than the fact that she had given herself wholly to Phoenix. It had not been as frightening as she thought it might be. She had always feared the day she would first sleep with a man. She prided herself on being fiercely independent and a brave soul. She gave everyone the impression that she was strong and capable and that she feared nothing – it was not true. She feared there would be pain when she gave herself up completely but she was more afraid of showing this fear than of the actual pain itself. She did not want to be perceived as weak. It had come as a pleasant surprise to her that it was not as terrifying as she had imagined it would be. She realized that the overwhelming love and passion she felt for Phoenix had taken that fear away and that she had wanted to feel and become one with him, even to the point of their bodies meshing. It was a surprisingly spiritual event and she could not deny that she felt closer to him than she had before.

'Thank you Great One,' she murmured. 'I am eternally grateful for meeting Phoenix. Please keep him safe.'

She could hardly bear not knowing what was happening within the borders of Ebondeen. She looked down at his signet ring and kissed it tenderly.

'Take care my love.'

⌘

Phoenix was weary and his horse was beginning to falter from exhaustion. He had to stop and feed and water the poor beast. He knew that every minute he delayed could mean the end of Ebondeen, but at the same time if he did not care for his horse and his own well-being then he would never get there. He rested as long as he could before mounting up and urging his trusted ride along. He felt a little anxious at what he would find when he finally got to Neverend Forest. He had heard stories of the brutality of the Northmen. Their daring and fearlessness was the reason for their success. Phoenix had heard that they did not fear death as they believed their death was determined by their gods at the time of their birth. This made them invincible and a force to be reckoned with. Raiding the southern kingdoms was nothing new. The first Northmen had ventured across the seas and raided as Early as the eighth century and had created fear wherever they went. Their attacks had died off toward the end of the eleventh century as castles were more fortified and raiding was not as easy as it had been in the past. However, every now and again a new tribe of Northmen would take up the challenge and venture south again. For years Griswold had avoided their raids – now it was simply a matter of time before they came. He had to protect his villagers before they got there and the best way to do it was by helping Conall Macphaid. He kicked his horse harder, urging the animal to give its last ounce of effort.

⌘

Thorfinn took the frightened little boy and carried him in his strong arms. The child could not have been more than ten years old. He was small for his age and wiry. Thorfinn guessed that food was scarce in his family. He felt a moment of conscience using the child for their own ends. He shook it off as he thought of the harsh winter facing all the families in his tribe. If they did not raid successfully then everyone would suffer, and as Earl he would be responsible. He hated doing this but it was necessary. He would make sure no harm would come to the lad, although he did not tell the boy's mother that.

She looked on, hatred reflected in her eyes. She was terrified for her son and what would happen to him. She had hugged him fiercely before Thorfinn had taken the boy whispering urgently, 'do everything he tells you to.'

Now they stood below the huge castle wall where the drain flowed. It was dark and the only light they had was the moon shining silently, hanging in the sky like a big, round ball. Two men tied a rope around the metal grate while another two chipped at the stonework with a rough chisel and mallet. When they were satisfied they had removed enough stone the men pulled on the rope. They grunted with the exertion, feeling encouraged when they heard the metal beginning to scrape against the loosened stone. They whispered to one another to keep the soldiers of Ebondeen from discovering them. Finally the grate gave way. Thorfinn peered into the small drain lighting the dirty, damp passageway with a lamp he quickly lit. The boy would just fit but it would be a tight squeeze.

'Don't let us down lad,' he said to the terrified young boy. 'Your mother is counting on you.'

'Please don't hurt her sir,' the young boy stammered. 'I promise I will do everything you asked.'

Thorfinn swallowed hard. He had threatened the boy's mother with death if the young lad failed. It was an intimidation tactic but he needed the boy to believe her life was in danger for their plan to work.

'That's up to you, young man,' he patted the boy on the shoulder then lifted him into the dark tunnel.

'Don't forget to turn out the lantern before you get to the end of the drain.'

CHAPTER 16

THE BOY

THE YOUNG boy inched his way forward on his stomach through the drain. The stench made him gag several times and his progress was slow. He kept thinking of his mother and felt a huge weight of responsibility on his skinny shoulders. If he failed then those men would kill her – he must not fail. He felt the skin on his elbows rubbing raw as he crawled and he shivered as his clothes became damper the further he crawled. When he saw the end of the tunnel he quickly extinguished the lantern, waiting in the darkness, allowing his eyes to adjust to the dark. He felt something crawl over his back and he had to clamp his hand over his mouth to stop the scream escaping from his throat. He quickly moved toward the dim light that showed him the exit. He needed to get out of this small claustrophobic space. He gulped in the fresh air when he got to the drain opening, like a drowning man. Then he waited to see if anyone was around. This was the riskiest part – if he were discovered sneaking into the castle then he would jeopardise his mother's life. When he was certain there was no one watching the drain he slipped silently from the smelly cocoon into the castle courtyard. He stayed in the dark shadows and crept around the edge of the walls, pressing himself into the wall each time a soldier passed. He had to get to the kitchens and find the passageway that led to the underground water source. The castle at Ebondeen had this secret passage in the event of a siege. This ensured that there would be fresh water should the castle be in lock down as it was right now. He knew about this passage as his mother worked in the kitchen at the castle before their village was raided and she knew of its existence. He snuck through the door and into the warm kitchen. All was quiet due to the midnight hour. In a few hours it would be bustling with cooks and servants readying breakfast for Lord Macphaid and his family. He quickly took some straw lighting it on the still warm oven and lit his lantern again – he would need the light.

He entered the larder as his mother had instructed him and found the small door under one of the shelves. He pulled it open carefully hoping it would not creak. Then he crawled through it and pulled it closed behind him. He was glad for the lantern as it was dark and eerie. The stone walls loomed above him and there were steep steps that descended deep into the earth. He could feel the cold creep up the further down he went. At last he came to the bottom of the steps and it opened out into a large cavern. There was a large clear lake of water. So his mother was right. There was a water supply under the castle and it had to come from somewhere. He skirted the edge of the lake peering into the water looking for where it flowed. He could see the water gently flowing near one section of the wall. Then he made his way quickly back up the stairs and across the courtyard to the drain.

Thorfinn waited anxiously for the boy to return. They would wait another fifteen minutes and if he was not back they would have to assume he had been caught. They would have to leave as once the boy talked half of Ebondeen's soldiers would descend on them. He paced up and down the side of the wall. Time was ticking by. A scuffling noise coming from the drain alerted him to the boy's return. He sighed in relief. Although they had used the boy to carry out the task he had been anxious for him to return safely. He did not want this child's death on his conscience. He smiled to himself – the other Northmen would say that Siobhan had made him soft and in a way it was true – she had brought out the softer side of him he had not known existed.

He helped the boy out and covered him with a cloak when he noticed how the child shivered from the cold.

'Good work, lad. What did you find?'

'There is a water supply under the kitchen. The water flows out at the side of the wall.'

'Well done,' he patted the boy's shoulder and he flinched ever so slightly.

'Don't be afraid, boy. Your mother will be safe I promise you.'

The hour was getting late – they would have to move quickly before daybreak. Thorfinn selected three of his soldiers who were fishermen in Kaldakinn when the raiding season was over. They were good swimmers and he needed them to find the opening to the underground water source. The men crept around the castle to where they believed the kitchens were situated based on the lad's mother's description. Then they took off their heavy cloaks, sword belts and leather shoes. They waded into the cold water feeling with their feet as they went. They went under the water many times feeling and testing the wall with their hands.

'It's too dark,' Niels said after coming up for the tenth time. 'Even if we find the opening we cannot attempt it in this water – we will need daylight to see anything at all.'

'That is a great risk,' Thorfinn said.

'No more than trying to swim in the dark. We have no idea how long the tunnel is – the risk is greater if we do it at night.'

'You're right,' Thorfinn relented. 'Come back here just before daybreak and then wait till there is enough light. You should be concealed from the soldier's sight if you stay close against the wall.'

They made their way back to the camp of men who eagerly waited for news of the impending siege. They were restless and the thought of waiting another whole day was not well received.

'Patience men,' Thorfinn encouraged. 'Save your strength, for tomorrow we will raid Ebondeen.'

CHAPTER 17

INFILTRATION

'IS THERE any word from Phoenix?' Conall Macphaid asked his chief advisor.

'No my Lord, there has been no word at all.'

'Damned coward! I knew I could not count on that woman's word. They had no intention of ever helping us. If we get out of this mess Griswold will have to answer for their lack of aid.'

'The savages are getting more and more brazen each day. We spotted scouts circling the castle. They are looking for a way in my Lord.'

'Will they find one?' Conall asked.

'I doubt it my Lord. We have our men up in the battlements with oil and arrows ready. The gate is barricaded with a secondary wall of carts and wagons. There is no other way in unless they fly in on dragons. Already we have shot down a creature trying to breach our castle walls.'

'Well, be prepared for anything,' Conall advised. 'If they get in we are all doomed.'

'Yes my Lord.'

Conall was concerned for his daughter as she had not had enough time to escape before the Northmen landed on their shores. He could not bear the thought of what would happen to her if these men invaded. Death would be the best thing but he knew that as a beautiful young woman she would be used by the Northmen first and she would wish they had rather killed her. He felt helpless to protect her.

Dammit Phoenix, don't let us down he silently prayed.

He did not realize that the creature his men shot down was the Monwing carrying a note from Phoenix pledging their support – a note he would never receive.

⌘

Balfour and Struan and a large contingent of men rode toward Ebondeen. They knew they were about to fight an epic battle – they hoped to be there before daylight. Struan felt a measure of excitement stirring in his belly. For years he had trained with his sword but he had never used it in an actual battle. He recognized that in his excitement there was also a measure of fear and anxiety. He did not want to die. He was not even forty years old and had a whole life to live. He thought of Ceinlys and the life he could have had with her. He still felt a dull pain when he thought of her but for the first time, facing real danger now, he felt something else – the desire to have a family and love in his life again – a desire to leave a legacy. He would have to make sure that he had that opportunity.

⌘

The three Northmen waded back into the water, silently and stealthily. The sun was shining down and the water had changed from a deep, dark void to a shimmering blue. They submerged numerous times looking for the tunnel that would take them to the underground water supply of the castle.

'I've found it,' Niels spluttered excited. 'I can't tell how long it is though.'

They were silent for a few seconds. Each man knew they could very well be swimming to their death. If the tunnel was too long they would drown before ever getting to the end. They were all well trained in swimming and often dived for fish and food in Kaldakinn but this was different. They did not know these waters.

'May the gods be with us,' they murmured to each other.

Niels tied a long piece of twine to his ankle. The fourth man who had accompanied them would stay in the water and when the twine was tugged three times in succession he would know they had reached their destination safely. That would be his cue to head back to their camp and tell Thorfinn that the siege would go ahead as planned that night.

The men all took deep breaths readying themselves for the big swim. Then one by one they dived under and headed up the tunnel, using their arms and legs to propel them through the water. Niels felt as though his lungs would burst, the burning sensation that gripped his chest sucking the last drop of oxygen from his body.

Relax or you'll use all your oxygen. The gods are with us, we cannot fail he mentally willed himself as he swam as hard as he could. When he thought he would not be able to go another inch he spotted light.

Thank the gods, there was an opening.

He spluttered and coughed as he broke the surface of the water, gulping in air as though it would be his last breath. The two other men surfaced and the three of them took a moment to catch their breath, each heaving and gasping for more. Then Niels tugged the twine hard three times. He waited to feel it tugged before he cut it from his leg. The message had been relayed. They searched the cavern looking for a place to conceal themselves. They would have to hide all day until midnight before they could put their plan into action. It was going to be a long day.

⌘

Thorfinn and the other Northmen prepared themselves for battle. It would not be long now until they finally got to raid the castle at Ebondeen. Their patience over the last few weeks was finally going to pay off. It would be a good and successful raid – he could feel it in his bones and he felt the smile and favour of the gods upon them.

⌘

Balfour and Struan concealed themselves in Neverend forest surrounding Ebondeen castle. They would wait for Phoenix and try to formulate a plan of action. They had found where the Northmen had made camp – along the banks of the river that harboured their long boats. There were more than they anticipated. They had no idea how they were going to get to Conall Macphaid with these men scouting the castle. If push came to shove they would have to attack from the rear – the element of surprise being their greatest weapon. Now all they could do was wait for Phoenix.

⌘

Isabel paced up and down – she could bear it no longer. How could she just sit here while her husband and uncle went into battle when she could easily be another warrior on their team? Pretending everything would be all right was killing her – she knew that Phoenix would be furious with her for disobeying his request but she could not help herself – she would deal with his anger later when this was all over.

She pulled out a piece of parchment and scribbled a note to her parents – she prayed they would understand her reasoning – just another party to explain her actions to when this was all done. Her mother had been equally headstrong when she was even younger and so she should understand her driving need to go. She pulled her cloak around her shoulders, picked up her bow and arrows and strode out the cottage to her horse. If she rode through the night, she would get to Ebondeen early the following day.

⌘

Dusk began to settle over the grey stone walls of Ebondeen. The beautiful orange and pink streaks that painted the sky were no indication of the horror that was about to befall.

Phoenix surveyed their surroundings, watching as the Northmen gathered their weapons and made ready for battle.

'Something is going down tonight,' he whispered to Balfour and Struan. 'Do you see the way they are grouping themselves and preparing their weapons? Their leader is dividing them into camps. I think they are waiting for nightfall.'

'How do you think they plan to get in?' Balfour asked. 'We have scouted the castle and it is fortified.'

'I don't know but they must have a plan. That makes them the most dangerous enemy to anticipate – one who has the ability to overcome obstacles and persevere through. I have heard these Northmen fight like no other – death is an honour for them.'

'What are we going to do?' Balfour looked worried.

'We have no choice but to surround them and when they make their move we will have to attack from behind. They will certainly not be expecting it and it just may give Conall Macphaid a chance at surviving their attack. Balfour you need to get back to our men and let them know what our plan is.'

Balfour nodded. They had brought the men who had been trained from Griswold and they were waiting deeper in the forest so as not to alert the Northmen of their presence. Tonight their training would come into play and he prayed it was sufficient to face these fearless men.

⌘

Niels and the other two men could hear all the movement happening within the kitchen. They waited just behind the secret door that led to the larder. Once dinner was over and the cooks retired for the night they would make their move and set their plan into action. Their limbs felt sore and stiff after the icy water and sitting in hiding all day. They looked forward to the siege – this is what they had been taught to do since they were just young men. Now all they had to do was wait patiently for the midnight hour.

CHAPTER 18

THE SIEGE

EBONDEEN

THORFINN and Erik checked their shields and sharpened their swords. It would not be long now till they plundered the castle. Finally their dream of raiding the south was becoming a reality. They did not talk – each man was lost in his own thoughts. Neither of them worried about death or the possibility of it. They were taught as young warriors that battle was a man's right and his destiny. The gods were the ones who decided your fate so there was no point worrying about it – if Odin wanted you in Valhalla then nothing you could do would ever change that outcome. This made them completely fearless. Instead, Thorfinn thought about Siobhan and how beautiful she was – he missed her and could not wait to see her and feel her warm body next to his again. She would be delighted with the riches he hoped to secure on this raid – they would be set for winter as they would be able to trade with some of the other northern clans. Erik thought about his future and how exciting it had suddenly become – a whole new world had opened up to him and he would learn so much about these southern people after the raid. He hoped to attain some books that would broaden his knowledge as he was hungry to learn new things. Most of the men sought treasures and wealth from these raids but Erik hoped to gain the knowledge and wisdom his father had spoken about. That was his dream, his goal.

Besides knowledge there was just one other thing he yearned for. Someone to share his life with, someone he could love beyond himself. He had not met her yet and he wondered how on earth he ever would as Kaldakinn was a village of just a few hundred people. None of the young maidens had captured his attention, though they had certainly tried. Perhaps he would meet someone from the south as his father had done all those years ago when he had saved his mother.

Bring her to me Odin, please – I will be forever grateful he thought as he prepared himself for battle.

⌘

Phoenix, Balfour and Struan watched the men. They had prepared themselves and now they seemed to be waiting for something – but what? Their men were ready waiting to move at Phoenix's command. The Northmen gathered up their swords and shields and started to move silently toward the castle. Phoenix and his army moved along the tree line of the forest mirroring their moves, equally silent.

'What are they doing?' Balfour whispered alarmed.

'They seem to be dividing into three different groups,' Phoenix said. They are heading for different parts of the castle.

The Northmen moved in different directions – one group heading for the drawbridge and the outer gate. The other two groups headed either side of the main gate. Phoenix watched as ten men in each group waded into the water and swam silently across the moat toward the wall. They scrambled up on the muddy banks, positioning themselves below the battlements of the castle.

⌘

'It's time to move,' Niels said as they carefully pushed open the little door into the larder. The kitchen was quiet and they crept out into the warm room. Each man grabbed a piece of crusty bread and wolfed it down followed by some ale they found. They peered out the kitchen door to the courtyard. It was quiet but they knew that soldiers and watchmen were posted at the gates and on the walls. They slipped out into the shadows, moving stealthily around the outer walls toward the main gate. They found cover under one of the many wagons that had been pushed together as an extra barricade should the gate be breached. Ebondeen would not expect the attack to come from within its walls.

Now all they had to do was wait for the signal.

⌘

The Northmen on either side of the main gate began to shout – horrible war-like cries that sent a message of fear into the quiet night air. The soldiers on the battlements shouted orders as chaos erupted. Arrows were lit and they endeavoured to shoot the wild men below, to no avail as they pressed themselves against the stony walls.

'Get the oil,' the order was issued.

Another group of Northmen across the river taunted the soldiers who fired on them, deflecting their deadly arrows with their shield wall.

Phoenix and his army watched the game of cat and mouse.

'Should we attack?' Struan asked.

'No we wait – as yet they have not breached the castle and we don't want to alert them to our presence or they will turn on us and we will become the victims. I don't like our odds if that happens.'

'What are they doing? Why are they trying to draw attention to themselves?'

'Because they are trying to create a diversion,' Phoenix said. 'They have something planned. Watch the group who have gathered near the main gate – they are being silent – that is where they plan to breach the castle.'

⌘

Niels and his men moved quickly the moment they heard their kinsmen's war cry. Soldiers ran through the courtyard toward the battlements to assist with the boiling oil. This gave the three intruders the opportunity to scramble under the wagon and head toward the portcullis and outer gate. Ten soldiers manned the huge main gate, which they believed to be impenetrable. It did not take them long to run them through with their swords – Thorfinn's plan was genius – the element of surprise had worked. They lifted the portcullis quickly and efficiently and lowered the drawbridge opening a way for the swarm of Northmen to enter the castle protected by their shield wall.

The Northmen stormed the castle, the steel of their swords glinting and their haunting cries echoing off the stony walls.

'We must go now,' Phoenix said urgently as he and his army spilled from the forest, running headlong toward the castle drawbridge, swords drawn.

⌘

Conall Macphaid had woken with the first cries they had uttered and he knew they were coming. He ushered his daughter ahead of himself toward his chambers. He had to protect her no matter what. He felt fear at what would inevitably take place but more than that he felt intense anger – Phoenix had let them down. If they survived this then Griswold would pay. He and Catriona hid beside his huge canopied bed, crouching low on the floor. It did not take long for them to come.

His door was kicked open and Thorfinn filled the frame, massive and intimidating. Behind him, stood two other Northmen, equally intimidating. Conall put his finger over his lips indicating to Catriona that she should be quiet. Thorfinn entered the room, his gaze roaming the room.

'I can see you old man,' he said in his deep, booming voice. Get up and we will not harm you. I assume you are the Lord of Ebondeen?'

Conall stood, holding his sword in front of him placing himself between the huge Northman and his petite daughter who still crouched behind him.

Perhaps he won't see Catriona if I stand, he thought hopefully.

'Yes, I am Lord of Ebondeen. Please just take what you want, but don't hurt my people,' Conall said, trying not to let his fear show.

'We certainly will take what we need, but just how many of your people get hurt depends on you and your soldiers. Sit down,' Thorfinn waved to a nearby chair. He complied.

'So who do we have here?' he looked over at Catriona who looked so pale he thought she might faint.

'No one, it's just a serving maid, who was spending the night with me,' Conall lied. He hoped his lie would protect his daughter.

'In that case you won't mind sharing her with my men,' Thorfinn said as he grabbed her by the arm and pulled her up off the floor. Conall leapt off his chair, face flushed and angry.

'Please,' he begged, 'don't hurt her.'

'So who is she really?' Thorfinn asked. He lifted Catriona's hand laying it in his huge palm. 'Her hands have not seen a day's work as a servant. This is your last chance to be honest with me.'

'She's my daughter.'

'She'll be coming with us. We need more beautiful women in Kaldakinn and my son needs a wife.'

'Please, no,' Catriona begged, fear reflected in her eyes.

'No,' Conall shouted, jumping to his feet and running at Thorfinn. Even though Conall was far smaller and older than Thorfinn, his fury gave him added strength. The two men fell to the floor, arms around each other as they rumbled, a mass of arms and legs. Thorfinn punched Conall hard but the instinct to protect his daughter overrode his pain. He hardly flinched. He straddled Thorfinn and wrapped his hands around the Northman's neck squeezing as hard as he could. He wanted to kill this man who had come into his home uninvited with the belief that he was owed something. Slowly his hands began to lose their grip and his strength began to fade. He could hear Catriona screaming his name and he felt momentarily confused.

Now is not the time to feel faint Conall, he chided himself.

He looked down, a sword protruding from his chest, red liquid flowing from him like tears as he swayed sideways. Thorfinn pushed him off and looked gratefully at the Northman who had saved his life. Catriona slumped to the floor beside her father crying uncontrollably. The young Northman moved to pull her away but Thorfinn stopped him.

'Give her time to say goodbye,' he said hoarsely.

This was not the outcome he had wanted. He wanted to negotiate with the old Lord to see whether they could discuss a mutually beneficial agreement for both parties. It was not to be.

⌘

Phoenix and his men had almost reached the castle. They breathed hard from running. Before they crossed the drawbridge Phoenix raised his hand cautioning his men. They needed to approach with care. They could not do much now to help Conall against the invasion but they could ensure that these men never came to Griswold.

'I have a plan,' he said outlying his idea to them.

Balfour and Struan headed away from the castle toward the Northmen's camp. The rest of Griswold's army followed Phoenix toward the castle to fight off the men.

Balfour and Struan quietly made their way into the camp. They found women and children under the guard of two Northmen. They hid in the murky shadows and crept toward the long boats, the water lapping against their sides as they gently bobbed on the river. Balfour pulled himself over the side and dropped onto the deck floor. Struan did the same on another boat. Then they took some rag that had been doused in oil for their arrows and lit it. Silently they slipped back over the side into the water and swam along the river bank to safety. The boats began to catch alight and thick black smoke rose into the night sky as the wooden long boats formed a burning mass of timber. The two Northmen guarding the women and children ran to the edge of the water yelling.

'Get Thorfinn back here now,' the one shouted to the other as he helplessly watched the boat burn. Left on his own he was no match for Struan and Balfour who sent him to Valhalla to meet Odin. The women and children, once untied fled into the forest.

⌘

Erik saw the flames coming from their camp as he fought on the battlements. Their boats were alight. He ran his sword through the soldier and made his way down. If their boats burned they would be stuck in Ebondeen for many months and their people would starve in Kaldakinn over the winter. As he made his way through the fighting mass of men he came face to face with Phoenix. They stood on the drawbridge facing each other, a moment of admiration and respect passing between them, some unspoken recognition that each was an heir to their own kingdom. Erik nodded at Phoenix who acknowledged him in return. Then they began to fight, sword hitting sword, the metal sparking and clanging as they battled it out. They were equally matched in ability and strength. Both wanted to win. Erik tried to concentrate on the battle in front of him but his mind kept wandering to the burning boats and what it would mean for his people. It made his resolve stronger. Phoenix too was thinking of other things – namely Isabel's sweet face and the memory of being one with her. He did not want to lose her. It strengthened his resolve. As each man battled, their will to live matched; another force would make the choice for both of them – mapping a new course for them both.

⌘

Catriona fought the rough hands that dragged her kicking and screaming from the castle walls. She was terrified. She looked back at the burning castle that had been her home, her last thoughts of her dead father. The warriors holding her either side pulled her along, her feet stumbling on the uneven rubble. Her mind was numb and her body in shock. Thorfinn had raced ahead to the boats with some men to try and quench the flames. Still others raided the castle for treasures and loot.

'Stop struggling woman,' the one Northman growled at Catriona.

It was the last thing he said as an arrow pierced his chest. Struan stepped out of the shadows his sword drawn.

'Let the lady go,' he said.

The Northman launched himself at Struan his sword waving in madness, a lethal force. They battled it out sword upon sword, the metal echoing through the night air as it clashed. Struan did not see the tree root behind him in the dark as he fought his huge attacker. His foot twisted on the gnarly root sending him to the ground in excruciating pain.

He held his sword out in front of him as he tried to scramble to his feet. The Northman advanced his sword sweeping in an arc as Struan scrambled backward. The blow caught him just below the knee. He screamed in agony as his left limb was severed from his body. Then he passed out.

⌘

Erik and Phoenix stood eyeball to eyeball as they danced on the drawbridge, their swords rhythmically playing a tune. Both were beginning to tire, but each had more than enough incentive to fight to the death. The end came suddenly and unexpectedly. It was an arrow shot from the battlements by one of Conall's soldiers that caught the young man in the left side. He slumped to his knees, surprise registering on his face. The other young man caught him to himself and dragged him across the drawbridge out of firing range. He saw the pain on his face as he tried to catch his breath.

This is not how this battle should end.

They stared at one another, eyes locked; the one breathing heavily while the other tried to stem the bleeding with his hands. He would have given anything to kill this man but now his only thought was to save him, the true horror of war dawning on him. Somehow he recognized that he could so easily have been the one drawing his last breath and in that moment he felt one with this foreigner.

⌘

Isabel could see smoke billowing from Ebondeen and hear the battle as she dismounted her horse in the forest. The sun was up and the devastation was immense. She pulled out her bow and an arrow and moved along the edge of the forest scouting for her husband and her uncle. She could not see Phoenix but she could see Struan lying on the floor bleeding, a Northman standing over him readying himself to run her uncle through with his sword. Instinct took over as she fitted her arrow and released it as fast as she could, sending the deadly weapon hurtling through the early morning air, silently seeking its target. The Northman grunted as the arrow penetrated his chest. He dropped his sword and fell to the ground alongside her uncle. She ran as fast as she could toward them. She dropped to her knees, cradling his head as she shook him. He groaned and she sighed in relief. She ripped fabric from her cloak and bound his severed limb tying it tight just above the bloody flesh. For the first time she noticed Catriona standing helplessly in shock.

'Help me to move him into the trees,' she commanded the young woman. Catriona did not respond. Isabel stood up and slapped her hard on the face.

'You need to help me move him now.' The young woman nodded numbly coming out of her stupor. They dragged Struan to the trees and made him as comfortable as possible.

'Stay with him,' Isabel ordered. 'If I don't come back get him help.'

She still could not see Phoenix. She scanned the men fighting on the drawbridge, looking for his dark hair. She felt afraid, desperate to know he was safe.

Then she saw him. He was with a Northman. Her heart stopped in her chest and her legs moved before her brain could tell her what to do. She ran as fast as she could toward him – toward her love.

'Get away from him,' she screamed as she dived onto the unsuspecting Erik sending them both rolling through the leaves. Erik had not expected a tiny woman to attack him and he was caught off- guard.

Isabel picked up her bow which had fallen near her and pulled an arrow from her quiver aiming it at The Northman. He was covered in blood. She looked at Phoenix sprawled on the ground and aimed, her hand shaking. Then she released the arrow. She dropped to her knees next to him and lifted his head.

'Don't leave me please,' she sobbed as she held him. The arrow protruded from his body – the thing that had brought them together but would now separate them forever.

'Belle, you came,' he whispered opening his eyes.

'You're going to be all right,' she sobbed 'Just don't talk. I will get you help.'

'No, don't leave me. You made me so happy and for that I thank you. Be happy Belle, live your life and know that I love you – more than anything in this world.'

'You promised me you would be with me no matter what. Stay with me Phoenix – I need you, I love you. Remember you said we had a whole life to live together,' she sobbed, her tears dripping on his chest.

'I'm sorry,' he spluttered before the light left his eyes and his body went limp. Isabel buried her head in his chest and let out an anguished wail. He was gone and they had only spent one night together as man and wife – there would be no more. She would never feel his strong arms around her again or his sweet kisses on her lips.

How can life be so cruel?

She felt strong arms pull her to her feet and she struggled as the arms pinned her down.

'You killed him,' she sobbed anger and rage fuelling her.

'Shh... it's going to be all right,' Erik said as he hoisted her over his shoulder.

CHAPTER 19

DESOLATE

IT WAS a bloody battle with great losses on both sides. The Lord of Ebondeen was dead as were many of his soldiers. Phoenix's army suffered losses too, the greatest being the Lord of Griswold himself. The Northmen lost two of their long boats and some men. Struan lost his leg, his life hung in the balance. He had only been saved by Balfour who took Struan and Catriona and rode back to Sherbrooke to Aislinn and Drew Williams. They were the only people who could help him now. Phoenix's body was on the way back to Griswold with the remaining survivors. Balfour looked haunted, as though he had failed Phoenix. He wanted to shout out his fury and pain but could not as he had to attend to Struan. He was determined that at least one of them would survive.

Aislinn was shocked to see Struan so mutilated. She was also terrified knowing Isabel had gone to the battle – she only prayed her daughter had not arrived in time. She had sent Regent and Nuada after her when she had found her note. She feared how Isabel would respond when she found out that Phoenix was dead. She had withdrawn when she thought he was going to marry Catriona but how would she deal with his permanent loss? Would she ever recover from a grief so huge?

She felt deeply afraid but she could not dwell on it now – they had to operate and save Struan's life. Someone had tied a tourniquet around his knee which had helped but now there was infection to worry about and they had to amputate his leg properly to ensure against it. As she cut away the drenched material trepidation filled her heart. She recognized the fabric. It was from Isabel's cloak. Isabel had tied the tourniquet. She had been there in the midst of the battle.

Great One please let her be alive – let her be safe!

She worked with Drew as they operated and stitched, trying to keep her mind from filling with images of her daughter being mutilated or captured. How would Struan cope? He was such an active man and sword fighting was his passion. Now he would be crippled and his movement limited.

You've had your revenge Gwen – you've hurt those closest to me, she thought as she stitched Struan's wound.

Catriona was fine but in shock. She was devastated by her father's death and now learning that Phoenix had been killed was an added weight. She was surprised to hear that he had married Isabel before the battle and that stung a little too, knowing she had been betrayed in more ways than one. Still, she was grateful that Aislinn and Drew had opened their home to her – she could not go back to Ebondeen just yet – it was not safe.

⌘

Gwendolyn wiped a tear from her eyes. She could not believe that in just a few months she had buried her husband and now her son would soon follow. She would not accept that her devious marriage agreement was the reason he was dead. Instead she blamed Isabel Williams and the Great One.

'They hate me and they are trying to punish me. They are the ones who have brought this calamity on our bloodline. I will make sure Isabel that you suffer for what you have done to our family and in your suffering your mother will suffer too. It's time she paid for what she did to Daemon.'

⌘

The Northmen would be delayed. They had planned to attack Ebondeen's neighbours after this raid but now they would have to spend weeks building some new boats. There was not enough space on the existing six boats to get the men back and to load up their raided treasures and supplies. They chopped and prepared wood from Neverend forest. No one stopped them. The survivors of Ebondeen had fled to the hills till the Northmen left and all that was left of the burning ruins was being daily ransacked. Summer was coming to an end and the foreigners worked around the clock rebuilding their vessels. They had to return to Kaldakinn before the fjords froze up.

Isabel felt trapped. She was locked up in a section of Ebondeen castle that had survived the fire. She felt heartbroken and crushed at the loss of Phoenix. She had nothing left to live for now. She did not fear for herself – she had lost her will to live and did not care what they did with her.

Maybe I should join him and just end it all.

The temptation was there but then she thought of her parents and brothers and how it would hurt them beyond measure.

No, I will wait till the time is right and I will kill the Northman who killed Phoenix. I will have my revenge, my love. He won't get away with what he's done to you, I promise, she silently vowed.

To pass the time she scratched words onto the stone walls of the castle that would provide clues that she had been there.

⌘

Autumn broke through the warm summer days with beautiful orange and red leaves that shimmered like liquid gold. Nuada and Regent had not found any sign of Isabel. They had watched the castle at Ebondeen but could not get into it due to the Northmen who had taken up temporary residence. They had not seen her at all.

Aislinn and Drew were devastated by her disappearance. They assumed she was dead but the lack of closure and not knowing what had happened to her made it more painful. Struan's leg was beginning to heal and Catriona had taken it upon herself to care for him since he had saved her life. She wanted to stay busy, to keep her mind off the loss of her father and home. She was helping Struan to heal emotionally and in return he was doing the same for her.

The Northmen prepared themselves to set sail. They had to return to Kaldakinn before the snow fell and the fjords iced up. If they failed, their people would not survive the icy winter. The new ships were not as sturdy as their existing longboats as they had been hurriedly built, but they would be sufficient to get them back home.

Erik carried Isabel over his shoulder and gently put her onto the boat. He tied her to the side of the boat to ensure that she would not fling herself overboard. He had made a point of visiting her every day that she was in captivity. He had tried to tell her many times that he had not killed Phoenix, but she would not talk or listen to him. She just stared at him vacantly, hatred in her eyes.

'Please, let me go,' she begged each day.

'You may not believe this, but I am keeping you safe by taking you with me. If I release you now there are at least ten men here who would claim you for themselves. The only reason they have not touched you is because I am the Earl's son. You will be safe with me, I promise.'

He gently wrapped a fur pelt around her shoulders.

'You will need this in the months to come. It's going to get pretty cold where we are going,' he said.

He rubbed the scar that ran down the side of his right eye. He had been lucky. She had almost killed him with that arrow when she had found him with Phoenix. It was fortunate for him that Isabel's grief had made her aim less than perfect. The arrow had grazed the side of his head and now he had this scar to show for it. It made him look even more rugged and handsome. It was a reminder to him not to underestimate this woman. She was beautiful and strong-spirited – everything he had yearned for in the woman he wanted as a wife. Still, she hated him and her heart clearly belonged to another. He had been torn in two. A part of him wanted to let her return to her family, but another part urged him to take her with him. He had been captivated by her the moment he saw her. There was something different about her and even though she hated him, he could not bring himself to let her go.

'Are you going to tell me your name or am I going to have to name you myself?' he smiled.

She glared at him, her grey eyes cold. For days he had tried to find out her name but she had stubbornly refused to give it to him.

'All right then, Helga it will be.'

She spluttered, furious with him and through gritted teeth growled, 'Isabel, its Isabel.'

Erik laughed delighted at his little victory.

'Welcome aboard Isabel. I meant what I said, I will not hurt you and you will be safe.'

She looked at him uncertain, fear in her eyes. His heart ached for her. She was so young, had lost the man she loved and was about to be thrust into a world that would be so foreign to her. He would not let her down.

The ships cast off and headed down the river back toward the open sea where the journey back north would begin.

CHAPTER 20

DENIAL

ISABEL felt sick – violently sick! The rolling motion of the boat left her feeling weak and green. Erik was worried about her. Many times she had to lean over the side and vomit and she looked pale and drawn. She did not manage to keep much of her food down and he was worried that she would fade away before they got to Kaldakinn. They had been at sea for a full moon and the weather was getting quite cold, unusually early for the autumn months. There had even been the occasional sleet. They hoped to hit the fjords in the next day or two where they would be better protected from the elements. He sat down next to her and noticed her shivering. He pulled her closer to his body, covering them with his fur cloak. She tensed and tried to pull away but he held her tight.

'I know you don't want me near you, but you will freeze to death if you don't let me keep you warm,' he growled. She was one obstinate woman.

'I don't care,' she moaned 'Death sounds pleasurable compared to the way I am feeling. It would be preferable to this sickness and being kept captive by a bunch of savages.'

'That may be so, but your baby doesn't deserve to die this way.'

'What are you talking about,' she spat out.

'I've seen this before many times with women in our village. That is the advantage of living in close community – everyone is part of an event like a baby being born or someone dying. Your culture seems to have a more separate way of living – the Lord lives in his big castle and all his people live in surrounding villages. It is not like that with our people. We all live together, eat together and do life together. I know what a pregnant woman looks like and how sick she can be.'

Isabel kept silent. She had not thought about being with child. He couldn't be right. She and Phoenix had only spent one night together. Surely it couldn't have happened that fast?

It is just the motion of the boat that is making me so sick.

'I'm not pregnant,' she said defiantly.

'Yes you are and if you were honest with yourself you would recognize that there have probably been changes in your body.'

She felt the world spin, her mind in turmoil and it wasn't the motion of the boat. He was right, she had noticed that her breasts were tender and her monthly womanly cycle had not come. She had been too distraught to notice it at the time but now it all made sense. This should have been the happiest day of her life but instead all she felt was terror at bringing a child into the new and unknown world she was going to be a part of.

'Don't worry Isabel,' Erik said seeing her fear. 'I promise I will not let anyone harm you or this child.'

She did not believe him.

⌘

'We found something Aislinn,' Regent said. 'There are signs that Isabel is alive. We found words she carved into the stone at Ebondeen castle. We think the Northmen have taken her captive.'

Relief overwhelmed her but was quickly replaced by fear for her daughter. 'How will we get her back?'

'We will rescue her but there is no way to do that till Spring. The fjords will be frozen over with winter and there is no possibility of reaching her till they are thawed.'

'What if she doesn't survive that long?' Aislinn cried. She knew there was nothing they could do but it pained her that they had to sit helplessly by.

'She's a strong woman Aislinn. She will be fine. The Great One has promised to keep an eye on her in the Mirror of Time. He assures me that she is fine and that no harm has come to her. He has set a protector over her although the young man in question does not know it yet. He believes that the gods have destined him to care for her. It doesn't matter what he believes though – the gods he prays to are the same as the Great One – he just thinks differently that's all.'

Aislinn wasn't sure she understood what Regent was saying, but she did know that the Great One had never let her down before and she believed him when he said Isabel was protected. It gave her a measure of peace and hope that she would see her daughter again.

⌘

The boats sailed into the fjords and the elements seemed less fierce. Isabel was grateful that it was calmer and that the icy wind was not as bitingly cold. She had to admit that the scenery was magnificent, the steep mountains rising out of the aquamarine water like giant monoliths. She had seen nothing like it before.

'How much longer till we get to your village?' she asked Erik.

'We should be there in about three days if all goes well,' he said. 'My mother comes from the south just like you Isabel – she will like you and she will help you. She's a good woman.'

'Was she kidnapped too and forced to marry your father?' she asked sarcastically.

'No, she was kidnapped by another clan. She escaped and my father found her nearly frozen to death. She chose to stay with our people.'

He handed her a strip of dried fish and she wrinkled her nose.

'You must try to eat something Isabel – it is not good for the baby for you to starve yourself.'

She took the fish and bit off a small chunk. She chewed and swallowed before her throat threatened to close and push it back up.

It began to snow lightly and small wet flakes landed in her jet black hair making her look even more beautiful. He brushed away a flake gently and she flinched smacking his hand away from her face.

'Don't touch me,' she snarled. 'You killed my husband and I won't forget that.'

Erik sighed deeply. 'I didn't kill him Isabel.'

'Of course you would say that but my eyes told a different story. I saw you leaning over his body. I saw his blood all over you.'

'I was trying to help him Isabel. I don't know if you have noticed but we Northmen don't use arrows except for hunting food. We fight with swords and shields. Besides the arrow was in his side – if I had shot him, it would have hit him in the chest.'

She was silent. It was true – not one of the men she had seen from this clan carried a bow or arrows. The only bow and quiver of arrows on this boat was hers, and Phoenix had been shot in the side. She was confused.

'Why would you help him – you were fighting against us?'

'It's true – I was fighting him, sword against sword and I probably would have killed him if it had come to that. It's war Isabel- he would have killed me if he had the chance. I believe in clean fighting and I respected him while we were battling it out, as he respected me. The battle was pretty evenly matched – he was a good swordsman but neither of us got the chance to see who would win. He was shot down by an arrow from the battlements. I dragged him away in the hope of helping him. I would never kill a wounded man – there is no honour in that.'

'You are asking me to believe that Conall Macphaid's men shot Phoenix. Why would they do that? Phoenix was helping them.'

'I don't know, but there were a lot of men fighting and we were outside the castle walls. Perhaps they were trying to kill me. I am truly sorry Isabel.'

Erik unconsciously rubbed his scar. Her eyes filled with tears as his words sank in. It was easier believing that these savages had killed Phoenix – what was she to do now with the truth? Logically it all made sense but the only way she would survive this was if she hated him – it was still their fault that any of them were at Ebondeen that night – if they had not raided then she and Phoenix would have been on their honeymoon, beginning their life together.

'I don't care what you say,' she said turning her back on him. 'You may not have shot that arrow but it was you who brought us to that battle in the first place so you may as well have killed him yourself.'

Erik lifted his hand to touch her shoulder then thought better of it. He let it drop to his side. She was in pain and he understood her need to blame someone. She would need time and she would have plenty of that in Kaldakinn in winter – there was nowhere else to go, there was nothing but time.

⌘

Kaldakinn

Siobhan's concern was growing – the men should have returned weeks ago and winter was setting in earlier than usual. The first snows had already begun and their supplies would not last for more than half the winter. It was imperative for them to trade with the other clans. She stood in the sleet and looked out to the horizon willing the longboats home.

Come on Thorfinn – where are you?

She felt afraid for the first time – usually the men were back well before winter began from raiding. This trip was so uncertain – the distance to the south and the opposition they would face was all new territory – she prayed that they would return soon. Many of the other wives had come to her seeking reassurance and while she had tried to sound positive she felt alone and afraid. She had to be strong for them – she could not give up hope yet.

⌘

'We have a problem,' one of the men shouted to Thorfinn, pointing out toward the fjord.

Thorfinn could see that the water had frozen over – the narrow section between two steep cliffs through which they were sailing. It was not a big section and the ice was not very thick but it was enough to prevent their long boats from sailing through. They could see the open water ahead where the fjord opened out into the bigger lake. They had not expected the waters to be frozen yet, but the weather seemed to have a mind of its own. Thorfinn cursed under his breath. This would further delay them – a delay they could ill afford.

'We have to break it up. If we can get through this section then we should be able to get home.'

The men clambered over the side of the boat onto the ice carefully testing the thickness while holding onto the side of the boat.

'Be careful,' Thorfinn said. 'We will take turns breaking it up– too many of us on the ice will cause it to collapse. It wouldn't do to lose men to the ice when we are so close to home.'

The Northmen knew the danger of cracked ice and the chance of survival should a man fall through into the water. If you didn't freeze to death in a matter of moments you could drown being trapped under the ice as the ice moved on the lake. It was not a pleasant way to die.

The men took turns breaking the ice and opening a way for their boats. Erik was taking his turn chipping at the hard crystals with his axe. His hands were frozen and his muscles ached. He had been at it for a while before Niels took over from him.

'Go and warm your hands,' he said to the young man hitting him affectionatelyon the back.

Erik pulled himself back into the boat and went to get his cloak. He hoped Isabel was all right. The sooner they got her to Kaldakinn the better. She was not accustomed to this cold.

He found her seat empty.

Where is she? Perhaps she feels sick again.

He searched the boat quickly and could not find her. Then he noticed her bow and arrows were missing. She was making a run for it. Once they were out on the open water he had untied her – now he wished he hadn't.

Silly girl – she will freeze to death out there if she doesn't fall through the ice first. What is she thinking?

He growled in frustration. He scanned the horizon searching for her. She was hard to spot as she was wearing the white fur cloak he had provided her but movement caught his eye in the distance. He hopped out the boat and told his father where he was going.

'Be careful Erik, the ice is not very thick,' his father warned.

He moved slowly trying not to rush after her. He was trained to listen to the ice beneath his feet – any shifting or cracking sounds told a story. He shuffled after her hoping that she would not do something rash. He knew what she was thinking. She was heading for the end of the steep cliffs hoping that the land would open out and provide her a way out of the icy river bed.

He was gaining on her as he was used to negotiating the slippery ice but she was completely out of her depth. She had almost reached the edge of the fjord when he heard the sound of cracking ice. It was not under his feet as he was still on the thicker part of the ice. It was Isabel who was in danger.

'Isabel' he called urgently.

She turned surprised by the panic in his voice.

'Don't move,' he shouted, 'the ice is cracking.'

She froze unsure whether to believe him or not. Was he trying to trick her?

The ice started to form little cracks all around her feet. She looked up fear written all over her face.

'Erik, help me,' she begged as the ice gave way beneath her plunging her into the icy water. She could not breathe it was so cold and her head submerged beneath the water freezing her mind and body. She could not think or fight and the heavy coat dragged her down.

She thought of Phoenix and relaxed. This was meant to be.

I will be with you soon my love.

Strong arms reached down and pulled her up to the surface. Erik lay on his stomach and gripped her tightly under each arm. Isabel spluttered and coughed up the water she had swallowed. Slowly he pulled her out and they lay side by side catching their breath.

'What were you thinking?' he finally yelled at her, relieved he had managed to rescue her but furious with her at the same time.

'Of all the stupid things to attempt Isabel – where were you hoping to run to. You would have died within the day out in the cold.'

She started to cry – great big sobs. He noticed she was shivering uncontrollably.

'Come we need to get you back to the boat before you freeze to death.' His voice softened at her distress.

Her lips were purple and she shook violently a combination of the cold and the shock. He pulled off her wet cloak and wrapped her in his. Then they slowly made their way back to the boats. The men had managed to break through the ice and some of the long boats were already heading into the open fjord.

'My bow and arrows are gone,' she lamented.

'That is the least of your problems,' he chided her gently lifting her back into the boat.

'I'm tired,' she said flopping down onto the boat deck.

'No Isabel, you cannot sleep now. That is the cold taking over your body. We need to warm you up.'

He pulled her close to himself and shielded her with his cloak. Gently he began to remove her wet clothing.

'Stop, what are you doing?' She tried to fight him off but her hands were numb and her limbs would not co-operate.

'Relax,' he growled 'I am just getting the wet things off. I'm not going to hurt you. You are very lucky – if it had been winter I would have been unable to rescue you.'

He pulled her closer into his body, her sheer slip not much of a barrier between their bodies. Then he wrapped his cloak around them both. Her head rested on his broad chest and she could feel his strength beneath her.

'Is this really necessary?' she said feeling uncomfortable.

'Yes, we have to get your body temperature up and this is the only way to do it out here on a long boat. My body will warm yours.'

'As long as you don't get any ideas,' she said sleepily. He could not help smiling at her remark – even when she was half frozen to death she had fire in her and it was very attractive. He cradled her as she finally slept, warming her and protecting her and the child that was growing in her womb. He felt the stirrings of something he had never felt before – for any woman and it felt good.

CHAPTER 21

A WHOLE NEW WORLD

KALDAKINN

'I SEE them,' Siobhan shouted as the first long boat came into sight. The women cheered in delight – everyone was beginning to fear they had been lost at sea or taken captive by the Southerners.

They watched the boats drawing closer with each row and they could hear the cheers and cries of the men coming from the boats. There would be great celebration in Kaldakinn that night.

Thorfinn held her close and breathed in her scent.

'I have missed you, beautiful woman,' he said kissing her longingly.

'I have missed you too. I was beginning to get concerned.'

'We ran into some trouble after our raid. Two of our boats were burned and we had to build new ones before we could come home.'

'Where is Erik? Is he safe?'

'He is well but a little preoccupied with a pretty woman he brought back from the south.'

'He kidnapped a woman?' she asked horrified. 'That does not sound like the son I know. Why would he do that?

He knows how I felt being captured and taken from my homeland as a young woman.'

'We could not let her go. She was the wife of one of the Lords and he was killed. We needed her to ensure our safe departure from the south. Don't worry, he has not harmed her – if anything I think he is quite taken with her and views himself as her protector.'

'That sounds more like Erik,' she smiled, 'but promise me Thorfinn that if she wishes to return home that you will take her back to the south when you go raiding next summer.'

'I give you my word,' he said pulling her close again.

⌘

Griswold

Gwendolyn stood at the graves of her son and her husband. She looked across at two more graves – one was her father's grave and the other belonged to Daemon. Four men she adored – all gone way before their time. It was not right for one person to lose everyone important within a few years. She felt overwhelming grief that threatened to swallow her into a bottomless pit – why was she being punished? Did the Great One hate her so much? Legion had assured her that the Great One only knew how to love and forgive but she had not seen that at all. Why had he not rescued them all if he loved them? Surely he could do that if he was so powerful. She would never forgive him.

She was also very angry. Balfour had given her a letter that Phoenix had drafted before they went into battle. She pulled it out and read the words her son had penned.

Dear Mother,

If you are reading this letter then I am gone. There are a few things we never got to resolve between us and I don't want to leave this world without saying what needs to be said. I know that the marriage arrangement was forged by you. I discovered the truth and despite your treachery I choose to forgive you for deceiving me. I have to believe that you did it with the best intentions for Griswold and that it was nothing personal against Isabel. There is one thing I would ask of you – to reach out to Isabel and welcome her into my home at Griswold. You see, Isabel and I were married the day before I went into battle – I ask your forgiveness in deceiving you this way but I saw no other way out and could not bear the thought of a loveless marriage. I need you to do this for me as she is the rightful heir to Griswold and as my wife she is the Lady of Griswold now. Nothing would make me happier than you welcoming her into our home. Mother, we may not have been close while I was growing up but I want you to be happy – to find peace and live life fully again. It is my greatest and last wish.

I love you

Phoenix

Of all the words Phoenix had penned Gwen could only assimilate that he had married a Williams. She could not believe he had deceived her so. She would never welcome Isabel Williams into Griswold castle. Only over her dead body would that woman ever be Lady of Griswold. She did not see the words of love that her son had uttered or the words of forgiveness; so great was her hatred. It was her final moment of loss – the defining moment of who she had finally become.

⌘

KALDAKINN

Kaldakinn was unlike anything Isabel had ever seen before. The entire village was nestled below the mountains on the edge of the fjord. With winter setting in it was covered in light snow and the ground was muddy and soggy from the rain. It was a contrast of immense beauty and space conflicting with the knowledge that you were trapped by the snow with nowhere to go. The homes were simply constructed of wooden timber beams and the walls filled with wattle and daub. They had thatch roofs which was the one familiar thing to Isabel as her grandfather was a thatcher. Erik was correct in saying that it was a close knit community. There was the great hall where everyone gathered to feast with the Earl and his family. Even the animals were a part of the living conditions, only separated at the end of each home in a byre. A large fire kept the room warm and was used for cooking, the smoke escaping through a hole in the middle of the roof. Isabel felt completely out of her comfort zone. Erik took her into the sleeping quarters which were separated from the great hall by hanging fur pelts and thick wooden posts.

'This is where you will be staying Isabel.' He indicated a rough box bed that was filled with straw and covered over with fur pelts.

'Thank you,' she said sitting on the edge of the bed awkwardly.

'Come, I will show you around the village,' he volunteered. He took her cloak and gently wrapped it around her, insulating her from the icy cold air that would greet them when they stepped out of the hall.

He took her around the village showing her all the things that were new to her, explaining things as he went along. There was pride in his voice as he explained his culture to her. Isabel could not help but notice the

Northerners staring at her – as though she was a freak of nature, an atrocity or disease. She was certain that many of the women glared at her with intense dislike in their eyes. Many of the men stared at her with undisguised lust and instinctively she pulled her cloak tighter around herself as though to protect herself and her unborn child. It was not surprising that they stared – she looked so different to these people with their fair hair – hers was raven in contrast and she stood out as the outsider.

'Can we go back now?' she asked Erik when the stares became too much. 'I'm really tired.'

Erik took her back to the hall and settled her on the bed offering her some goat's milk. She sipped the unusual milk, forcing it down and thinking of her child. She had to learn to eat what these people ate for her child to get the nourishment it needed. There was no option to be fussy. Then she closed her eyes and fell into a deep sleep.

She awoke with a start – it was dark and all was quiet. She felt afraid when she realized that someone lay beside her – too close for comfort. She turned her head and came face to face with Erik who gently snored next to her. What was he doing in her bed? She felt angry.

How dare he take advantage of me this way!

Her natural instinct was to push him out the bed but then she remembered they were sleeping in a large hall where others also slept. She bit her tongue and instead she watched him as he slept. The scar on his face was healing nicely. She resisted the urge to touch it. She looked at his strong jaw that was covered with beard and then let her gaze travel up to his straight nose. He looked peaceful as he slept and she could not help but admit that he was a very handsome man.

Stop it Isabel – he's a monster – Phoenix is dead because of these men.

'Is everything all right?' he murmured not opening his eyes. She jumped in fright, embarrassed that he knew she was watching him. Did he have a sixth sense?

'I'm fine, just surprised to wake up with you in my bed.'

He chuckled and opened his eyes – the intense blue colour drawing her in.

'I'm not in your bed Isabel – rather you are in my bed.'

'But you said this was my bed,' she whispered angrily.

'And it is. What do you think this is – an inn with private accommodation? The only place for you to sleep was here in my bed. Besides it is safer for you here – you saw how people looked at you when we went out today and I know it made you uncomfortable. My mother had the same problem all those years ago when she first arrived here – the women hated her and many wanted her dead – it took a while for them to come around.'

'Wonderful,' she replied sarcastically. 'It is totally inappropriate for me to share your bed. My husband has only been dead for just over a moon.'

'People in our culture aren't concerned with how things look Isabel. We are not as conservative as you when it comes to our sexuality. Most of the men here would expect me to take you whether you agreed or not.'

She went silent and he could see fear cloud her grey eyes.

'You have nothing to fear from me Isabel. I promised I would protect you and I will. I will never force myself on you.'

'Thank you,' she whispered.

'Now get some sleep,' he said closing his eyes again.

She watched him a little longer as his breathing deepened and he fell back into sleep. He was an enigma – unlike the other Northmen she had seen on their trip from the south. The other men on the boat seemed rough and uncouth. Erik had spent some of their days on the boat paging through some of the books he had taken from Ebondeen. The men had laughed at him and teased him relentlessly but he had just smiled and turned his attention back to his book. There was something different about him – of that she was certain.

⌘

Isabel woke to the bustle of the morning preparations for breakfast. The hall was filling up with people and children played around the fire-pit. Her nasal passages felt clogged from the wood-smoke. She was not used to smelling like a fire-pit. She had a desperate urge to wash, to freshen up, to somehow start the day clean. She threw her legs over the side of the bed and sat upright, untangling her long hair which had knotted during her sleep. She had slept surprisingly well on this crude bed. She shivered briefly. Her clothing was not suitable for this climate. She pulled on her cloak and headed out into the great hall. She felt the stares that followed her as she left the hall and made her way to the water's edge. She kneeled down and cupped water in her hands, gasping as she washed her face with the icy water. She felt their presence behind her before she saw their reflections in the blue lake. She tried to turn but was grabbed by the back of her neck, her head forced down into the water. She gurgled and fought, her arms flailing in an attempt to push herself up. They were trying to drown her.

Her lungs began to fill with water as she swallowed mouthfuls. Black spots formed before her eyes and her mind went fuzzy. Then they pulled her out of the water and threw her down on the muddy sand. She saw the fur boot coming and managed to shield most of her face with her arms as she was kicked. She grunted in pain as she felt her nose begin to bleed.

'Leave Kaldakinn before it's too late. You've been warned.' The voice was a woman's and as they walked away Isabel could see that there had been four of them – young women – probably shield maidens who had given her the beating. She lay on the ground coughing and wiping the blood from her nose. She was grateful they had not kicked her in the stomach – at least her baby would be safe. She tried to pull herself up but nausea overwhelmed her and she slumped back on the sand.

'Save the gods,' Erik growled when he found her bloody and bruised on the sand. 'Who did this to you Isabel?'

He scooped her up in his arms as though she were a feather and carried her back to the great hall.

'Lie here,' he commanded as he left to get some water. He returned with water and a cloth and gently wiped the blood from her face. Then he rubbed herbal salve onto her bruises which were beginning to show, angry purple marks around her eye and nose. She flinched, the pain of the bruises becoming evident.

'I'm sorry,' he said worried he was hurting her.

She smiled reassuringly, letting him know she was all right.

'You must not leave the hall alone Isabel. I thought I had made it clear that some people want you dead here.'

'I guess I figured that in a village full of people no one would attack me in broad daylight.'

'You are not safe at any time – is that clear,' he growled.

'So I am to be a captive again simply because strangers don't like me?'

He softened, seeing her frustration.

'It will get better Belle, I promise – it will just take time.'

She froze – Phoenix called her Belle – that was his special name for her. Her heart ached, the wound of loss ripped opened afresh.

'Don't ever call me that. Do you understand?' she said coldly. She pushed him away 'Leave me alone.' She curled up in the foetal position and turned her back on him.

Erik sighed. He did not understand this woman.

Chapter 22

Bruised

Lionsgate

The Great One watched Isabel, his heart aching for the young woman. She had endured a lot of pain for one so young and now she felt alone and afraid. He would have to send her a sign, something to encourage her and give her a hope for the future. There was no way to send anyone to be with her as winter was well and truly set in and the fjords were freezing up. He would send her a message in a dream.

⌘

Sherbrooke

Aislinn and Drew tried to focus on the medical practice and Heart and Home, but it was difficult. Isabel was constantly in their hearts and on their minds. The feeling of helplessness that surrounded them was frustrating and left them anxious.

Regent brought them news of Isabel whenever he could.

'The Great One says she is fine. She has arrived safely at Kaldakinn and is being cared for. She has the protection of the Earl and his son.'

Regent did not tell them of Isabel's beating. It was pointless worrying them more.

'Thank you,' Aislinn kissed Regent on the cheek. 'Please thank the Great One for watching over her – it does help us to know he is looking out for her.'

⌘

KALDAKINN

'How are you feeling my dear?'

Isabel opened her eyes to find a beautiful woman with long braided hair sitting on the edge of her bed.

'We have not met yet as so much has happened since your arrival. I am Siobhan, the Earl of Kaldakinn's wife and Erik's mother.'

Isabel pulled herself upright in the bed and groaned at the shooting pain in her neck which was also bruised from being held under the water.

'Take it slowly,' Siobhan chided. 'I think Erik has told you that I too came from the south. I understand what you are going through and how foreign and frightening all this must be for you.'

'They killed my husband.' The revelation came out unexpectedly and Isabel began to sob, deep painful bursts that bubbled up from her heart. It was the first time she had really let out her grief and she sounded like a wounded animal as it poured out of her in rivulets. Siobhan held her and let her cry.

'I'm sorry,' she said. 'I know the pain you are going through. My husband was killed too when I was taken.'

'Why have you stayed with these people?'

Siobhan knew the question was coming and that Isabel would very possibly not understand the answer.

'They are not as evil as you imagine Isabel. There are good men and women who live in our clan. Life is different here – much harder than the life you lived back home. Survival is our first priority. We only raid so that we can survive the harsh winter. We are locked in by the frozen fjords and we have to provide for our people. I stayed because I found a people who learned to love me despite our differences. It took time and it was hard in the beginning but once they accepted me I had a family. I had nothing to go back to – and I fell in love with Thorfinn.'

'Those women tried to kill me.'

'I know and there will be consequences for that if we find the perpetrators. We will protect you. Erik tells me that you are with child.'

'Yes.'

'Then that is what you need to focus on and look forward to – you have a future and that child is part of it. I have taken the liberty of bringing you some clothing – I noticed the clothes you had are not suitable for this climate. I have also provided some larger sizes for when your belly begins to grow. '

'Thank you.'

'We would be very honoured if you would join us in the great hall for dinner. Thorfinn would like to officially welcome you to Kaldakinn. The invitation and hospitality of the Earl will go a long way in keeping you safe. Not many would dare to cross him.'

Isabel changed into the clothing that Siobhan had given her. She touched her belly gently – it was just beginning to swell – the flat stomach she was used to looking a little more rounded than usual. Siobhan was right – she did have a destiny and a future – and she owed it to this baby and Phoenix to protect this child no matter what. She would do whatever it took to survive this winter and get back to her family.

⌘

The atmosphere in the great hall was festive and the air thick with smoke as the meat roasted over the fire-pit. The men drank vast quantities of mead – a rich alcoholic beverage made from honey. Isabel sat between Siobhan and Erik at the table. She sipped on water as she could not drink the mead. It was hard not to feel the community spirit in the moment – it felt like a large family dinner as the families chatted and laughed. Thorfinn tapped his goblet and stood.

'It is with great joy that we return from the south after a successful raid. It is good to be home with our families.'

Cheers erupted from the people as they toasted their raiding success and the favour of the gods.

Thorfinn continued. 'I have the honour of welcoming Lady Isabel of Griswold who is our guest in Kaldakinn this winter. I expect you will all welcome her and offer true northern hospitality while she is with us.'

There was a stunned silence all eyes on Thorfinn, mixed emotions displayed on the faces of the clan.

'To Isabel,' Thorfinn raised his goblet. The villagers waited momentarily then raised their glasses. 'To Isabel,' they all chorused. To refuse the Earl's toast would have been unwise. Isabel could tell they were complying with his request but she knew deep down that it did not change things – if anything they hated her more now.

'Let's take a walk,' Erik suggested. He sensed her discomfort after his father's toast.

It was good to get out of the hall even though it was freezing outside. Their breath sent up clouds of vapour as they walked.

'How are you feeling?' he asked.

'I'm not sure. Honestly I feel like I have been thrown into deep water and no matter how hard I try to swim I can't seem to stop the feeling that I am slowly drowning.'

'It will be all right Isabel – I promise. Time has a way of changing people's feelings – the villagers of Kaldakinn will get used to your presence and they will accept you. We are not used to visitors this far north and they are set in their ways, protective of our people, but they will soon come to realize you are not a threat.'

Isabel laughed, a hollow sound.

'It's ironic isn't it? It wasn't even my choice to be here. Anyone would think I came sailing in with an entire army behind me ready to conquer Kaldakinn. I can deal with the curiosity but it's the young women I am afraid of most,' she admitted. 'I think many of them are furious that you are protecting me and for some reason they seem to think I belong to you. Why haven't you married yet Erik?'

'I guess I am a little more idealistic than the average Kaldakinnian male,' he smiled. 'I do want to get married and have a family – more than anything, but I want the woman I marry to be my best friend, someone I want to be with the rest of my life. My parents have great love for one another and that is what I want too. I just haven't found that woman yet.'

'I know what you mean,' she said. 'My parents have that kind of love too and it is special – once in a life time...' her voice trailed off wistfully.

'Was that the kind of love you and Phoenix shared?'

'I think it would have been if he had not been killed. My chance at that kind of love is gone – all I have are memories now and this child who will be the focus of my life.'

She sounded sad, lost, momentarily a little girl.

'You are so young Isabel – there will be time for another love,' he said hopefully.

'No, I don't know that I will ever be able to love anyone as much as I did Phoenix. I don't know that I ever want to give my heart that way again – it is too painful when there is loss.'

He stopped and turned her to face himself. He tucked a stray strand of hair behind her ear and then gently traced his finger over her bruised face.

'Don't shut your heart off to the world Isabel – that will be more painful in the long run – to lose greatly means you have loved greatly and to experience great love, even momentarily is a gift.'

'It's time we got back,' she said suddenly feeling a level of intimacy in his touch that made her uncomfortable.

CHAPTER 23

THE GIFT

SHE WALKED through heather on the side of the hill and the purple flowers shimmered in the late afternoon sun. It was beautiful, the golden warmth reflecting off the colours of the countryside. Below her the fjord was turquoise blue with the icy waters that had melted. She felt happy, winter was over and Spring was in full swing. Then she saw him coming toward her. He had a smile on his face and her heart leapt in her chest. He had that effect on her. She ran to him and flung her arms around his neck, kissing him deeply, every fibre of her being feeling electrified.

'Isabel I love you,' he said.

'I love you too Phoenix,' she replied kissing him again.

When she pulled away it was not Phoenix she was kissing but Erik that held her in his strong arms.

'Let me go,' she shrieked pummelling his chest with her fists.

'Isabel it's okay, you are allowed to love me – you are not betraying him.'

He let her go and she turned catching her breath, her emotions confused.

When she turned back he was gone and the Great One stood before her, smiling, his arms outstretched. She fell into his arms and buried her head in his chest.

'I don't know what to do, help me,' she begged.

'He will give you a gift Isabel and it will remind you who you are and what you were destined for. Take it from him and let him protect you and your child while you are here. I have sent him to you to for the next season. There are others who want you dead besides some of the villagers in Kaldakinn. You need Erik right now.'

'What about Phoenix?'

'He is with me in Lionsgate and one day you will be reunited with him again. Right now you have your life to live and much to give still.'

Suddenly she was standing alone on the hillside in the warm sunshine –the Great One, Phoenix and Erik were gone.

She woke, her heart pounding in her chest. This was no ordinary dream. It was extremely vivid as though she had really been on the hillside. She stared up at the ceiling and took a deep breath. She sat up, careful not to disturb Erik sleeping next to her. Something was in her hair – she ran her fingers through it and pulled out a small piece of heather.

That's impossible – it's winter and there is no heather.

She realized her dream had greater significance – it was the Great One sending her a message. Her grandfather always talked about the Great One's ability to communicate through dreams. She loved hearing his stories of adventures against Legion before he became a changed man. Now he was letting her know that he was with her and that she had a future. She lay back down on the bed and pulled the fur over her body. She felt peaceful for the first time since she had arrived at Kaldakinn. Erik was right, everything would be all right.

⌘

Winter was well and truly set in. The snow was thick and the fjord iced up completely. Children played on the ice, the animals were confined to the byres and life seemed to slow down in Kaldakinn. There was not the productivity that happened during the summer months. Isabel spent many hours reading and explaining things to Erik about life in the south and farming methods. He was absorbing every detail, hungry for knowledge. She had been at Kaldakinn for over a moon and her face was back to its normal hue, the bruises a distant memory. There had been no further incidents as Siobhan and Erik made sure she was never alone. Her belly was just beginning to show and for those who knew no better they had no inkling of the baby she carried. She was about four moons along and she was grateful the nausea and sickness had passed. Now she felt constantly hungry and devoured everything she could gratefully. At the back of her mind she feared the day she would give birth. She had always hoped her mother would bring her baby into the world – someone who knew what to do and would support her. The thought of giving birth to this child with strangers assisting her was terrifying.

'Isabel I have something I want to show you,' Erik said entering the great hall. He had little white flakes of snow on his shoulders and in his hair and he shook himself and stamped his feet as he entered.

Isabel sat around the fire-pit with Siobhan who was preparing a skin ready to make into a garment.

'Your mother is showing me how to prepare a hide,' she beamed at him, proudly lifting the pelt she was working on.

'We'll make you into a Northman yet,' he laughed. 'That looks pretty good I would say. Do you mind if I steal her away for a moment Mother.'

'Go on you two,' Siobhan smiled. Her son was falling hard for this woman – it was very obvious to her – the love in his eyes and his manner around her. She hoped that he would not be hurt in the process.

Erik pulled Isabel up by the hand and wrapped her cloak around her shoulders.

'The weather is pretty brutal out there.'

She pulled the fur closer and followed him out, curiosity getting the better of her.

'Where are we going?'

'You'll see,' he replied mysteriously.

She followed him through the huts to the grain store. It was a large building that housed all the food stores for winter. Right at the end of the building was a smaller room where some tools and benches were set up. He ushered her in through the low doorway.

'Erik why are we here?'

'Close your eyes,' he commanded placing his hands over her face so that she could not see. I have something I made for you.'

She closed her eyes and waited.

The sound of a sickening thud and Erik grunting in pain brought her back to reality in a moment. His hands slid from her face as he fell to the floor. Her eyes flew open and she spun around to find herself face to face with a Northman who towered above her slim frame. He blocked the doorway preventing her escape. He was in his mid-thirties his long hair pulled back off his bearded face. He had seen war many times as his face was scarred and a tattoo ran down one side. She glanced down at Erik who lay on the floor. Fear flickered in her eyes as she tried to keep her voice calm.

'What have you done to him? '

She moved toward Erik, her concern for him overriding her fear. He grabbed her by her wrist pulling her toward himself.

'What do you want?' she asked the fear returning.

'I have been watching you Lady Isabel and I fancy you for my own. In Kaldakinn we men take what we want and I have noticed that the evnukk has not proved himself man enough for you. I will show you what a real man is like.'

Isabel tried to pull away but he cornered her in the room. He grabbed her other wrist, pushing her down onto the wooden bench trying to kiss her. Isabel bit him hard and he yelped in pain, slapping her hard across the face to subdue her.

'Please don't do this,' she begged.

'You're a wild one,' he laughed further aroused by her fighting spirit.

'Touch her once more and I will kill you.' Erik's voice was icy cold.

The Northman turned around to find Erik holding a bow, the arrow aimed straight at his heart.

'Now evnukk, let's not be hasty. You can't blame a man for wanting a piece of this beautiful woman. I wouldn't be human if I didn't feel some attraction for her.'

'Get out Gunnar, and if you ever attempt this again, I will kill you.'

The man shuffled out of the room, wiping his bleeding lip as he went. He glared at Erik as he passed hatred in his eyes.

'Are you all right,' Erik asked concerned that he had hurt her.

'I'm fine, thank you Erik. Let me look at your head, you're bleeding. It was a small cut on the side of his head and Isabel dabbed at it with her sleeve stemming the flow.

'It doesn't look too deep,' she murmured. 'Why did he call you evnukk, Erik?

'The men call me that because I don't rape women or force them. It is their way of making me feel less than a man.'

'Don't ever feel that way,' she said as she gently dabbed his wound. 'If anything that makes you more of a man.'

He grabbed her hand and held it tight, closing his eyes. His heart pounded in his chest. She affected him in ways he had never encountered and it was sheer agony being so near to her yet unable to have her.

'Thank you,' he said letting her hand go.

'So why did you bring me here?'

He had forgotten the surprise with all the drama. He smiled – it was something he had worked on for weeks and he hoped she would like it.

He picked up the quiver covered with grey fur and handed it to her. It contained eight arrows perfectly crafted. Then he handed her a bow made from elm.

'I hope it's all right. I had to read some of the books from Ebondeen to make it as similar to the one you lost. Your bows are a little more elaborate than our hunting bows here.'

She turned it over in her hands, feeling the familiar strength of the wooden weapon beneath her hands. She was speechless – moved by his thoughtfulness and all the effort he had gone to craft it for her.

'Why did you do this for me?'

'The gods came to me in a dream Isabel. Odin himself told me to make you a bow, to remind you who you are and what you are destined for. I wanted you to have something that reminds you of your home.'

She had heard those exact words. She thought back to her dream and the Great One's words.

Then she saw it. Engraved on the bow was the head of a lion. She had seen this engraving before. It was the symbol on the gates of Lionsgate. Her mother had told her all about the place the Great One and Ziah lived, every detail. When she was fourteen her parents had taken her there and she had seen it for herself. She ran her fingers over it.

'Why did you engrave this?' she asked.

'I don't know. I have never seen a creature like that but that is the creature I saw in my dream – the one Odin told me to carve on the bow.'

'It is a lion Erik.'

'A lion; what is that?'

'Lions are strong and fierce and they protect their young ferociously. They symbolize courage and leadership.'

'Well then this lion is a perfect symbol on your bow – you are all those things Isabel. Odin is trying to send you a message.'

'No Erik, I think the Great One is sending me a message.'

'The Great One; who's that?'

She laughed at his confused expression.

'It looks like we have some other differences between the North and South to discuss.'

She hugged him touched by his gift. She thought of her dream and how he had received his instruction to make the gift in a dream. It was too much to be coincidental.

'Thank you Erik, I love it.'

CHAPTER 24

CHALLENGES

EBONDEEN

STRUAN had offered to return to Ebondeen with Catriona. There was much that needed to be done in rebuilding the castle and she did not want to face it alone. His leg was healing nicely and he was learning how to adjust to his new life.

'We've done some research Struan, and we've discovered through Drew's medical journals that a French surgeon named Ambroise Pare developed artificial limbs that have become very successful over the last one hundred years. Would you be willing for us to construct a limb for you? It would give you greater freedom to move around,' Aislinn had told him.

He had been delighted with that news. They were working on his new limb and he looked forward to the day he would use it. In the meantime his leg needed to heal completely and he would help Catriona as best he could. Balfour had offered to bring some men from Griswold to help restore the castle. He watched the young woman as she stood at her father's grave, tears running down her face. The rough wooden cross was all they could construct in the aftermath of the raid.

'We will get him a proper headstone, I promise,' Struan said to her.

She helped him as he hopped on his crutch and they headed back to their horses. He tried to pull himself up into the saddle and slipped as the horse moved. He fell on the ground and swore.

'Damn this leg, I will never be a man again.'

She dropped down beside him and grabbed his shoulders.

'Don't say that. You are more than a man – you saved my life and I can never repay you for that.'

'I'm sorry Cat, I would do it all again if I had the choice. Your life is more important than my leg. Thank you for being here for me the last few months.'

He gazed at her sweet face and his heart stirred. He felt his stomach flip. He had not had these feelings since Ceinlys died.

'Come on let's get you back on that horse,' she said pulling him up.

⌘

KALDAKINN

'What do you mean Father?' Erik bellowed, incredulous at what he had just been told.

'It is the custom of our people Erik.'

'He tried to rape her, he attacked me. Doesn't that mean anything?'

'He would not be the first man to fight over a woman here in Kaldakinn.'

'I can't believe you are allowing this,' Erik fumed.

'He is following the correct custom Erik, as you well know, by approaching me for Isabel's hand in marriage. His clumsy attempt at forcing her earlier was a mistake he has apologized for. You know that unless someone else contests it by asking for her hand I cannot deny him.'

'What about what she wants? Does he even know that she carries another man's child?'

'No and it is early enough for that not to be a problem. The child will come in the summer months when he is raiding so he will be none the wiser when it is born. As for her consent, you know that as Earl I have the right to decide what is best for a maiden in Kaldakinn.'

Erik stormed out the hall – he needed to clear his head. Isabel would rather die than be given to Gunnar in marriage. He knew she would never agree to it. He was angry with his father. He had the power as Earl to change the laws but he was a traditional man in many ways and believed in the system they had for living in harmony in the village.

Back in the hall Siobhan looked at Thorfinn, disapproval written all over her face.

'Not you too, woman,' he groaned.

'You promised she could leave if she chose to in the spring. Now you are allowing Gunnar to ask for her hand in marriage. I don't understand you sometimes.'

'You will understand in time Siobhan – my decisions may not make sense to you now but they will. I need you to trust me.'

'I hope you know what you are doing Thorfinn,' she said as she left to find her son.

He paced angrily up and down the beach, muttering to himself and yelling to the gods.

'Erik, you need to calm down,' Siobhan patted her son on the shoulder.

'She is not ready to marry someone and certainly not that brute Gunnar.'

'I know, but Gunnar has the right to request her as his wife. That is the custom here. Your father cannot deny him his right as a man.'

'So that makes it all right then? I can't believe you are defending his actions Mother.'

'No it does not. Gunnar would be the worst thing that could happen to Isabel. Someone else would be much better suited to her – someone who cares about her – someone like you.'

She let the insinuation hang in the air.

'You do care about her don't you?'

'Yes, I do – I've never felt this way about any woman before, but I promised I would never force myself on her. I want her to love me the way I love her – I don't want her marrying me because she has no choice and I don't want to marry a woman who doesn't love me.'

'Then you need to convince her that it is in her best interest to marry you and the only way to keep her and her child from harm. She may not love you the way she did her husband, but she does like you and she feels safe with you. Fight for her Erik, and if she does not have feelings for you when spring comes then let her go back to her people. If she marries Gunnar she will never be free again. Think about it son – it is the only solution. You are the only one who has the ability to save her.'

⌘

'I'm sorry Isabel; I was as shocked as you when he petitioned for your hand in marriage.'

'I won't do it – I would rather die first than have that man touch me. Help me Erik – help me get away from here please.'

'I would if I could, but we are snowed in Isabel and you would die out in the cold.'

'There has to be a solution. I can't marry him.'

'There is another way but it won't please you,' he said cautiously.

'Anything has to be better than marrying Gunnar.'

She listened as he outlined his plan her face revealing mixed emotions of fear, gratitude and confusion.

⌘

'So you wish to petition for Lady Isabel's hand in marriage,' Thorfinn said, his son standing before him. 'You are aware Erik that Gunnar has already made this request and that this will require you to fight him. The winner will earn the right to wed Isabel.'

The men in the hall cheered. They loved it when there were marriage petitions as the contenders had to fight for the maiden. Winter was always a little drab but this would add a bit of adventure and entertainment.

'I understand and agree to the terms.' Erik said.

The men slapped him on the back. 'Good luck evnukk,' they teased. 'It is about time you fought for a woman.'

Isabel was horrified to learn that Erik would have to fight for her.

'What if he beats you Erik? Then I have no choice but to marry him. I swear I will drive an arrow through my own heart before that happens.'

'I don't plan to lose Isabel. Will you trust me? I promised to protect you and that baby and I will.'

'When will the fight take place?'

'Tomorrow morning.'

'So soon,' she said dismayed.

⌘

'You planned this all along, didn't you?' Siobhan asked him as they readied for bed.

Thorfinn smiled as she brushed her long hair.

'Of course I did,' he replied. 'I've seen how our son has looked at her from the day she boarded the long boat. He is so noble that he would never have asked her to marry him and come spring she would have left and he would be left heartbroken. He just needed Gunnar to nudge him in the right direction. I knew that he would never stand for him marrying Isabel.'

'What if Gunnar beats him tomorrow,' she asked afraid.

'I have fought with Erik and Gunnar many times and I know what they are both capable of. Gunnar is strong but he is impulsive and fights for the wrong reasons. Erik on the other hand is clever and can read his opponent. He is fighting for love and that gives him the edge. Don't worry Siobhan, he will win tomorrow, I'm sure.'

'What if she wants to return to her family in spring? His heart will be crushed. Have you considered that?'

'I have and it's a possibility, but we have time and feelings can change. If he loves her he will fight for her Siobhan – that's how great love is born.'

⌘

Isabel struggled to sleep. She was fearful and she felt helpless regarding her own future. It was an awful feeling having others decide your fate.

'Great One,' she whispered, 'you said that I have a destiny and a future. Please don't let anything happen to me or my child. I know you can hear me and I trust you will take care of me.'

'Your god is probably sleeping Isabel, as you should be,' Erik whispered to her, his eyes still closed. He had caught her out again.

'How can you sleep at a time like this?' she whispered annoyed.

'If I don't get some sleep then I won't be in any state to fight tomorrow. Stop worrying now and go to sleep. I believe Odin has set me as your protector and so I am not afraid to face Gunnar.'

It took her another two hours but finally she fell into an exhausted sleep. She woke in the morning to find their bodies entwined. Her head was on his broad chest and his arms encircled her protectively.

She lay dead still, hardly daring to breath. She felt embarrassed and tried to wiggle her way carefully out from under his arm.

'Don't go yet,' he murmured enjoying the feel of her curves next to him.

'I'm sorry,' she said pulling away from him.

'I'm not,' he smiled sleepily and she blushed.

'I'm scared Erik.'

'Don't be – I won't let anything happen to you.'

He sat up and swung his legs over the bed. Then he pulled off his shirt and reached for a clean one. Isabel tried to avert her eyes but it was hard not to notice his strong back and arms and the tattoo that travelled down his shoulder and arm.

'It will all be over soon,' he said pulling on his shirt.

CHAPTER 25

THE FIGHT

THE MEN formed a circle outside the great hall. There was great anticipation for the fight and they took bets on who would win. Isabel could not bear the thought of watching it and stayed within the hall. She paced up and down like a caged animal, twisting the signet ring Phoenix had given her.

'It is time,' Thorfinn said to her.

'I don't want to watch thank you.'

'It is custom in Kaldakinn for the maiden to attend the fight. It is an insult to the men fighting if she does not attend Isabel.'

'It's barbaric.' The words slipped out before she could stop them.

'That may be your opinion but we shall follow the custom and you will attend.' He ushered her out the door to the chanting men.

Erik stood in the circle, opposite him was Gunnar who smiled leeringly at Isabel as she approached with Thorfinn. She glanced nervously at Erik and he nodded reassuringly at her. Neither man looked afraid of the upcoming fight. Thorfinn ushered her to a bench and then stepped into the middle of the circle.

'Gunnar, Erik, you know the rules of the fight. There are to be no weapons – your fists will settle this dispute. The last man standing will win the hand of Lady Isabel.'

He settled himself on the bench alongside Isabel.

'Let the fight begin.'

The two men sized one another up as they danced around the makeshift ring. Gunnar made the first move, running at Erik like a tornado. Erik side-stepped him and he sprawled face first into the mud. The men laughed and jeered. He pulled himself up and spat out a mouthful of mud, disgust on his face.

'Come and get me evnukk, if you have the balls' he taunted Erik. All the men began to chant 'evnukk, evnukk, evnukk.'

Isabel felt humiliated for Erik but the young man did not seem bothered by Gunnar's jibes. She cringed when the first punch was thrown, squarely on Erik's jaw. She thought she heard his bone crack. She closed her eyes, nausea threatening to overwhelm her. How could Thorfinn sit here so composed watching his son get beaten by another?

Come on Erik, don't let him hit you she willed silently.

Punches were traded back and forth between the men as they slipped in the mud. They were both beginning to tire and Isabel wondered whether they would ever give up. Gunnar wiped his bloody nose with the back of his hand as he staggered toward Erik ready to attack again.

'I am going to enjoy ravishing her body when I win this fight. Think of me with her Erik,' he laughed, an ugly evil laugh.

It was too much. Erik let out a growl, driven to fury by his taunts. He grabbed him around the chest driving him to the muddy ground. He straddled him and punched him relentlessly until the men had to pull him off the now unrecognisable Gunnar.

'Enough Erik,' his father said sternly.

Gunnar lay unconscious and bloody in the mud and Erik shook off the men who held him back. His fists were grazed and bloodied and his one eye was cut and swollen. He looked over at Isabel.

She could not sit there any longer Leaping to her feet she staggered away from the men before she vomited, her stomach cramping in revulsion. These people were animals!

⌘

Erik found her in their sleeping quarters. She looked pale and sad.

'Are you all right,' he asked.

'A lot better than you,' she said trying to make light of the circumstances.

He touched his swollen eye and then grimaced in pain.

'Here let me look at it,' she said making him sit down. 'My Mama and Papa did teach me a thing or two about basic medicine. You will need to have that stitched up if you don't want a nasty scar.'

Erik erupted in laughter.

'What's so funny?' she asked.

'The woman who shot my face with an arrow is worried I might have a little scar from a split eyebrow.'

She smiled at the irony of it. She cleaned the wound and rubbed some salve around it before stitching it up.

'There, that should heal nicely,' she said. He took her hands in his and looked up into her eyes.

'I'm sorry you had to watch the fight. I know it was hard for you.'

'I'm just glad you are all right. I thought you were going to kill him and that made me afraid. I've never seen you so angry and out of control – for a moment I did not know you."

'I don't know what overcame me. I remembered how he tried to hurt you and the thought of him doing that to you again made me so angry. When he expressed his intentions I just lost control.'

'Well thanks to you that won't happen now.'

'Isabel I know you haven't even had time to grieve for Phoenix and I know you loved him with your whole heart, but the only way I can keep you safe is for you to marry me. I promise I will not take advantage of you and I will treat you with the utmost respect. When spring comes I will help you return to your family if you so wish. That is my promise to you. Will you marry me and let me protect you and your child?'

Isabel was silent. She did not hate this man. Oh, she had certainly tried but he had saved and protected her countless times in the last few moons. He was the only way she would survive her time at Kaldakinn. She trusted him when he gave her his word. For the last moon they had shared a bed and not once had he forced himself on her. He had certainly had plenty of opportunity to and no one would have blinked an eye if he had.

'Yes,' she whispered 'I will marry you Erik, for the sake of my baby.'

His heart ached. He did not delude himself that she loved him but it hurt that she only wanted him for her child's sake.

'That's it then – I will make arrangements,' he said as he left the room.

Isabel lay in bed confused. Had she done something wrong? Erik had not returned and chose to sleep out in the great hall. She looked over to the empty side of the bed and rubbed her hand over the fur where he usually slept. A tear slid from her eye and she wiped it away. She felt strangely lonely.

⌘

GRISWOLD

Gwendolyn stood in her father's spell chamber, the musty air pungent. It was twenty-four years since she had been into this room – it had been locked up after Daemon's death and she had ordered that no-one touch it. Every time she thought of entering she lost her courage and her heartache would return, so she had put it off year after year.

'Why don't you go in there and sort out your father and brother's things?' Legion had asked her more than once. 'Perhaps it would help you to finally get closure.'

But, she could never do it – until now. Daemon had used this chamber after her father's death and so some of the spell books and items belonged to him. She ran her finger over the open spell book, tracing a line in the dust as she did so. The spell caught her eye. She whispered the words as she read, 'FEAR NUA.'

Gwendolyn was horrified as she read through the ritual. Her father had a spell to harness greater wisdom and power to become a new man by the murder of a baby. She thought back to the night Phoenix was taken. Daemon said it was a man from the North who had stolen the child. Why did her father have this spell open? The Northman must have broken into his chambers to get access to the spell. Her father must have known it and followed Daemon and the man to Skull Hill where he laid down his life for Phoenix and Daemon. She quickly closed the huge book with a bang, sending dust flying. She moved over to the writing bureau and sat down on the chair. There were quills and old parchment and some spells half-finished on his desk. She browsed through the paperwork finding nothing of interest. Then she saw the drawer. She pulled at it but it would not budge. She tried a little harder but it was clearly locked. Curiosity got the better of her as she rummaged through the bureau looking for a key, sending papers scattering as she did so. She could not find one.

CHAPTER 26

CEREMONY

KALDAKINN

'DO WE really have to go through all this fuss,' Isabel moaned to Erik.

'It is tradition in Kaldakinn Isabel, and while I realize our marriage is merely a front to keep you safe, we still have to let the villagers believe it is genuine. They will know something is wrong if we don't follow the traditions of our people. Besides I am the son of the Earl and they will expect it to be a great celebration.'

'I understand Erik, but a week-long celebration is a bit extreme don't you think?'

He laughed. 'Not here in Kaldakinn. If you hadn't noticed there isn't much to do here in winter and this gives the villagers an excuse to indulge in large quantities of mead.'

'All right then. When will we be married?'

'Marriages always take place on Frigga's day to honour the goddess of marriage.'

'You people and your gods – I don't know why you believe in so many of them. I have always believed that following the Great One is the only way to live in this world. I don't think I could ever believe all the things you do.'

'I don't expect you to understand Isabel – I know it is all new to you, but you are here in Kaldakinn now and you need to respect our beliefs. The people will be very offended if you shun the gods and talk about this Great One. Believe what you wish, but keep it to yourself if you want to remain safe. Our people will do anything to protect the gods and please them.'

'All right Erik, I will do as you say.'

Isabel still felt uncomfortable with the wedding rituals that would take place. Still she had to follow the custom. It was four days till Frigga's day and there was a lot to do before then. Erik had not returned to their bed since he conquered Gunnar and Isabel felt more confused than ever.

'Why is Erik sleeping on the bench in the hall?' she asked Siobhan one morning while they were washing clothes.

'Erik only shared his quarters with you to ensure your safety Isabel. Now that you have been pledged to him in marriage no one would dare attack you and so you are safe. He will stay in the hall till you are married then he will return to your bed.'

Isabel felt relieved. She thought she had offended him.

'Erik may appear strong and indifferent Isabel, but he has a tender heart. Please don't take advantage of that and hurt him,' Siobhan said.

Isabel felt shocked at the direct challenge.

'I have made no promises to Erik, Siobhan. He knows how I feel and I certainly have not led him on in any way.'

'Good then there should be no problems.'

⌘

FRIGGA'S DAY

The day dawned clear and crisp, the rain gone for the moment and Isabel felt relieved. She did not relish the thought of standing in sleet and snow to get married. Custom dictated that marriages took place outdoors in the elements of nature – something to do with the gods being present and invited to the ceremony. Isabel did not understand it all and she had no wish to learn about it either.

Siobhan and some of her ladies came in and helped her to get ready. They poured her a steaming bath which they scented with herbal oils. Isabel sat in the tub with her eyes closed inhaling the scent of lavender. She looked down at her belly and protectively cupped it in her hands. She had a small bump which could be mistaken for womanly curves but she knew her body had changed and was filling out. She thought of Phoenix and looked at his signet ring. Their wedding day had been equally rushed as this one but she had been so happy and so sure about the future. Now she felt nervous and had no idea what lay in store for her. She trusted that Erik would keep his word, but she really did not know him at all.

She finished bathing and stepped out the tub wrapping herself in a warm fur. There was no special bridal clothing in Kaldakinn. She pulled on a grey woollen tunic that fitted her form perfectly. Then she slipped her feet into the deerskin boots. Finally she placed a white fur coat around her shoulders. She had been instructed to leave her raven hair loose as only married women braided their hair. Once she was married the women would pull her aside and braid her hair for her husband.

'You look beautiful Isabel,' Siobhan said carrying a large item in her arms.

'What is that?' Isabel asked.

'This is the bridal crown; it has been in our clan for generations.'

The headpiece was made of woven straw and wheat and garlanded with flowers.

'Here let me put it on.'

Isabel felt strange with the unusual crown but she did as she was told.

'Now you are almost ready. Just one more thing; this is my youngest son Sveinn. He will represent your kinsman and will carry a sword which you are to give to Erik during the ceremony.'

Isabel nodded and smiled at the boy who could not be more than twelve. He blushed as he smiled back shyly. She had seen him around the great hall but had not realized he was Erik's brother. It seemed like everyone was related when you lived in a community where everything was shared.

'Thank you Sveinn. It would be an honour to have you represent my family since they can't be here. I hope we can be good friends.'

The young boy smiled broadly. She had found an ally.

Isabel walked beside Sveinn to the circular stones that were considered sacred ground. She shivered, half from the cold and half from fear. She felt guilty as though she were betraying Phoenix in some way.

There's no going back now. I'm sorry my love, I have to do this for our child, Please forgive me.

She could see Erik standing waiting for her and his blue eyes smiled as she approached. He looked strong and handsome in his woollen tunic and flecked fur coat.

The ceremony began with the seer calling out to the gods, inviting them to attend. Isabel watched fascinated as the villagers called out to Thor and Freyja. Then a goat and a sow were brought out before the people.

'It is with honour that we sacrifice these animals to our gods Thor and Freyja. May their blood make us one with the gods and bring fertility to both Erik and Isabel.'

Isabel glanced at Erik, panic in her eyes.

They aren't going to kill the beasts right here are they?

Erik could see the horror on her face. Perhaps he should have told her what to expect but knowing Isabel she would have refused and that would have caused all sorts of problems with the clan. He gripped her hand tight and squeezed it warning her to keep silent.

She gasped when the first animal's throat was slit and she thought she would faint when they caught its blood in a clay bowl. She tried to look down at the ground. Her head felt faint and her heart pounded in her chest. She wanted to vomit. The squeal of the sow was the last thing she remembered. Her legs buckled under her as she started to fall. Strong arms caught her up and held her close.

'Isabel,' he whispered into her ear. 'It will be all right. Trust me.'

It took a few moments for her to regain her composure and she looked at the villagers apologetically.

I can't believe I have to pretend that I'm the abnormal one. These people are not human. Her thoughts assailed her.

She thought the worst was over after the sacrifice until the seer dipped fir twigs into the animal blood and began to sprinkle them with it. Then he sprinkled the villagers speaking the gods' blessings over them. Isabel felt repulsed and she shuddered as the droplets sprayed her face and her tunic.

I'm sorry Great One. I know you are probably horrified by this all. Please forgive me, she thought.

Erik stepped forward and presented Isabel with an ancestral sword.

'This was my grandfather's sword. He would be honoured for us to have this today. I give this to you Isabel to put in safe-keeping for our first-born son.'

Sveinn stepped forward and handed Isabel the sword that represented her family.

'Erik I give this sword to you as a token of my father's trust in you to care for and protect me.'

Erik took the sword and smiled at her.

Then they exchanged metal rings with one another and holding hands on the hilt of the sword they pledged their lives to one another. It was bizarre for Isabel marrying someone she admired but did not love. Deep in her heart she felt sad. Erik felt sad too. He loved this woman but she would never be wholly his. It was not what he hoped for.

'Now for the fun part,' he said to Isabel.

'You mean being sprinkled with blood wasn't the fun part?' she asked trying to be humorous. Erik looked wounded by her response and shook his head.

'Maybe one day you will understand our customs.'

'I'm sorry Erik. What happens now?'

'The bridal run. The women and the men race back to the great hall and whoever arrives last has to serve the ale and mead all through the night.'

'Are you serious?' Isabel asked.

'I am,' he shouted as he sped off. Chaos erupted as men and women bustled to get to the hall, slipping and sliding on the icy ground as they went.

Isabel arrived at the hall out of breath and laughing. It had been fun. The women had no chance against the men who cheered loudly, delighted to be served for the night.

Erik was waiting for her at the entrance, his bared sword across the entryway.

'I have to lead you into the hall to make sure you don't stumble,' he told her. 'It is a bad omen if you fall.'

Once they were inside Erik took his sword and plunged it as hard as he could into the central wooden pillar. Isabel noticed that there were many gashes in the pillar.

She looked questioningly at him.

'The depth of the scar will determine the luck of the marriage,' he informed her.

'So how are we doing then,' she asked amused.

'Looks pretty good to me,' he smiled.

They took their seats at the table and the bridal ale was brought to them. Isabel had to serve Erik as a symbol of her wifely devotion. He took the cup and made the symbol of Thor over it, moving his hand in a T-shaped pattern. Then he made a toast to Odin and sipped the ale. He passed the cup to Isabel and all eyes were on her.

He leaned over and whispered to her, 'Make a toast to Freyja.'

'I can't do that Erik,' she whispered back 'I cannot toast a god I don't believe in – that would be wrong.'

'Isabel, you have to. They will not understand if you do not. Just do it,' he growled.

'Is there a problem?' Thorfinn asked.

'No,' she replied standing up. 'To Freyja.'

She sipped the ale and the villagers cheered believing that since they had drunk from the bridal cup their union would be recognized by the gods.

Isabel sat down, seething inwardly. She had been made to follow rituals that went against every fibre of her being. She felt dirty, tarnished.

The celebration went late into the night as the villagers feasted and danced. Isabel felt sick when the dinner came – meat from the animals that were sacrificed. She tried to pick her way through it but her stomach turned. All she wanted to do was put her head down and go to sleep – to forget about everything for a few hours.

Erik could see she was tiring so he went and spoke to his father. Thorfinn tapped his goblet and the room quietened down.

'Erik is anxious to get his bride to bed.' Everyone roared with laughter and the men whistled. Isabel felt mortified.

'As is custom three men and three women will lead them to their quarters by light.'

'What does that mean?' Isabel asked him worried.

'Don't worry they won't be staying.' The look of relief on her face made him laugh.

They were escorted to their room and the witnesses made sure they entered and stayed together. Once they were alone Isabel sank onto the bed, exhausted. Emotionally it had been a hard day. Added to that were all the strange rituals she had endured – rituals she did not understand.

Erik helped her remove her cloak and he took a damp cloth and wiped a few spots of blood that had dried on her face. She washed her face and hands.

'Here's a clean shirt,' he said handing her a new garment. She felt self- conscious. Although they had shared the room he had never seen her undress as he always left when she changed. Now she had no choice as there were witnesses who would question him leaving their chambers. She could not bring herself to sleep in the bloody tunic she wore. She needed to get every reminder of that bloody sacrifice off her body.

'Thank you,' she said quietly.

He turned his back to allow her some modesty and she felt extremely grateful. She did not understand this man – she had yet to figure him out. Sometimes he was so gentle and sensitive, but she had also seen the brutal side of him when he had mercilessly punched Gunnar, not that she felt sorry for the brute. At times he was so hungry for culture and knowledge and yet other times he embraced what she thought was a dark belief. She dressed quickly and then climbed into the bed. He removed his shirt. She was afraid to admit to herself that she found him very attractive. She noticed a necklace he was wearing. She had not seen it before. It was a wooden eagle, beautifully carved on a leather thong.

'Where did you get that?' she asked.

'My father made it for me when I was a boy. Legend has it that Odin can change shape into an eagle and that he soars over the earth and looks down on the world.'

She looked away, embarrassed that she was staring.

'He carved it beautifully,' she said. She felt so awkward. She had shared this man's room for weeks, but never as his wife.

What were his expectations?

'What now?' she asked tentatively.

'You get some sleep,' he answered. 'I will not lie to you Isabel – I find you very desirable and I would love to be with you, but I have promised that I will never force myself on you and so I will honour that. If you ever want to change our circumstances then it is up to you. The gods have seen fit to put us together and so for now that will be enough for me.'

Isabel did not understand why his statement goaded her. She assumed it was because of all the rituals she had undergone during their wedding. She could not bite her tongue, even though her head told her to stay silent.

'The gods did not put us together Erik,' she scoffed. 'You took me from my homeland against my will and brought me to this awful place. I have gone against everything I believe in marrying you today. That ceremony was a bloodbath and goes against everything I believe. I will not allow you or your people to turn me from the Great One. You may want me to sell my soul to the devil, but I won't let you.'

'Then perhaps you are not the woman I believed you to be Isabel. You're too afraid to explore and discover other cultures, to be open to learn from others who think differently to you. That's a pity – I thought perhaps you were more adventurous. I obviously made a mistake.'

'Erik...' she said trying to defend herself.

Go to bed Isabel,' he said coldly, turning his back as he extinguished the light.

CHAPTER 27

DISCOVERY

SHERBROOKE

AISLINN and Drew took the wooden limb and fitted it to Struan's leg.

'How does that feel?' Drew asked. 'It will take some getting used to and might even cause severe pain until your leg adjusts to it.'

'It feels strange but I am grateful to you both for giving me my life back. Thank you.'

Aislinn hugged her brother, glad to see him smiling again. It had been a difficult time for Struan and he had suffered depression for a while after the battle that took his leg.

'How is Catriona settling in back home?' Aislinn asked.

'It's been hard – everything reminds her of her father and she misses him terribly, but we have tried to cheer each other up. Have you had any news of Isabel?'

'Regent keeps us posted – the Great One has assured us that she is safe and being cared for but I still feel anxious. He has not told us any details other than she is fine. Come now,' Aislinn said to her brother, 'let's get you up on that leg trying it out.'

Struan wobbled as he tried to walk but shouted triumphantly when he managed to move a few steps.

'What are your plans now?' his sister asked.

'I will return to Ebondeen. Catriona has asked me to be her advisor as she feels completely out of her depth and I feel I can assist her in running her lands.'

Aislinn smiled – her brother did not seem to realize that his eyes lit up when he spoke about the young woman. It would be good for him to find love again – he deserved to be happy and since Ceinlys had died he had been lonely. She hoped he and Catriona would find each other through this tragedy.

⌘

GRISWOLD

Gwendolyn had not been able to shake her curiosity regarding the bureau drawer since she had been in her father's chamber. She had tried everything possible to open the drawer to no avail. She desperately wanted to know what was in there.

She had systematically been sorting the room out and found no keys that fitted the lock. She sat at her dresser brushing her hair, thinking about her father and Daemon. She missed them both but particularly her brother. She had kept his saddle pouch all these years hanging from her mirror above her dresser. She remembered the awful day they brought it to her after finding it in Grimwood Forest. She had been determined that she would not forget him or what Aislinn and Drew Williams had done to him.

She pulled the pouch from the dresser mirror and held it in her lap. Tears flowed from her lids. She opened the empty bag and peered inside. There had been nothing all those years ago when the pouch was returned and the theory was that thieves had stolen the coins Daemon would have carried. She drew it closed again and rested it on her dresser. She was interrupted by Maeve, her lady in waiting and she brushed her tears away quickly, replacing them with her composed face.

Maeve helped her dress, lacing her corset.

'Could you get the pearls from my dresser please?' Gwen asked her.

Maeve plucked the shiny beads up accidentally knocking the pouch off the dresser onto the stone floor. She gasped, afraid at her mistress's response. She knew how precious that pouch was to Gwendolyn and no one was ever allowed to touch it.

'I'm sorry Mam,' she stuttered not sure whether to pick it up or leave it on the floor.

'Leave me,' Gwen barked rushing over to the pouch. Maeve fled the chamber.

When the pouch had fallen Gwen could have sworn she heard metal hitting the floor.

How was that possible? The pouch was empty.

She peered into the leather bag again and saw nothing. Slowly she ran her fingers over every inch of the bag feeling for any irregularities. Then she felt it – a hard object, metal she presumed. She turned the pouch inside out and when she inspected closer found a secret compartment. She tugged at the loose stitches prying it open. Inside she found what she was looking for – an old key.

⌘

KALDAKINN

Isabel felt bad. She and Erik had gotten off to a rocky start in their marriage. It had been a week since the wedding and although they pretended to be the happy couple when they were amongst the villagers they hardly spoke a word when they were alone. It seemed that Erik had decided to shut himself off from her and she felt lonelier than ever. She knew it was her fault – attacking him on their wedding night and accusing him of being a brute when all he had done was protect her since she had been here, had been uncalled for. She had also attacked his gods and mocked them. She knew that was wrong. She would never believe in Odin and Thor and however many others there were. Her belief in the Great One was too strong, however she would have to respect his beliefs while she was here.

She wanted to make it up to him somehow. She rose from her bed and headed out quietly into the great hall. Everyone was still asleep. Pulling on her cloak she left the hall, her fur boots crunching in the snow. She headed for the little room next to the grain store. She had not been back there since Gunnar attacked her and she shuddered at what could have been but Erik had once again come to her rescue. She moved the bench around and placed it near a table. Then she dusted it clean and set about readying her plan.

⌘

'Where are we going?' Erik asked as she led him by the hand through the village.

He had been taken aback when Isabel had told him she had a surprise for him. He had resigned himself to the fact that they would live as strangers even though they were wed. He had even convinced himself that it was what she wanted. He felt angry and hurt at her accusations and to protect his heart he decided to distance himself emotionally from her.

'If I tell you it wouldn't be a surprise then,' she laughed.

They got to the door of the little room and he looked at her questioningly.

'I hope you don't have Gunnar in there ready to hit me over the head again. If you want to trade me in as a husband you just have to say so,' he joked.

'Nothing like that,' she smiled. It was good to have the light-hearted banter back again – she had missed his friendship. She hadn't realized how much she needed it till it was gone. She knew now that she did not hate him or blame him anymore. Without him she would not survive the winter in Kaldakinn.

She led him into the room and he looked surprised at what was set out. She had packed a picnic of salted meat and some bread. There were some nuts and honey too. The table had been set out beautifully, decorated with candles she had found and some winter twigs sculpted into a star shape.

'I thought we could have a picnic. This is my way of saying I'm sorry Erik. I said some horrible things to you and I know I can never take them back, but I hope you can forgive me, that we can start again.'

He sat at the table and she sat beside him.

'I'm sorry too,' he said. 'I should never have brought you here Isabel – I should have made sure you got back to your family, but I was afraid that if I didn't lay claim to you that some of the other men would rape and kill you. I thought I was protecting you at the time but I see my decision was selfish.'

She touched his arm gently; she appreciated his honesty with her.

'Can we be friends again?'

'I would like that,' he smiled.

'I have something else for you,' she said leaping up from the table. She rummaged in a leather pouch and pulled out a book, one he had not yet seen.

'What is it?' he asked.

'It is a book of stories about the Great One,' she said. 'I thought that maybe you could read it and understand why I follow him. In return I promise to learn and listen to your many stories about Odin and the other gods – a truce so to speak and an opportunity to learn more about each other's culture.'

'I agree. I am willing to learn about this Great One. New knowledge is always good. Thank you Isabel.' He raised her hand and kissed her palm tenderly. She felt strangely stirred by the intimate gesture.

'How is the baby doing?' he asked.

She took his hand and placed it on her belly. He smiled feeling the roundness that was becoming evident.

'It won't be long till I start to show. What will the people of Kaldakinn think?'

'They won't think anything Isabel. We will address this when the time comes. I want you to know that I will protect this child as if he were my own.'

'Thank You Erik, you are a good man.'

⌘

GRISWOLD

The key turned in the lock and Gwendolyn let out a sigh of relief. She hesitated briefly before pulling open the bureau drawer. She was afraid at what she might find. The drawer creaked as she pulled it open, it was rickety and old. Inside was a leather book with Daemon's initials inscribed on the cover.

So this was not father's secret drawer but Daemons. What could he possibly have wanted to hide here?

She pulled out the worn leather book and opened it up. It appeared to be a journal, Daemon's handwriting filling the pages. She ran her fingers over the words as though they would somehow magically connect her to her long lost brother. Then she began to read.

I am finding it harder by the day to keep up this charade father has concocted. Pretending to be Doctor Drew Williams is giving me mixed feelings. I am realizing more and more what I missed out on as a child and I am trying not to feel resentful. Father is playing a dangerous game and I hate lying to Gwen and Legion....

She flipped further on in the diary and read more.

I am falling in love with Aislinn Hamilton. I never planned for it to happen but I can't help myself. I don't know what to do – she thinks I am Drew and has no idea I exist. I will have to make a plan. I don't think I can live without her....

Gwen could not put the book down. She had not realized how her brother felt. Clearly he had been torn between their father and his love for Aislinn.

I lied to Gwen again today but I had to protect her. Father took Phoenix to Skull Hill where he planned to sacrifice him so that he could gain greater power and wisdom – an evil spell. We fought and I had no option but to kill him. He was mad and wanted to gain power over Griswold. I told Gwen that a Northman tried to poison them and stole Phoenix but it was not true – it was our father. I have turned into a monster and can only hope for forgiveness. At least Gwen will always remember father with love.....

Gwen let out a sob. She was shocked by this entry. All these years she had believed her father had saved Daemon and her child – she had been so grateful for his sacrifice and had viewed him a hero. Now she felt horrified at the truth. He had wanted them all dead. She felt angry that Daemon had lied to her. The number of times she had climbed Skull Hill to put fresh flowers on father's grave and to talk to him made her feel sick. He deserved none of it.

She could not read any more of the diary. She had to process what she had learned, her wounds opening afresh and memories flooding in. She took the book and headed back to her chambers.

What have I done to deserve this?

CHAPTER 28

HOPE RENEWED, HOPE DESTROYED

KALDAKINN

THE WINTER seemed to drag – it was dark most of the day and Isabel hardly got outdoors now. Her belly had started protruding and the villagers whispered to themselves speculating on when she had fallen pregnant. Some said she was carrying twins while others believed she was pregnant before she came to Kaldakinn. They felt sorry for Erik believing that he would father a bastard child. Erik did not let it bother him. His father made it clear that Isabel and Erik had been together before they left Ebondeen and that he felt it his responsibility to wed her and raise their child. Isabel fumed at all the rumours.

'Why can't we just tell them the truth – that I was married and my child conceived before my husband was killed?'

'To protect your baby Isabel. The Northmen will not want another Southerner in our clan. You are a woman so they believe you can be tamed and kept in check by your husband – you are not like our maidens who are more independent. They believe you are softer and weaker. If your child is a boy they will view him as a threat to their children. They will worry that he will rise up as he gets older and become Earl one day as he is in our family line. For this reason they will try to kill him if they believe he is not my child.'

She was shocked – they would actually try to kill her baby. She agreed it was best that they make the villagers believe that he had taken her by force at Ebondeen and then dutifully agreed to marry her when she found out she was pregnant. She hated the lie but she would do anything to protect her child.

They lay in bed that night and Isabel read her book. Erik too was reading – something they both enjoyed. Many of the Northmen could not read or write but Siobhan had made it her purpose to ensure that Erik was educated and she had spent many years teaching him. Now she taught those children whose parents requested it, but many Northmen still did not see the need for it and refused their children education. Many believed that living daily life was enough of an education and all they would need for the future. Thorfinn had supported Siobhan in her endeavour to teach Erik as he knew that the future lay in learning and exploring other cultures and that his son would need more than just farming and fighting skills. He wanted his son to become wise as he would be the next Earl of Kaldakinn.

Isabel let out a squeal.

'Are you all right? What's wrong?' Erik asked concern on his face.

'I'm fine,' she laughed. 'The baby moved Erik – I felt it.'

She placed his hand on her stomach and they waited patiently for the child to stir again. It came, a small butterfly movement under his hand.

'Did you feel that?' she asked.

He grinned and the joy on his face said it all. She realized that he was as excited as she.

They lay next to one another feeling the baby moving in her womb, each movement more exciting than the one before.

'He's active,' Erik said smiling.

'So you're sure it's a boy Erik?' she teased.

'I know it is Isabel. He is Phoenix's legacy and will carry on his line – it will be a boy.'

Isabel smiled at the huge man lying next to her. He knew what to say to make her feel loved and she leaned her head on his shoulder. He had been a good friend to her the last few months and she appreciated it so much.

⌘

EBONDEEN

Struan was getting the hang of his wooden leg. Aislinn was right – it was extremely painful wearing it and he could only do so for a few hours each day. He still had dreams that he could run and often he woke feeling as though his leg were still there. He could even feel his toes. Drew had warned him that this was quite common for amputees and that in time it would go away.

Struan enjoyed his work at the castle – he felt useful to Catriona and was well liked by the villagers as he had ensured their homes were rebuilt after the raid. He had organized for Mac and Eion to come and re-thatch the homes that were burned. He realized most of all, that he enjoyed spending time with Catriona. He felt that she had helped his heart to mend. He did not delude himself though – as much as he loved her he was not the man for her – at twenty-three she was much younger than his thirty-nine years. She deserved a man who was whole, not an invalid who would become more and more of a burden as he aged.

'There you are,' she said entering the room where he was working. 'Would you like to come for a ride with me? I need to go and see the Smith family and drop off some herbs for their sick child.'

'Why don't you ask young Angus to join you?'

She looked surprised by his suggestion. Angus was one of the soldiers in her father's army. He had not held much rank but after the raid and some daring bravery he had been made an officer. He was in his late twenties with sandy brown hair and blue eyes – not a bad looking man but not anyone Catriona wanted a relationship with.

'Why would I want him to come with me? It's you I would like to ride with Struan.'

'You are young Catriona and you have your whole life ahead of you. It's time you got to meet some young men who could possibly be suitable as husbands one day. I have seen Angus looking at you and he would make a good match.'

She looked at him incredulous. Her face flushed crimson.

'Since when did you become my father?' she said sarcastically.

'I'm just thinking of your best interests Cat.'

'No you are not Struan – you are a coward,' she taunted.

He pulled himself up on his wooden leg, his face angry. He took a step toward her to grab her shoulders but she side-stepped him sending him lurching forward off-balance. He crashed to the floor and cursed as he did so.

'Struan,' she cried dropping down beside him. 'Are you all right? I'm so sorry I shouldn't have done that.'

'Leave me alone Cat, I'm just a useless cripple. You don't have to pity me – I refuse to be a burden to anyone.'

'Is that what you think, you stupid man? Your leg is not the problem Struan. It's your blindness that hinders you. I do not pity you, nor will I ever. Don't you know that I am in love with you? I don't want to be with anyone else, but you are too scared to admit you feel the same way ....'

She did not get a chance to finish the sentence as he pulled her to him kissing her hard on the mouth, weeks of passion pouring out as they locked bodies.

Dear lord he loved her so much.

⌘

GRISWOLD

Gwendolyn opened the journal again. She had not read it for weeks since the last revelation of her father's treachery. She had gone through many emotions, anger being the greatest, followed by seething hatred for the man, disappointment at Daemon's secrets and even fury that Legion had died and left her to deal with all this alone.

Now she was ready to read more.

Drew and Aislinn have left Griswold – I am devastated as I had hoped to get Aislinn alone to reveal my identity. The last few weeks I have spent with her riding and getting to know her have made me the happiest I have been in a long while. I know Drew's my brother but I don't have any ties to him – father made sure of that when he and Doctor Williams kept us apart. I have decided to follow her to Sherbrooke and convince her to marry me. I don't know how I will do that but I do know that I will do anything to make her mine...

Gwen skipped further along reading about her father's plans to have Drew and Aislinn burned at the stake for witchcraft. If he had succeeded none of the events would have unfolded as they had – Daemon would be alive today. She felt that anger burn her belly again. Her father couldn't even get that right. She flipped the page.

I finally have a plan – I can't let Aislinn marry Drew. Gwen has told me that they are getting married soon. I know that she will not choose me over him – she doesn't even know I exist though we have shared kisses. If I want her as my wife then I have to take her- I have to become Drew Williams. A fresh start away from all this madness seems appealing to me – I am only sorry that when I kill Drew, and he is believed to be me, that it will hurt Gwen more than I wish to think about. Maybe in the future I can make things right with her. If all goes according to plan this will be my last entry as Daemon. Soon I will become Drew Williams....

Gwen looked at the words which blurred on the page in front of her. This was even more painful than her father's betrayal. So Daemon had planned to kill Drew and take his identity. She remembered Aislinn's letter declaring that Daemon had tried to force himself on her and she felt nauseous. She would have responded the same way as the young woman if she had been in the same circumstances. She shut the journal and threw it across the room angrily. All these years the different men in her life had played her – she did not know any of them. Her father and Daemon had deceived her, Legion had chosen Aislinn and Drew over her and she did not know her son because she had fought for justice for a cause that was a farce at the expense of her relationship with Phoenix.

'I hate you all,' she screamed.

She hated Aislinn even more now even though she understood why she had killed Daemon– if she hadn't bewitched him then none of this would have happened – she would have known her son and spent the last twenty years being his mother. It was all Aislinn's fault.

CHAPTER 29

THE SIGN

LIONSGATE

THE GREAT ONE looked in his Mirror of Time. Across many miles and kingdoms many things were happening. He always marvelled at the cycle of life and death and how people were affected by them in different ways. They all felt isolated and alone in those moments – as though they were the only person in the whole world going through that experience at that moment and yet they were all tied to one another through invisible energy – waves that connected them even though they were unaware of it all. He could see Struan and Catriona planning their wedding at Ebondeen, Gwendolyn wrestling with her demons in Griswold, Aislinn and Drew caring for children with no parents and bringing new children into the world and finally Isabel who fought for her values and beliefs in a world that was strange to her in every way. They all were linked and would all meet again one day. They would work it out – he was confident.

⌘

KALDAKINN – EARLY SPRING 1649

Isabel felt enormous – she was nearly eight months along. She walked in the sunshine with Erik at her side. She had missed the warmth on her face and although there was snow on the ground and the fjord was still frozen, little plants had pushed their way through the ground with bursts of green energy. It was the most beautiful sight she had ever seen – signs of life and promise in the white wonderland she had grown so sick of.

She had been itching to get outdoors with her bow and arrows, to have a chance to practice. She felt really rusty. Erik had agreed to take her up the hill to see if they could hunt some food and she felt really excited. She panted as she climbed, the weight of her baby pressing on her lungs. He held her hand, balancing her and helping her to climb the slippery slope.

'Shh...' he stopped dead in his tracks. He indicated a deer a few hundred metres from where they stood. It was searching for some of the little plants to eat. It was a beautiful animal, its coat thick and shiny against the white hill. Running water gurgled as the snow melted and an eagle called as it soared on the wind currents over the fjord. For a moment Isabel felt at home and she was surprised at how happy she felt.

Erik signalled her to get her bow ready. She pulled out an arrow and slowly loaded it. She stretched her arm back, trying to remember all her training to take the perfect shot. She had the animal in her sights and she knew that her aim would be perfect – she had lost none of her skills. The bow felt like an extension of her arm. The deer, sensing danger, looked up staring her straight in the eye, almost daring her to take the shot.

Isabel lowered her bow.

'What's wrong?' Erik asked surprised.

'Nothing,' she smiled. 'I guess I am just happy to be alive today and I think that deer should enjoy spring a bit longer. It's been a long winter for everyone.'

He laughed and hugged her.

'I think becoming a mother has made you soft Isabel. I like it – it suits you. I guess there will be no fresh venison tonight. You've obviously taken a liking to our salted pork.'

She turned her nose up and pulled a face and he laughed loudly.

They walked down the hill back to the village hand in hand like two old friends.

⌘

'Close your eyes, I have something for you,' Erik said to her. Isabel was resting on the bed and he was standing at the door, the fur pelt curtain pulled aside by his big frame.

She giggled and closed her eyes.

Erik grunted as he moved something heavy.

'What are you doing?' she laughed.

'You can open them now.'

Isabel opened her eyes and gasped. There in the room was a wooden crib, carved out of yew and perfectly created for her baby. On the head and base of the crib was the same lion that Erik had carved on her bow.

'Oh Erik, it's amazing,' she said wiping tears that escaped her eyes. 'When did you find time to do this?' she asked.

'I have been working on it a while.'

'I can't tell you what this means to me. Thank you so much.'

She wrapped her arms around him and rested her head on his chest. Erik inhaled the scent of her hair and his heart ached. For seven months he had lain next to this woman and he had kept his promise not to touch her, but it had been hard – he wanted her more than anything – he loved her more than anything.

'I want you to be happy Isabel.'

'I am,' she said and was surprised to realize that she actually was.

⌘

Spring came quickly once the sun was out. The snow gave way to green hillsides and the Northmen readied their ships for the next raiding season. Children played on the beach and there was the sound of life again in the village. Isabel enjoyed getting out each day, practising hitting the targets Erik had created for her. She had lost none of her skills with the bow.

'When do the men leave for raiding?' she asked Erik.

'They will leave in a week – It will give them time to get to the south before the summer.'

'I want to go Erik. I need to see my family. I cannot go another whole winter before I see them. They deserve to know that I am safe.'

'Is that wise Isabel? It will take weeks to get there and your babe is due to be born in just over a moon. You need to be here amongst the women when that happens.'

'I want to be with my family Erik.'

'I know you do, but it is not possible Isabel. I will get a message to your family and invite them here if they wish to see you. I give you my word – they will be safe. Then you can all return the following spring. The child will be older then and better able to travel.'

Isabel was upset. The timing for this baby's birth could not have been worse. She would have to spend another long winter in Kaldakinn before she could return home – she felt her happiness slip away – she did not think she could endure it.

⌘

It was two nights before the long boats were due to sail to the south. Isabel tossed in her bed, her mind in turmoil. Erik would be leaving in a couple of days – he would not even be here when she gave birth – her protector would be gone and her child would possibly be in danger. What if someone tried to kill her baby?

Eventually she fell into a deep sleep.

She was holding her baby, a beautiful boy and he looked just like Phoenix. She cuddled the child and nursed him and she felt peaceful. Suddenly she became aware that she was not alone – she was surrounded by snarling wolves, their teeth bared, saliva dripping from their snapping jaws. She screamed for someone to help her but there was no one – everyone was away raiding. The wolves advanced and as they did their faces changed. One became Gunnar who leered at her, another was Gwendolyn who spat at her. Then the maidens who had attacked her advanced. She tried to protect her baby as they pulled at the screaming child, kicking her to the ground. She looked at the baby lying so still – he was covered in blood. They laughed at her pain. She kneeled over the child scooping him into her arms and holding him close. That is when she noticed it – blood on her hands. Her child's blood was on her hands – it was her fault that she could not protect him. She saw Phoenix and Erik watching from afar – they shook their heads and turned away from her.

'Don't leave me,' she sobbed reaching out to them but they moved further into the mist.

'I'm sorry, I'm sorry....'

'Wake up Isabel,' Erik gently shook her. 'It's all right you are having a nightmare.'

Isabel sobbed as he held her close, whispering to her reassuringly. She reached up and pulled his head down claiming his lips, hungry to be one with him. Erik was caught by surprise but responded to her needs. He could taste the salt from her tears and his desire to protect her deepened. He caressed her cheek as he kissed her, his heart bursting inside his chest.

Save the gods, I want her so badly.

Isabel opened her eyes, shocked to find her lips locked with Erik. She pushed him away shakily.

'I'm sorry,' she spluttered embarrassed. 'I thought you were Phoenix.'

Erik drew away – she may as well have slapped him it hurt so much. He thought she was finally giving her heart to him – instead she was still dreaming.

'No I apologize,' he said huskily. 'You were having a nightmare.'

'Yes I remember,' she said.

'Are you all right, you seemed very afraid?'

'I'm okay,' she replied. 'Thank you Erik for being my friend.'

She had established the boundaries again – they were friends and no more – she had made that perfectly clear. His heart felt crushed as he tucked her under the fur pelt.

'Go to sleep Isabel. You have nothing to be afraid of.'

⌘

GRISWOLD

Gwendolyn could not sleep. She looked out the window at the dark sky lit with millions of stars. It looked so peaceful out there – so ordered – as though each star knew its place and function. Just as she thought this a shooting star leapt across the sky, disturbing the serenity.

No, not even the sky was ordered – there was always something that would change the balance of nature.

She felt as though her world was spinning out of control and she felt helpless to change it. Her father and brother had tried to change their circumstances and it got them both killed. She had tried to manipulate Phoenix's life with the marriage agreement and it had sent him to his death. Deep down she knew she was responsible but she was not ready to admit it. She still blamed Isabel and Aislinn for everything that had turned sour in her life.

Balfour had been away at Ebondeen helping to re-establish their community. Even Catriona had moved on, marrying Struan Hamilton – just another twist of the sword in her side. The Hamilton's always got what they wanted – it wasn't fair.

Isabel Williams had not been seen since the day of the attack on the castle and Gwendolyn felt a mixture of perverted justice and sadness the she would not be the one to get her pound of flesh. At least Aislinn and Drew

Williams would know the pain she felt at losing a child. It gave her some comfort.

⌘

KALDAKINN

She met with the boy up on the hillside, away from prying eyes. He listened to her earnestly his eyes growing large as he nodded his head vigorously. She made him promise secrecy and he felt excited that she trusted him with such an important task. Out of everyone in the village she had chosen him. He'd had a secret crush on her for a while now and would do anything for her. She thanked him with a kiss on the cheek and he blushed, delighted that she loved him too.

⌘

The men packed the long boats and checked the sails. There was great excitement at the upcoming journey. Isabel watched Erik as he carried food supplies and weapons to the boats. His muscles rippled as he lifted the heavy load and she could not help but admire his handsome form. He noticed her standing on the dock.

'Be careful you don't get knocked over,' he said hugging her. They had kept up the front of showing physical affection in front of the villagers so that their marriage would not be questioned.

'Where will you be raiding? Has your father told you yet?'

'I'm not quite sure but we will head south again. Why do you seem so anxious Isabel?'

'My family lives in the south Erik. Of course I am concerned.'

'I promise you we will not raid Sherbrooke Isabel. Your family will be safe from us.'

'It is more than that Erik. I want you to promise me you will not raid Ebondeen again – those people will have just got their lives back together again.'

'Isabel you are making this very difficult. My father will not take orders from you – he is the Earl and will decide where we raid.'

'Please Erik. I also want you to leave Griswold alone. That castle is my child's inheritance one day. If you raid it then you are stealing from him. Promise me you will not do that. Stay away from Griswold please.'

Erik cursed. She did have a point though – her son would rule over Griswold one day. He would have to convince his father to go to the lands east of Griswold and Ebondeen – to Cragshelm.

'I make you no promises Isabel but I will do my best to convince my father that there is more to gain by raiding elsewhere. Where is that book of maps, we will need it to help us navigate?'

One of the treasures he had taken on the last raid was a book of maps outlining all the kingdoms of the southern regions and he had studied it diligently throughout the winter.

'I will pack it with your other things,' she said.

'Now woman, let me get back to work – you are a distraction – a beautiful one I admit, but a distraction nonetheless.'

He kissed her forehead and sent her on her way.

Isabel waddled back to the great hall. She felt extremely uncomfortable and she could feel that her baby was beginning to drop lower into her pelvis. It would not be too long now.

Just wait a little longer precious one. You can't come just yet.

Isabel had been fourteen when she had first seen a baby born. Her mother had taken her along to a birth in the hope that her daughter would follow in her footsteps. Isabel could remember it as though it were yesterday. She was not a squeamish child – blood and battle did not usually faze her as long as it was real battle with both sides given equal opportunity. She could not bear fighting for the sake of trivial matters nor could she tolerate fighting where many attacked one. Her sense of justice was too strong. Childbirth however, was a battle she did not enjoy participating in, the mother screaming as pain ripped through her body, caused by an unseen adversary that was fighting to get its way out. The lack of control over the circumstances had frightened her – no body control as water and blood gushed, even the mother's bowels losing control as she pushed her child into the world. She did not remember the process as being beautiful – rather she thought it was messy and undignified and the thought that she would have to go through it in a few short weeks terrified her. No, she would rather fight a battle any day before giving birth.

⌘

The night was fairly festive. The men seemed more animated than usual – too much testosterone flowed as they hyped themselves up for their trip south. This was how they felt manly – the way they expressed their virility and stories flowed as they feasted together for one last time. The women served them and Isabel smiled.

There would be a lot of loving tonight in Kaldakinn.

'What time do you leave tomorrow?' Isabel asked.

'At first light. The earlier we leave the better. You do not have to get up to see me off. You deserve to sleep in – you certainly will need as much sleep as you can get before the baby comes.'

'But I want to,' she said.

'No Isabel, we will say our goodbyes tonight. You must take it easy – it would not do for the baby to come too soon.'

⌘

Erik was subdued when they were finally alone together.

'I will miss you,' he said longingly.

'I will miss you too Erik.'

'Promise me you will take care of yourself and the baby till I come back. Don't go off alone Isabel. I know things have settled down but there may still be people who would want to harm you or the child. I have asked Leif Gunnarson to keep an eye on you both – I trust him.'

'Thank you.'

They climbed into bed side by side.

'Can I hold you?'

'Yes,' she whispered.

His strong arms encircled her, drawing her head onto his chest. The baby kicked hard trying to find room and they both laughed.

'Someone's a little jealous I think,' she smiled.

'Isabel, there are some things I need to say before I sail. I never know when I go raiding whether I will be returning. That is for the gods to decide.'

'Don't say that Erik, it is not true. Your life is in your hands; your destiny is controlled by you. You have been reading the stories of the Great One – haven't you learned anything about faith? I will speak to him and ask him to keep you safe, to return you home to your family at the end of the summer.'

'Isabel, listen to what I am saying. '

He placed his finger over her lips to silence her rambling.

'The last eight months of my life have been the happiest in a long time. I do not regret marrying you. I want you to know that I love you and I love this baby as if it were my own. If circumstances had been different, if I had met you in another time I think you could have given your heart to me. I understand that we are just friends but for me you will always be the woman I have waited my whole life for. If this time is all we can have together before you go back to your family next summer then I would not change it for the world.'

Isabel did not know how to respond. He had declared his love for her. She knew he was fond of her but she had not known how deep his feelings ran. It was evident he was attracted to her – that passionate kiss they had shared after her nightmare had shaken them both in different ways but since then things had been back to normal between them and they had not discussed it.

'I don't know what to say Erik.'

'You don't have to say anything Isabel. I will always be here for you – it is up to you to decide where you want to go and what you want to do. I will not stand in your way once this baby is born.'

He was a good man, but she was confused. She still dreamed of Phoenix and she always woke from those dreams with a tender heart, a sadness that she could not describe. She doubted she would ever love that way again.

⌘

Early the next morning Erik kissed her forehead as she slept and slipped quietly from their room out to the dock that was bustling with men doing last minute preparations. His mother and father were having a long farewell, their arms entwined and their heads locked together as though they could not bear to be pulled apart.

'Take care Siobhan,' he kissed her gently.

'And you, may the gods be with you all.'

Siobhan hugged Erik and reassured him.

'Don't worry we will take good care of her and the baby. Just come home safely.'

The men climbed into the long boats, excitement reaching fever pitch. Their journey was beginning.

'FIRE, FIRE,' someone screamed pointing to a cart of straw that had gone up in flames. Pandemonium broke out. The men leapt from the boats and raced to the burning wagon.

'Quickly, before anything else catches alight.' They pushed the burning wagon as hard as they could toward the lake dousing the flames in spluttering clouds of smoke and steam as it went into the water. Then they pulled it out again and assessed the damage.

'How did this happen?' Thorfinn roared looking around at the stunned villagers. Nobody said a word or moved a muscle.

'This is not a good omen – a bad way to start a raid,' he growled. 'We will have to call out to the gods before we leave and ask for favour.'

The men all gathered in a circle and cried out to Odin asking for favour in battle and safety as they sailed.

Thorfinn sought out the seer. He was sitting in his hut waiting.

'I knew you would come,' he said.

'What does this fire mean?' Thorfinn asked. 'Is Odin trying to send us a message?'

'The fire was not a sign of doom. It was a distraction. Odin will give you favour on this journey but I warn you, there will be mountains to climb and obstacles to overcome. Many years ago I prophesied that the north and south would come together not in bloodshed but in love. That has only partly been fulfilled – you will see it happen – don't let your hunger for raiding and the spoils blind you to it or you will change the course of every man, woman and child in Kaldakinn.'

'How will this happen?' Thorfinn asked.

'The gods will show you the way – just follow the signs.'

Thorfinn left the old seer, frustrated. Many times he spoke in riddles and the path was not clear.

He boarded his long boat and gave the command to set sail. The boats slowly edged their way out into the fjord, the men waving to their women on the shore. Summer raiding had begun.

CHAPTER 30

HIDDEN

THE NORTH SEA

IT WAS hard work navigating through the fjords as the winds were not very strong due to the steep cliffs on either side. The men sang as they rowed, trying to buoy their spirits. The start of their trip had been marred by the fire and some of the men felt afraid – they worried that the gods did not look favourably on them as they embarked on their journey south.

Thorfinn had reassured them but some of the men were still divided.

Erik sat at the rear of the boat reading his map book. The day was coming to an end and the light would be fading soon – he wanted to read as much as he could.

'This is where we should head father,' he said pointing at a map.

'Where is it?'

'It is a kingdom called Cragshelm and it borders Ebondeen.'

'I thought we would go back to Ebondeen. They will be weak after our last attack and they fear us – it will make raiding that much simpler.'

'Is that wise father? We might be making a big mistake going there. Isabel has told me that Griswold has an agreement with Ebondeen that they will fight together against our people. Attacking either kingdom may mean greater losses amongst our men. It would be better if we attacked a weaker kingdom – one that would not be expecting it. I have looked at the map and we can sail upriver to Cragshelm.'

Thorfinn was impressed with the research Erik had undertaken. The young man had put a lot of thought into it. Erik held his breath hoping that his father would take the bait.

'All right Erik, I will trust you on this one. We will sail upriver at night as we need to pass through Griswold and Ebondeen and we don't want to attract any attention.'

Erik sighed in relief. Isabel's family and her baby's inheritance would be safe. He would not have wanted to explain it to her if his father had insisted they attack Griswold. Thorfinn was not fooled either. He knew Erik had other motives for negotiating the raiding target and he knew it was because of Isabel. Still, the seer had told him not to be greedy and to follow the signs – maybe this was a sign and if he changed it things could go wrong. For now, he had to trust the seer and the gods.

⌘

KALDAKINN

'What do you mean she has gone,' Siobhan paled.

'Her room is empty and her things are gone,' Leif said. 'I went to look for her to invite her for a walk as I thought she might be a little frustrated being cooped up in here but there is no sign of her. I have searched the hills and she is not there either. It is as though she has vanished into thin air.'

'She would never run away – not with her baby due to be born so soon. Are you sure she didn't go for a walk or to practice her archery?'

'I'm sure Siobhan.'

'Oh no! What if her labour has started early? We need to find her now. If anything happens to her, Erik will never forgive us.'

'I have combed the hills with some men, Siobhan. She is not there. We have even tried to track her but there are no tracks to follow. The villagers I have spoken to, have not seen her all day – if she had gone out for a walk then someone would have seen her.'

'Maybe the seer knows something.'

Siobhan sat opposite the old man and he smirked at her, his rotten teeth protruding from his face in a way that always frightened her. Thorfinn swore by his prophecies but she avoided him whenever she could. Now she had no choice but to seek his wisdom and knowledge.

'The young girl from the south is missing. Do you know where she is?'

'She is not missing. She is simply not visible to you.'

'How do we find her?'

'You have no way to reach her where she is going but there is one who can tell you where she is.'

'Give me a name.'

⌘

Sveinn sat opposite his mother, his face anxious and drawn. He knew he was in trouble by the way she looked at him with no-nonsense eyes.

'I have been told by the seer that you know where Isabel is, Sveinn. Is that true?'

The boy kept quiet, torn between being honest with his mother and the loyalty he felt to Isabel. He had promised her he would keep her secret.

'Sveinn, I am not angry with you but I am deeply concerned about Isabel's safety. Do you know that her baby is due to be born any day now?

The boy paled. He was twelve – what did he know about when babies were due? He had no idea her baby was about to be born when he made his promise to help her. Now fear showed on his face.

'Tell me what you know,' Siobhan said. He nodded his head.

⌘

The North Sea

The night was still and some of the men drank mead while they ate salted fish. Others dozed on the decks of the long boat. They felt one with the universe as they bobbed up and down on the sea. The wind had picked up and the sails flapped gently in the wind.

Erik leaned back and looked up at the stars. It was beautiful, the world they lived in. Isabel's god- the Great One, and his god Odin may be very different in many ways but they both believed their god created everything and what a magnificent job they had done.

Maybe they did it together, he smiled at the thought, two such opposite gods coming together to make something beautiful.

His thoughts were interrupted by loud cursing and voices shouting at the other end of the long boat. He leapt to his feet, ready to break up a squabble between two men who had consumed too much mead. Instead he found himself face to face with Isabel who had been pulled from behind the barrels of food.

'Isabel,' he said shocked to see her on the boat. 'What are you doing here?' he shouted furious with her.

She knew he would be angry when she set her plan in motion but his sheer fury scared her.

He grabbed her under her arm and dragged her away from the curious men.

'You're hurting me,' she squealed.

'I should put you over my knee right now and spank the life out of you woman,' he hissed.

'Don't you dare,' she challenged her eyes flashing at him.

They eyed each other, each refusing to back down. Finally he let out a frustrated sigh.

'What were you thinking Isabel? We will be at sea for a full moon – what if the baby chooses to come before we reach land?'

'I guess that is a chance I am willing to take. I did not feel safe at Kaldakinn without you Erik. Besides, I want to see my family – I cannot endure another winter in Kaldakinn with them thinking I am dead.'

'So you are willing to risk your life and your child's life?'

'It is my decision Erik. That is why I had to stow away – I knew you would never agree to it.'

'How did you do it? You were fast asleep when I left.'

'No, I wasn't. As soon as you left I got up. While you were busy loading the last few items I created a little diversion to distract you all.'

'The fire was your doing?' he asked incredulous. 'Do you know how much fear that put into the men? They thought the gods were giving us a sign of impending doom.'

'I'm sorry; I didn't mean to alarm anyone. I just needed a few minutes to get onto the boat unnoticed.'

'Who helped you then?' he asked curious.

'Nobody,' she lied.

'Isabel, there is no way you could have executed this plan alone. So who did you beguile into helping you?'

'Sveinn,' she said reluctantly.

Finally he laughed. 'My twelve year old brother set the fire. You have bewitched him Isabel. Ever since the wedding he has been sweet on you. Seriously though, I am concerned that you will not make it to the south. I think we need to turn back.'

'No Erik,' she grabbed his arm imploring him with her eyes. 'Your father will be very angry – besides I want to go to the south.'

She was right. Thorfinn was very angry. He remembered the seer's words that there would be many mountains and obstacles and it seemed they faced the first one already. He was torn between returning one boat to Kaldakinn and continuing to the south. The men grumbled and threatened to mutiny if he returned to Kaldakinn. He was caught in a no-win situation.

'We should throw her over the side,' one Northman suggested. He quickly kept quiet when he saw Erik glaring at him.

'I don't want to return to Kaldakinn,' Isabel defiantly told Thorfinn.

'So be it,' he said, 'but if this baby comes then we are not responsible if you or the child dies.'

Isabel agreed, relieved that the men could get back to their mead. She did not enjoy being the centre of attention.

CHAPTER 31

THOR'S WRATH

LIONSGATE

THE GREAT ONE and Ziah watched Isabel.

'She is strong-willed that girl,' he said to his son.

'She reminds me of Aislinn all those years ago when we fought against Legion. Do you know Aislinn challenged him to his face – she even told him that she pitied him?'

The Great One laughed. 'I bet he did not appreciate that.'

'Will she be all right father – will she make it before her baby comes?'

'She is going to face some very tough trials Ziah, but she will discover much about herself and the ones she travels with. Don't worry she is stronger than even she knows.'

⌘

AT SEA

One day rolled into the next and Isabel felt her nausea return. They had been on this god-forsaken ocean too many weeks – she had lost count eventually, but she prayed that it would come to an end soon.

'How much longer Erik?'

She felt like a whale, her body clumsy and awkward now. She did not want to alarm him but she had been having cramps in her lower back and she could not find any way to be comfortable. When she sat down she ached and when she stood all she wanted to do was get down on her hands and knees.

If only Mama were here!

'It should only be a day or two till we sight land and enter the river mouth. Cragshelm is further west than Ebondeen or Griswold, so it will take us a couple of days to reach it up the river. How are you feeling?'

He could see her discomfort – she had not complained once the last few weeks even though there had been limited food rations and she had not slept very well. He had tried to make her as comfortable as possible giving her his cloak every night to sleep on. It was not much but he knew she was grateful.

'I am all right, but I won't lie to you, I am looking forward to getting my feet on solid ground again.'

'That makes two of us,' he smiled.

⌘

GRISWOLD

Gwendolyn stood on Skull Hill looking at the four graves in front of her. Four men in her life – and she had outlived them all. Usually she felt grief-stricken when she came here, but today she just felt disdain. All her life she had done what these men wanted – she had sacrificed herself for all of them. She had married Legion because her father was afraid he would lose his position as chief wizard, she had lived through hell with Legion in the early days of their marriage, constantly fearing him. Even Daemon had consumed her life – she had sacrificed her life and marriage for him, always wanting justice to be done, only to discover that his life was a lie. It cost her time with Phoenix – and he too had stabbed her in the back marrying Isabel Williams. They were all selfish men. It was time she lived for herself – made her own decisions. Since Isabel had disappeared she was the only living relative to the Lord of Griswold and that made her the next in line to rule. She knew that Phoenix wanted Isabel to inherit, but that little witch had done nothing to deserve this castle or the title of Lady – she and Phoenix had only been married a few days before he was killed – who would believe her? Besides she had vanished which left Gwen the ruler of Griswold.

⌘

The weather began to close in, the soft, puffy clouds becoming dark and angry. The sky changed from blue to deep purple and the wind picked up, blowing in angry gusts. The sail shook violently and the men scrambled to lower it. Isabel tried to stay out of the way as they manned their stations. The wooden hull shook and groaned beneath them as wave after wave smashed the side of the boat. Isabel shivered in her damp clothing, her dark hair plastered to her head. Her knuckles were white as she clung to the side of the boat.

'Sit down Isabel,' Erik shouted over the roaring wind. 'It is not safe for you to stand.'

She tried to shelter herself as best she could but the boat rolled and tossed as the storm hit. This was the first storm they had encountered on their journey and Isabel felt really afraid. Now she understood why the Northmen feared storms at sea and why they believed the gods were angry.

Odin must be in a really bad mood. Please Great One, let us get through this in one piece.

She unconsciously held her swollen belly as though to reassure the child within that she would keep it safe.

Lightning snaked through the sky, followed by deafening thunder. Thor was on the warpath, striking his hammer as his chariot sped across the galaxy. The men called out to him begging for mercy as they tried to keep the long boat on course.

Isabel felt more afraid than she had in a long time. She closed her eyes as though to block out the reality, then she felt it, a popping sensation followed by warm fluid trickling down her thighs.

No, this can't happen now.

Now she was truly afraid. She remembered the birth she attended with her mother. She had been surprised when a water-like fluid had gushed from the woman. Her mother had explained that the birth was getting closer and that the fluid around the baby was draining. The woman had given birth only a few hours later. She could not have this baby now, not in the middle of a storm on a boat. She groaned inwardly. She tried to remember everything her mother did at the birth but it was all fuzzy – it was not the most enjoyable experience for her and she had just tried to focus on getting through it instead of all the details.

A sharp pain squeezed her abdomen, causing her to catch her breath. It remained for a while before it let her go and she breathed relieved at the reprieve.

It will be all right, I will make it.

The waves grew fiercer and larger as the storm bore down on them in full force. It was a reflection of what was taking place in Isabel. Her calm day had turned into a frenzy of pain as contraction after contraction assailed her body. She moaned audibly now and Erik looked at her worried.

'Isabel, what's wrong?'

'It's the baby – he's coming,' she gasped as another pain came.

'Are you sure?' Erik asked hoping she was wrong.

'Erik, I'm sure – my water has broken and the pain is fierce.'

He dropped down beside her on his knees and cradled her, she squeezing his hand through yet another contraction. They did not see it coming and it caught them by surprise, the huge wall of water that lifted their boat and turned it on its side, dropping the men out the side one by one like chess pieces scattered off a board.

Isabel plunged into the water, her arms thrashing as she tried to keep afloat. The pain in her abdomen increased causing her to lose her breath. Then she fainted.

CHAPTER 32

WRETCHED

THE BOAT could not be salvaged and most of the men were hauled out of the water by the other long boats. Thorfinn scrambled on one of the boats searching the water frantically for Erik, shouting his name over and over till he was hoarse. There was no response. He sunk to the deck his head in his hands. How would he tell Siobhan that their son was gone, taken by Aegir, the god of the sea? The seer had promised them they would be safe but now they had lost some good men – he had lost his son and Isabel was gone too. How would it all be okay?

The storm passed as quickly as it had hit and the boats bobbed on the calm waters as the sky lightened. The thick mist began to lift as the sun broke through the clouds, revealing the shoreline a few hundred metres away. The wild winds had buoyed them to land sooner than they expected. The men cheered, bailing water out of their long boats. They had lost one boat and five men besides Isabel and Erik. Although they were glad to be near shore there was still a sombre air. The omens for this trip had not been good and they were anxious for what was yet to come. Thorfinn hoped there would be no more obstacles or mountains to climb.

⌘

She spluttered and then vomited, the salty water emptying from her stomach. She lay on sand and the sun shone on her. Then the pain came again and she remembered. She looked over at Erik a short distance from her. His head was bleeding and he lay so still.

Wake up Erik she willed. *Wake up!*

She dragged herself over to him and shook him. He did not respond. She shook him harder and then realized she was screaming at him, tears running down her face. She slapped him hard on the face and he groaned.

'Stop,' he whispered.

'Thank you Great One,' she croaked.

Erik pulled himself up and looked at her. 'Are you all right?'

He coughed trying to clear his lungs.

'I'm fine,' she lied. 'How did we get here, I don't remember anything?'

'I pulled you up when you went under and managed to hang on to a piece of the ship that had broken. That is all I remember.' He got to his feet and helped her up – they clung to one another trying to get their bearings.

'Where are we?' she asked.

'I'm not entirely sure but my guess is that we are on the shores of Griswold. According to the maps I studied the river should run from the ocean through Griswold and Ebondeen up to Cragshelm.'

'We need to get to a village,' she said 'This baby is not going to wait.'

They began to walk, holding one another for support.

Isabel knew something was wrong the moment she felt the pain come. She doubled over screaming as she held her belly.

'Lie down,' Erik ordered. She was in too much pain to feel embarrassed or concerned about her dignity. He lifted her tunic to see what progress was happening.

'You're bleeding Isabel,' he said concerned.

She screamed again as another contraction came and then passed out as her body went into shock. Erik scooped her in his arms and ran. He had no idea where he was going – he only prayed to Odin that he would find someone who would help them and that they would be in time.

⌘

LIONSGATE

'She needs help father,' Ziah cried distressed. He had been monitoring Isabel constantly since she had been on the long boat.

'It's time to send a little coincidence their way,' the Great One said.

He always found it amusing when people believed in coincidence – he was the master of creating coincidental events – events he put into motion to help people out of sticky situations.

'Time to rearrange some plans. Don't worry Ziah, we will get her some help.'

⌘

GRISWOLD

Balfour did not enjoy taking orders from Gwendolyn. She seemed to thrive on giving them to him, as though she somehow resented him for having been Phoenix's best friend. He knew that she was aware that he had caught her out in her marriage agreement deception and she was trying to make it abundantly clear that she was now ruler of Griswold. He was not sure how much longer he would stay. The only reason he had not left and gone to Ebondeen was because of Isabel. Phoenix had made him promise that he would take care of her should anything happen to him. He feared what would become of Isabel if she turned up at the castle. It had been over eight moons since she went missing and he believed he would never see her again. Struan had made him an offer that was very tempting. He wanted Balfour to command the soldiers and train them. Ebondeen needed a strong army now that the Northmen knew how to breach their walls.

He had not told Gwen about his plans but he could not tolerate her attitude any longer.

They were out patrolling the river and the coast – they knew the Northmen would be back soon and they wanted to be ready for them. Last year's attack on Ebondeen caught them all unawares and they were determined not to let it happen again.

They saw him before he saw them – a wild man with a woman in his arms. He was not one of them – they could tell he was a Northman from the tattoo on his arm and his hair.

'Stop,' Balfour shouted as he advanced.

Could this be a trick? Are there a horde of Northmen over the rise waiting to slay us?'

The man kept advancing as though he were desperate.

'Stop,' shouted Balfour again, more forcefully, as the men drew their swords.

Erik stopped in his tracks.

'Help her,' he whispered pleadingly.

Her head rested on his chest and her dark hair covered her face.

'Who are you and where do you come from?'

'We are from the North, from Kaldakinn. Our boat capsized in the storm. Please she needs help.'

'What is wrong with her?'

'The baby is coming.'

The men looked alarmed at the information then seemed suspicious. Why would the Northman be travelling with a pregnant woman? The story seemed ridiculous and they looked around searching the surrounding landscape for his companions.

'There's no one else,' he said aware of their suspicions.

She groaned like a wounded animal. 'Erik,' she whispered, 'show them my ring. It was Phoenix's - he gave it to me when we married.'

Erik slid it from her middle finger and held out the palm of his hand, the signet ring visible. Balfour approached cautiously and took it.

'Where did you get this?' he demanded.

For the first time he looked at the woman in Erik's arms.

'Good lord, Isabel, is that you?'

'Balfour,' she nodded weakly, then passed out again.

'She needs help now,' Erik shouted. 'This child is Phoenix's baby and the heir to Griswold.'

His words sank in as Balfour mentally did the math. He was right; Isabel married Phoenix nine moons ago. This baby had to be his.

'Let's get her to the castle,' he shouted to the men.

Isabel did not remember much of the journey to Griswold – she lapsed into unconsciousness several times. She did remember hearing Erik calling her many times, urging her to stay with them and she remembered feeling his strong arms holding her, his heart pounding in her ear, her head on his chest as he carried her.

'How did she come to be with you?' Balfour asked Erik. 'We thought she was dead.'

'I was concerned for her after Phoenix died that the men would rape and kill her. The only way I could protect her was to claim her as my own.'

Balfour looked questioningly at Erik. 'If you've hurt her I will kill you.'

'Relax, I have not touched her –her heart is still with Phoenix I can assure you.'

Balfour tried to size up the man.

Was he the one who killed Phoenix? If he did I will kill him myself once this is over, I promise you Phoenix. I will still have your back – I will always have your back.

Gwendolyn heard the commotion in the court as the men arrived back from their patrol. What was happening – they should not be back so soon? She looked out the window and was surprised to see a man carrying a woman in his arms. Balfour led them into the castle.

She hurried down the stairs to the parlour where they gathered.

'What is the meaning of this Balfour? Who are these people?'

'It is Isabel and a man from the North. She is about to give birth and needs help immediately. Get the physician.'

'How dare you issue me orders? I don't even remember giving you permission to allow that woman into the castle – and with the enemy in tow – are you insane? Let her give birth to her bastard child outside these walls.'

'This is hardly the time to indulge your hatred for Isabel. This baby is not a bastard Gwendolyn, but Griswold's rightful heir.'

Her face paled as his words sank in, and he continued, twisting the knife a little deeper.

'Isabel is having Phoenix's baby. If you send them away and she and the child die the Northmen, who are already on our shores, will attack Griswold. The Northman who is with her has vowed to protect her and he has promised me that if we help her then their men will spare Griswold.'

'You would take the word of a savage – of the men that killed Phoenix. He was like a brother to you Balfour and you would betray him this way?'

'Believe me Gwendolyn, I would like nothing more than to run a sword through his heart but I also promised Phoenix that I would take care of Isabel and right now that is the more urgent issue. I am also thinking of keeping Griswold safe from a war against the Northmen. You did not see the devastation at Ebondeen last year and I doubt you would want to experience it firsthand. Added to that, is the fact that you are a woman and these Northmen have been known to lack in gentlemanly behaviour if you know what I mean.'

'All right, I will get the physician, but I warn you, Isabel and that child have no rights here.'

Isabel groaned again as another contraction came. The physician examined her.

'The bleeding has stopped which is a good sign that nothing major has ruptured. Things are progressing nicely Isabel,' he said. 'If all continues this baby should make its entrance in a few hours. Try and rest as much as possible between the contractions.'

'Please, I want Erik to stay with me? He is the only person I trust right now.'

The doctor looked surprised at her request. It was not common for men to be present at births. He shrugged and looked at the large man with the plaited hair and tattoos. He wondered how on earth she could find his presence reassuring – he found the Northman terrifying. Erik nodded and held Isabel's hand.

'It will be all right, you'll see,' he encouraged. 'I will stay with you; I won't let you go through this alone.'

She gave him a weak smile. She felt exhausted and could not believe all she had endured during her labour. She would have a story to tell her son one day of how they were ship-wrecked and almost drowned before being brought back to his father's childhood home. Isabel had seen how Gwendolyn had looked at her when she arrived – the hatred and blame in her eyes did not escape the young woman. After they had moved Isabel to a chamber she had left the young woman. Isabel had felt immense relief – that woman frightened her.

⌘

EBONDEEN

Aislinn and Drew sat at the dinner table with Catriona and Struan. It was wonderful to see them both so happy again. Aislinn marvelled at the twists and turns in life. She realized that as much as tragedy was unbearable and painful, it also sometimes yielded the most beautiful outcomes. Struan and Catriona had both lost much and yet through it all they had met each other and gained strength from one another. They would never have met had it not been for the battle that turned their worlds upside down. Every situation could open the way for joy and peace to prevail. One just had to look for the silver lining on every dark cloud. Their love was obvious to Aislinn and she smiled. Her brother deserved this.

'How is the leg going?' Drew asked. They had come to Ebondeen to check on Struan's progress and to spend time with them.

'It is getting easier the more I wear it. I guess my stump is feeling less sensitive.'

Struan had not told Catriona but he had been practising his sword skills in an old barn. He was determined not to be useless when it came to defending his wife should another attack take place. He would rather die like a man than see her abused by the Northmen. He had worked hard to become agile on his new leg and many times he had almost fainted from the pain, dizzy spells almost overcoming him; but he had persevered.

'Master,' a young boy stood at the door of the dining hall looking apologetic.

'Yes Finn?'

'There is a man at the door that seeks Mistress Aislinn. He says it is urgent.'

'Send him in immediately.'

They looked at one another, surprised. Aislinn hoped everything was all right at Heart and Home. They had left Maggie and old Doctor Williams in charge and their two boys Logan and Jaimie were helping them.

Regent stepped through the doorway and Aislinn leapt out of her chair, almost toppling it over.

'Is everything all right Regent?' she asked alarmed.

'I have news about Isabel. It is good that you are here in Ebondeen.' He smiled as he said it thinking once again how the Great One had organized another coincidental event.

'Is she safe?'

'She is safe but needs your help. The Great One did not tell you everything of her condition as he did not want you to worry when there was nothing you could do. She is at present in Griswold castle and she is about to give birth to Phoenix's child.'

They looked at one another shocked. Never had it entered their head that she would have fallen pregnant so quickly.

'How did she get back here – I thought she was in the North?'

'She was, but she stowed away on the Northmen's boats when they set sail.'

'Now why does her impulsiveness not surprise me,' Drew said.

'How long will it take us to get to Griswold?' Aislinn asked.

'If we leave now we can be there by early morning.'

Aislinn and Drew said hasty goodbyes to Struan and Catriona.

'The Northmen are already here,' Aislinn said to her brother. 'Send Catriona to Sherbrooke – she can stay in our home.'

He nodded gratefully and she hugged her brother close.

'Stay safe,' she whispered.

'You too.'

CHAPTER 33

REUNITED

GRISWOLD

THE NORTHMEN sailed up the river, the kingdom of Griswold on the one side and the Kingdom of Ebondeen on the other. Thorfinn was no longer sure whether they should continue upriver to Cragshelm or whether they should just attack the closest villages. He did not feel as enthusiastic about this raid as he usually did – his heart ached at the thought of his son lost forever. It was the way he died that made it so painful. A freak accident was no way for a warrior like Erik to depart this world. A Northman always wanted to die in battle, his sword and battle axe with him as this was far more noble and honourable than dying any other way. When a man died this way Odin adopted him as a son and took him to Valhalla to reside with him. Erik would never go to Valhalla now. Instead he would go to Hel, the realm ruled by the giantess Hel. It was a bleak place compared to Valhalla and those who died any death other than in battle would journey there.

The other men all waited for their Earl to make a decision. They wanted to raid and set up camp as soon as possible and growing dissention was beginning in their ranks.

⌘

'I can't do it anymore Erik,' she sobbed. 'Just put me out of my misery.'

'Yes you can Isabel. You are the strongest woman I know. You have survived months in a harsh, cold environment with people you don't even know; you have sailed for over a moon at full term and survived our boat sinking. You have even survived the loss of your beloved. This is nothing compared to all those things – you can do this. Phoenix would be so proud of you and so would your parents. Don't you dare give up on us all now.'

'It's taking too long – something must be wrong.'

'Don't be afraid. The Great One always has a plan. I've seen it from the stories I've read. He will rescue you and this baby.'

She was surprised at his willingness to acknowledge the Great One. They had not discussed their beliefs since they had made a truce to be more tolerant to one another and learn more from each other.

'What would Odin say?' she asked.

He smiled. 'Odin is the father of the gods and he is very wise, just like your Great One. He is also the god of magic and inspiration. He will find a way for someone to help you.'

'Thank you,' she squeezed his hand and he mopped her brow.

'Nothing can harm you Isabel, if you have two gods looking after you.'

⌘

Balfour knocked on Gwendolyn's chamber door. It was time he gave her the letter he had held onto for the last nine moons. He had kept it secret all this time as he did not know where Isabel was, but now he needed to do what Phoenix had asked of him.

'What is it?' she asked as he entered her chamber. 'Has the child been born yet?'

'No, it looks like it will be a long night.'

'Then why are you here?'

'I have been holding onto this letter for a while, but it is time that I gave it to you.'

He held out his hand, the parchment extended toward her. She took it from him and broke open the seal – Phoenix's seal, and read the contents.

This document serves to verify my marriage to Isabel Williams at Sherbrooke in the summer of 1948. She now becomes Lady Isabel and co-ruler of the Kingdom of Griswold. In the event of my death she is the legitimate ruler of Griswold and any children born of our union the heirs to the Kingdom of Griswold.

It was signed and stamped by Phoenix. Attached to the letter was a document showing the witnesses who attested to Isabel and Phoenix's marriage. She noticed Drew and Aislinn's marks as well as Mac and Imogene Hamilton's. That family were doing their best to steal her inheritance – she would have none of it.

She was not going to take this like a stray dog, kicked in the ribs when it tried to hang onto its bone. She was tired of being the underdog. It was her turn to rule Griswold. She deserved to rule after all she had put up with. She would not lie down and go away simply because Balfour presented her with a piece of paper.

'You can leave this with me,' she said curtly. She was barely hanging on to her anger.

'Just in case you are thinking of throwing it into the fire, I must warn you that Phoenix had two identical documents drawn up. Aislinn and Drew Williams have the other copy. Let's just say that after your marriage agreement forgery, he didn't quite trust you to do the right thing.'

'Get out,' she spat, her anger finally bubbling over.

⌘

Aislinn and Drew rode with Regent. Aislinn urged her horse on faster, kicking it in the ribs. The beast sensed her urgency and responded to her, straining forward, its nostrils flaring to draw in extra oxygen. They rode hard toward Griswold – Aislinn was desperate to be there for her daughter. She did not trust Gwendolyn to protect her – if anything she feared the woman may try to keep medical help from her. Isabel's death would solve a lot of Gwen's problems and would give her a measure of vengeance. She knew what it would do to Aislinn and Drew. Her hatred for them had never waned. What better way to hurt them than to hurt the one they loved the most?

⌘

Balfour headed back to the river. He had received word that seven long boats had been sighted sailing upstream. He had told Gwendolyn that if they helped Isabel that the Northmen would not attack the castle. The truth was that they had no idea that Isabel and Erik were even alive.

Somehow he had to get a message to Erik's father. Erik had given him the eagle pendant his father had given him as a child.

'Take care of it,' he said handing over the charm.

'I will. You take care of her,' he said indicating Isabel.

Erik nodded. 'I give you my word.'

He sat astride his horse and watched the boats approaching. He took the necklace and pushed it into a leather pouch. Then he tied the pouch around an arrow and pulled out his bow. His aim had to be perfect – if he missed the boat then the necklace would sink to the bottom of the river. He waited till the boats drew closer. He was extremely grateful for Isabel's training. She had taught him how to perfect his aim and he would need it more than ever now. He remained in the shadows of a large tree – he did not want the Northmen to see him till the arrow landed on their deck. Once it landed he would attempt to communicate with them. He pulled the bow string back and readied the arrow for flight. Then he waited for the perfect moment. The arrow released with a hissing sound and flew silently toward its target. Balfour had to take into account the pouch weighing the arrow down and adjust his shot accordingly – something else Isabel had taught them in training.

'An arrow is not just a weapon to kill,' she had said. 'It can be used for many things - to pin someone down or to send a message by attaching things to the shaft. The point is that you need to know how to shoot your arrow depending on what you are trying to achieve. Not all shots are equal. It is never good enough to settle just for bullseye – rather learn the technique of how to get your target – that is far more important.'

He watched the arrow arc into the air and descend over the first long boat. It landed on the deck with a thud leaving the men yelling for a shield wall. They waited for a wall of arrows to assail them. When nothing happened they looked at the lone arrow, noticing the pouch for the first time. Thorfinn picked it up and pulled on the drawstring. Then he pulled out Erik's necklace. He looked around frantically searching for where the arrow had come from. Balfour stepped out on the bank in full view of the men and shouted.

'Erik is alive. Come alone to the shore and we will talk.'

The Northmen urged Thorfinn not to go ashore alone but he insisted.

'They may have Erik prisoner. Besides if they wanted us dead they could have fired many arrows at us before we even knew they were there.'

He stepped ashore and moved toward Balfour cautiously, his hand resting on the hilt of his sword. Balfour noticed his stance and kept his hands out front.

'I just want to talk,' he said reassuringly.

'Where is my son?'

'He is safe at Griswold castle. We found him and Isabel on the beach. They were washed up after the boat capsized. He asked me to give you the necklace as a sign he is alive. Isabel is not in a good way – the baby is coming. He asked me to remind you of your agreement not to attack Griswold or Ebondeen. Attacking the castle now would put him and Isabel at risk. That is why I have come to seek you out.'

Thorfinn sighed. This raid was not going to plan. He thought of the seer's words and of the caution not to be hasty or greedy. The men would not be happy with his decision.

'All right, we will not attack Griswold or Ebondeen. I give you my word. When can I see my son?'

'I can escort you to the castle if you wish.'

'I don't think that is a wise idea. If I leave my men they may decide to attack surrounding villages while I am gone. It is better if Erik comes to me.'

'I will tell him, but I doubt he will leave Isabel until the child is born.'

'Then we will set up camp and wait for him. Do we have permission to hunt in your forest for food?'

'Yes you may take what you need. I will organize for some grain to be brought to you while you are here. That way there will be no need to raid the villages.'

'Thank you,' Thorfinn said.

Balfour left the men unloading their supplies and setting up camp. He hoped they would keep their word about not raiding the villages. Just in case, he would send a scout to watch their every move – he wanted to know if they went back on their deal. He would also send a message to Struan telling him of their agreement. He would need to be ready if everything fell apart, but it would be a relief for him to know that Ebondeen would not be attacked any time soon.

⌘

It was a long night and Isabel lapsed between exhausted sleep and painful contractions. The light was just beginning to come through the window as a new day was dawning.

'I don't think I can endure much longer,' she whispered to Erik.

'I wish I could take the pain from you Isabel. I would if I could.' His heart ached for her – she looked small and exhausted.

'I know. I could not have come this far without you. You are the greatest friend I have ever had.'

Erik smiled but his eyes were sad. He did not want to be her friend. He wanted to scoop her up into his arms and kiss her all over, to protect her and love her the way a man should love a woman.

'I will always be here for you.'

A knock at the chamber door interrupted their conversation. Balfour was at the door with two people – a man and a woman.

'This is Isabel's parents. How is she doing?'

Erik stepped aside to let Aislinn past. The woman almost ran him over in her haste to see her daughter.

'Issie,' she cried rushing over to the young woman who groaned. 'It's Mama. I'm here; everything's going to be all right.'

'Mama, you came,' she sobbed, relief overwhelming her.

Aislinn shooed all the men out of the chamber while she examined Isabel. It was as she thought. The castle physician was not experienced in childbirth and had not picked up that the baby was not progressing. She was not dilating as she should and Aislinn worried that it would have a negative impact on this child. She prayed that they would not have to cut her open as they had done for Gwen all those years ago. They had performed the same operation a few times more, but not always with favourable outcomes. It was one thing cutting a stranger open but Aislinn was not sure she or Drew would be able to cut Isabel open – she was their daughter.

'Drew,' she yelled. He entered a worried look on his face.

'Get me some caudle,' she asked. He nodded and left the chamber to get the warm, spiced wine that was sometimes used during childbirth to help the mother cope with the pain and relax. He knew that Aislinn was attempting to get Isabel to feel less stressed in the hope that her body would respond naturally and ready itself for the delivery.

Aislinn massaged Isabel and talked softly to her. She was desperate to know just what her beautiful daughter had endured all those winter months in Kaldakinn but now was not the time – she had to calm her, not remind her of what she had been through.

Drew brought the warm liquid and Isabel sipped it, grateful for the warmth and the tingling sensation it gave her. She felt calmer.

Everything will be all right.

She drifted off into sleep, exhaustion claiming her finally.

CHAPTER 34

THE EAGLE AND THE LION

THE NORTHMEN were not pleased with the turn of events. They grumbled amongst themselves. For months they had prepared themselves for the summer raids and now Thorfinn was hindering their plans. He was putting his family ahead of the clans needs. They felt frustrated.

'This whole journey has had a bad feel about it,' Gunnar said. 'The gods have shown us their displeasure – it is because of that woman from the south. Thorfinn and Erik have gone soft on her and she has brought disaster on us.'

The men agreed. They felt that Isabel had cursed their journey – the gods were clearly expressing their anger – Thor had almost killed them during that storm and now they were sitting on the river banks of two wealthy kingdoms twiddling their thumbs. They felt emasculated.

'We look weak to the people we are going to raid. They won't fear us after this. We need to do something about it.'

The more they talked amongst themselves, the greater their dissatisfaction grew.

⌘

She saw him in the distance – he had his arms open to her and he was smiling. She ran to meet him, desperate to feel him close once more.

'I've missed you,' she said as he held her. She could smell him again and her heart soared.

'I've missed you too, Belle.'

'Don't ever leave me again, promise me.'

He looked at her – his green eyes more vivid than she remembered. 'I wish I could stay with you my love, but you have got so much more to accomplish. You have our child to raise and one day you will find love again.'

'I don't want anyone else Phoenix – it is you I love.'

'I want you to be happy again Isabel. Love is right in front of you – I want you to take it, to love him the way you love me.'

'Who, Phoenix?'

He started to fade and she reached out trying to hold onto him.

'Please don't leave me,' she sobbed. 'Let me come with you.'

Her body shook violently on the bed as she dreamed.

'Drew,' Aislinn called urgently trying to wake her daughter. She was unresponsive, limp and cold to the touch.

'We're losing her,' Drew said listening to her heartbeat. 'Get me a blanket, we need to warm her.'

'She needs bloodletting,' the castle physician interjected.

'You are not touching my daughter,' Drew growled. Bloodletting was a common practice in their day – it involved puncturing an artery to allow the patient to bleed, the belief being that when blood was released the body would balance and health return. Drew did not believe this was sound medicine.

'It is the only way,' the physician persisted.

'Get out,' Aislinn said firmly, indicating the door. 'We will treat our daughter, thank you.'

'What are we going to do?' she asked Drew as he warmed her body.

'I am going to give her some Spirit of Hartshorn.'

Aislinn watched as Drew took out the small bottle that contained the ammonia solution obtained from the shavings of the deer horns and hooves. He waved it under her nose, hoping she would respond to the pungent smell.

Isabel felt as though she were floating between two worlds. She could see herself in the bed, her father and mother leaning over her.

What were they doing?

She searched for Phoenix but he was gone and she felt sadness overwhelm her. Then she saw two men in the distance. One looked familiar. It was the Great One, but who was with him? The other man looked younger, strong and determined.

'Who is he,' she asked the Great One.

'This is Odin,' Isabel.

'He's real?' she asked surprised.

The Great One laughed at her shock.

'It's all a matter of perception Isabel.'

'It's time Isabel,' they said in unison.

'Time for what?'

'Time to have your baby,' they smiled. 'He will have the strength and courage of a lion and the vision of an eagle.'

Then the strangest thing happened. Odin and the Great One merged, their bodies becoming one. Isabel shook her head, confused. Then she was alone again.

'Isabel, Isabel,' she heard her name called. She tried to find it but her mind was foggy.

'Isabel,' Aislinn called louder.

Her eyes flickered open. Her parents sighed in relief.

'You're back,' Aislinn smiled. 'You gave us quite a scare young lady.'

'I had the weirdest dream.'

'Right Isabel, it's time. Let's get this baby out.'

'That's what the Great One and Odin said.'

'Who's Odin?' they both asked in chorus.

'It's a long story,' she smiled. 'Let's do this.'

⌘

Erik paced up and down outside the chamber door. He was anxious ever since the castle physician had stormed out of the room shaking his head and muttering, 'They will be the death of that girl.'

Is she all right?

His stomach felt knotted and he had to restrain himself from bursting through the door and demanding to see her. He reminded himself that they were her real family and that although he was her husband it was in name only. Once this was over she would return to them and he would never see her again. He could not bear the thought of it. Then he heard it – the lusty cry of a baby. He smiled – she had done it.

The door opened and Drew stood there looking at the wild Northman who waited expectantly.

'She's asking for you.'

Erik strode into the room, unable to keep his relief in check any longer. She looked beautiful – as though the experience had awakened some new and hidden treasure within her. She smiled at him and indicated the infant that she cuddled.

'You were right,' she said. 'It's a boy Erik.'

'I knew he would be. He's beautiful Isabel.'

The infant had Isabel and Phoenix's dark hair and he slept soundly after his ordeal.

'Are you all right?'

'I'm fine, but glad it's all over. Erik, this is my mother, Aislinn, and my father Drew.'

'Thank you for getting Isabel here safely, Erik. She told us how you rescued her when the boat went under. We are indebted to you for bringing her home safely.'

Aislinn watched the huge Northman. In some ways he seemed wild, a fierce warrior, but then she saw how he looked at Isabel with such tenderness and she realized that he loved her.

Was Isabel aware of his feelings for her?

'I am glad it all turned out okay,' he said graciously. 'What are you going to call him Isabel?'

She had thought of naming him after his father but somehow the more she thought about it the more reluctant she felt - it was too bittersweet, too painful.

'I'm not sure. I'll have to think about it.'

'You just need to rest and get your strength back. There will be plenty of time to name the child,' Drew said.

⌘

Erik rode with Balfour toward the Northmen's camp. It would be good to see his father again. This raiding trip had certainly thrown obstacles in their path. He had been excited to venture back to the south but now he would lose Isabel and his enthusiasm for the raids had dwindled. All he felt now was sadness.

Thorfinn was delighted to see him, hugging him close, pressing his wooden pendant into the palm of his hand.

Erik tied it around his neck. He had worn it ever since his father had given it to him as a boy. Then they sat and ate together.

'What are your plans, father?'

'We will sail towards Cragshelm tomorrow, although the men are angry that we are not attacking Griswold or Ebondeen. It is another two days sailing to reach our destination.

'Father, I want your approval to stay at Griswold till Isabel is on her feet again. I feel it is my duty as her husband to ensure she is safe.'

'You are married to her?' Balfour asked shocked. He had not expected this. This could change everything regarding her inheritance of Griswold castle. The law of the kingdom usually stated that a woman forfeited her right to any inheritance when she married again. If Gwendolyn should find out about this then Isabel's child would be the only thing standing between her becoming the next ruler of Griswold.

'I think Erik is right Thorfinn. Isabel's child is in danger. Gwendolyn will stop at nothing to become the legitimate ruler of Griswold. Now that Isabel has remarried she has no legitimate claim to Griswold.'

'You believe this woman would try to kill her own grandchild?'

'She has always hated Isabel and her family. I think she would do whatever it took to remain the ruler of Griswold.'

'Then you must do whatever is necessary to protect them Erik – the rest of us will leave in the morning for Cragshelm.'

'Thank you father.'

⌘

Gwendolyn had heard that the baby had been born. She had hoped that Isabel would not survive the night. The physician had been confident that she would not make it but she had surprised Gwen yet again by not only delivering a healthy baby boy, but by being up and about sooner than expected. Curiosity made her want to see the child – he was the last remnant of Phoenix, but she did not want to see Isabel.

What am I going to do? I need a plan. Damn Phoenix for writing that document – I will not let them take my home from me.

⌘

Aislinn and Drew helped Isabel into the carriage. Catriona and Struan had sent it over to enable her and the baby to travel comfortably back to Ebondeen. The sooner they got her away from Griswold the happier they would be. None of them felt safe leaving her and the baby under Gwendolyn's roof. Balfour and Erik had confirmed this.

Gwendolyn had been furious that she was taking the child from Griswold. She had tried to convince Isabel to stay. She needed the child and Isabel in her court to put her plan into action.

The journey was slow as Isabel was still uncomfortable and sore. She was relieved when the carriage pulled up in the courtyard of Ebondeen castle. The last time she had been here Phoenix had been killed. She tried not to look at the place he had been struck down. Erik took her hand in his squeezing it as though to reassure her that he knew how she felt. She smiled at him sadly.

He's a good man.

Once in the castle Isabel settled the baby down for a nap and then headed down to the parlour.

'Would you like to go for a walk?' Erik asked.

'That would be lovely. I feel like I need to stretch my legs after being cooped up in that carriage.'

They wandered through the castle gardens. It was remarkable how Catriona and Struan had rebuilt the place. The last they had seen of Ebondeen it had been burning and ransacked by the Northmen.

'Your uncle has done a good job restoring the castle.'

'Yes he has, despite his disability. I am so glad that he has found Catriona – I guess that is the only thing about the raid that makes me happy – if he had not been here then he would not have met her.'

'I am sorry that it is so painful for you to be here Isabel.'

'It's all right – it won't be for long. As soon as the baby is strong enough and I feel more like myself we will head back to Sherbrooke. I'm just sad that I couldn't bring that beautiful crib you made with me.'

'I'm sure someone will find some use for it,' he smiled. 'So this will be the last time I see you?'

'I guess so. Thank you Erik for all you have done for me. I could never have endured any of this without you.'

'You are stronger than you believe Isabel.' He pulled her into his chest and hugged her.

'I have decided on a name,' she said changing the subject. It was getting too personal.

'What is it?'

'I am going to call him Griffin.'

Erik was surprised. He had thought she would call the child Phoenix. She could see the question in his eyes and she looked away.

'I couldn't call him Phoenix. It would be too painful, besides I have another reason for naming him Griffin.'

'I am not judging you Isabel. I was just surprised that's all. So, why have you chosen Griffin?'

'When I was a child my mother used to tell me adventure stories – I guess that is where my love of adventure and shooting a bow started. My favourite creature in the stories was always a Griffin.'

'I've never heard of a Griffin. Describe it for me.'

'Griffin's were strong and powerful. They had the body of a lion and wings and head of an eagle. I had the weirdest dream when I was in labour – I dreamed that I saw the Great One and Odin was with him. They told me that this baby would have the strength and courage of a lion and the vision of an eagle. I can't shake the dream – it was so vivid.'

'It's a sign Isabel, and I think Griffin is the perfect name for your boy.'

Erik felt honoured although he did not mention this to Isabel. He had carved a lion into her bow as that was the picture that Odin gave him but he also wore an eagle pendant his father gave to him. He felt that even if they would be apart, somehow their paths would cross again – they were connected even if she did not yet realize it.

CHAPTER 35

STOLEN

EBONDEEN

GRIFFIN was doing well – it was a week since his birth and Isabel was settling into the routine of no sleep and feeding the child. Erik had remained with her throughout the week and she had appreciated his friendship. She had not been able to tell her parents about her marriage to him – somehow she was not sure when the time would be right to do so – would they understand why she had married him? They believed in love and marriage – would her actions horrify them? She was not sure. They might insist that if she were married to him that she return with him to Kaldakinn and fulfil her pledge to him. She was not ready to do that. She planned to leave in a few days with her parents to return to Sherbrooke – they had been away from Heart and Home too long and were anxious to get back.

There was further exciting news. Catriona and Struan had announced that she was expecting their first child. Isabel was delighted for them. Struan deserved happiness and he would make a wonderful father, she had no doubt.'

'You have to promise that you will deliver this baby Aislinn,' Catriona said.

'I wouldn't have it any other way – you can count on me,' Aislinn smiled.

'We will miss you all when you are gone; it has been good having you here.'

'Well this baby gives us a good excuse to visit,' Drew said.

⌘

GRISWOLD

Gwendolyn smiled – her plan would come together, she had it all set in motion. Now was her time to not only become ruler of one of the biggest kingdoms in the southern world, but to finally destroy the Williams family and take her revenge. It would feel so good. To fulfil her plan she had to align herself with people she had feared in the past – people she believed were evil. How differently she saw things now. They were simply people who wanted things in life and would stop at nothing to get them – what was wrong with that?

She thought of the meeting she had with Elder Merek. Years ago, she had believed him when he threatened them with a reckoning. She feared what he would do to her family. Now, she needed him and she had the one thing he had wanted all these years – money and power. He had agreed to her plan in exchange for her word to build the sanctuary Legion had vetoed all those years ago. It would be bittersweet for Aislinn that the very man who tried to burn her as a witch would destroy her family twenty years later when she least expected it.

Now all she had to do was wait.....

⌘

NEW HAVEN

Cillian was torn in two. He had put the past behind him the last twenty odd years and now it was coming back to haunt him – to force him into a corner and dredge up all the old, painful memories. He wanted no part of it, but they left him little choice – co-operate or be exposed. He had tried to pick up the pieces of his life after his last run-in with Mac. He had moved to a new village, New Haven, and started afresh – he wanted to put the past behind him and look forward to a future. He had done that for twenty years and now a simple threat to expose his deeds to his community and to ruin his reputation left him in turmoil once again. On one hand he was tempted to take his chances and call their bluff. He would deal with the fallout if it came, but then another part of him could not find the emotional energy to start over and to defend himself.

What do I do?

⌘

EBONDEEN

Isabel settled the baby in its crib and watched him with a smile while he drifted off to sleep. What is was to be a child, carefree with no responsibilities. Isabel wished she could have the peace that this child did – he was unaware of the world around him, of pain and loss and choices to be made. He did not understand the sadness she felt when she looked at his face – of how he reminded her of Phoenix.

'Your father would be so proud of you Griffin. I wish you had a chance to know him little one.'

She tucked the quilt around the child and tiptoed out of the chamber. Erik was downstairs in the parlour.

'Will you take a walk with me?' she asked.

They wandered through the gardens in silence. The stars shone like little dancing jewels hanging from a midnight blue sky.

'You haven't told them, have you?' he asked.

'Haven't told who?' she asked.

'Your parents. They don't know we are married, do they?'

'No, but it's got nothing to do with you Erik, I promise. It's complicated. I'm not sure they would understand me marrying for protection. I need time to explain it to them and to share my story. I can't do that in one conversation. I know that Mama wants to ask questions, but that she is afraid of what she will hear.'

'Don't tell them Isabel.'

She was surprised and could not understand the twinge of hurt she felt when he said it.

'Why?'

'It is for Griffin's future. If you tell them that you married me you relinquish your right to the rulership of Griswold. Griffin is too young to rule now but you could until he is a young man. Balfour has told me that Phoenix left letters confirming your marriage and your right to Griswold should he die. If Gwen found out we were married she would do anything in her power to remove the last obstacle standing between her and Griswold.'

'You mean that obstacle is Griffin, don't you?' she asked horrified.

'Yes, we are worried what she will do to the child if she finds out. No one must know we are married.'

'All right Erik, I will stay silent. When do you plan to join your father?'

'As soon as you leave for Sherbrooke I will go to Cragshelm and meet up with the men there. I promise you we will not attack Griswold or Ebondeen. You can rest assured knowing Struan and Catriona will be safe.'

'Thank you Erik.'

She squeezed his hand in gratitude.

⌘

Cillian rode toward Ebondeen – his demons had been put to bed and his conscience pushed back in its box. He would do this last thing but he would make it clear that he would never be at their beck and call again. He wanted his freedom. All he knew was that he had to collect a parcel from Ebondeen and deliver it safely to Elder Merek. That was the only instruction he had received.

⌘

She tiptoed into the chamber looking from side to side, her ear cocked for any noise. She moved silently over to the crib where the child lay peacefully asleep. She looked up and whispered, 'forgive me,' before she reached into the crib and took the sleeping baby.

⌘

'Help, someone help,' she sobbed. Isabel stood over the empty crib, dread settling over her like a black cloud. Her baby was gone.

Gwendolyn's done this, I know she has. Why does she hate me so much?

Erik and her parents found her in a heap on the floor next to the crib, sobbing.

'He's gone, she's taken him.'

Erik was furious. He wanted to kill that woman. He hated seeing Isabel so broken.

'I'll find him Belle, I promise,' he said wrapping her in his arms. She did not chastise him for calling her Belle – somehow this time it was strangely comforting.

Aislinn knew what she had to do. She called for Ziah and the army of the Great One. It was time to battle with Griswold again.

⌘

Cillian was horrified to realize that his parcel was a living, breathing infant. He tied the baby in a sling against his chest and hauled himself into the saddle. He had to get the child to Elder Merek as fast as possible. The woman who took the child assured him that he had been nursed and she provided a container of milk with a medicine dropper to feed the child should it be necessary. He kicked his horse and headed for the rendezvous point. His conscience crept back like a thief in the night, the knot of tension returning in full force. He had not signed up for this.

Chapter 36

The Search

LIONSGATE

THE GREAT One and his son watched the events unfold. Gwendolyn had crossed the line – her hatred leading her headlong down a path of destruction.

'We must help Isabel,' Ziah said. 'Aislinn has called for our help father.'

'Take Aedan, Regent, and Nuada with you. Find Griffin, Ziah. I will deal with Gwendolyn.'

⌘

NEW HAVEN

Cillian handed the baby over to the old man. He felt sick at what he had been manipulated to do.

'Where are you taking the child?'

'That is none of your concern.'

'That's it,' he said. 'I am done with all of this. I want no more of your plan. If you wish to expose me then go ahead. I don't care anymore. I have lived my life in fear and bitterness the last twenty-odd years and I refuse to live that way anymore. If you need someone to do your bidding again then don't call me.'

'So be it Cillian,' Elder Merek said. 'Just remember that I know things that could destroy you.'

'Well then I guess we will have to trust each other because I know things that you have been involved in that would not be looked on favourably by those who seek your spiritual counsel. I think you have far more to lose than I do Elder Merek should all this come to light.'

The old man was surprised at Cillian's resolve. It was true – he did have more to lose should his involvement in this come out.

'I guess we should say our goodbyes then, as we won't be seeing each other again.'

⌘

Isabel pulled her bow and arrows out and lay them on her bed. She pulled on a pair of pants that Struan had found for her. They were a little loose around the waist as they belonged to one of the soldiers at the castle, but she didn't care. Her tummy was still swollen from carrying her child and had not returned to its original flat state so she could not wear her own trousers. She pulled on a tunic and tied the pants at the waist with a leather belt. Then she pulled on her boots. Lastly she grabbed a cloak as she headed out the door.

'Isabel, you can't possibly go with the men,' Aislinn urged her daughter. 'You are still healing from the birth. Doing this could cause you permanent damage. If you haemorrhage you may die from blood loss or you may never be able to have another child. Let them do their jobs – they will find Griffin.'

'The last time I was convinced to stay behind Phoenix was killed Mama. I was not there to have his back. If I had been there he may be alive today.'

'Yes it's possible Isabel, but you can't spend your life wondering what could have been different. You cannot know with certainty that he would have survived. Your baby needs a mother Isabel – you can make sure that happens by being here when he returns.'

'I can make sure that happens by going to find him Mama – nothing you say will convince me to stay. I am his mother and I am going to get him, besides he will need milk when he is found.'

Aislinn knew it was pointless arguing with her daughter. She had to remember that Isabel wasn't a child anymore. She left home as their daughter, hardly more than a child; but now she was a mother, a young woman and she had experienced things that Aislinn did not want to even consider over the last winter.

'All right, but take this mix of herbs. It will help with the pain and stop your bleeding. If you feel even the slightest bit sick you need to take it easy. Promise me.'

'I promise Mama,' she said taking the herbs.

'I will take care of her, I promise,' Erik said to Aislinn.

'I am coming with you,' Struan said.

'No Struan,' Catriona pleaded.

'So you think I am not capable because I have one leg? I have been practising and I am quite able to stand on my own two feet.'

Catriona smiled at his sense of humour despite her fear.

'Take care, and come back home safely,' she kissed him, realizing the futility of trying to dissuade him.

Struan, Erik, Balfour and Isabel rode out of the castle and across the drawbridge. They did not have much information to go on – only that a maid had taken the child and handed him over to a man at the edge of Neverend Forest. She said the man had headed toward the west.

'Why would he go west? Griswold's south of Ebondeen. It doesn't make sense,' Isabel said.

'I'm not sure Isabel, but my guess is that Gwendolyn would not have him taken to Griswold. She would know that's the first place you would look. We'll follow the tracks and see where they lead us.'

Erik studied the tracks left by the rider who had collected the child. He was used to tracking deer and other animals, as well as other Northmen who trespassed on their lands. It was a skill he was very adept at. Once again Isabel was grateful for the huge Northman.

'It looks as though he headed into the forest. It's going to be difficult to track him but hopefully he rode hard and fast as he had a baby that would need feeding. If that is the case we will be able to see the tracks as they will be deeper than a horse moving slowly. I can see a trail here,' he said pointing to the mossy ground.

They followed the single horse hooves through the forest along a track until they emerged from the huge trees. Struan pulled out a map and oriented themselves.

'The tracks continue in that direction,' Erik said looking into the distance.

'My map shows the kingdom of Haven. The closest village from here is New Haven but it is still a good half days ride.

'What are we waiting for then?' Isabel said as she kicked her horse into motion, galloping off in the direction Erik had pointed.

Her body ached as she rode hard toward New Haven. No one had warned her about the effects your body went through after childbirth. She had not realized that she would have incredible cramps in her uterus and that her breasts would feel ready to burst from all the milk that was accumulating. Erik noticed the discomfort on her face as he rode alongside her.

'Whoa boy,' he said catching onto her reins and slowing her horse down to a trot.

'What are you doing?'

'You need to take it easy Isabel. I think we need time to have a rest and let the horses have a drink. You need to release some of your milk too or you will get an infection.'

'How do you know all this?' she asked.

He laughed. 'You have to ask that after spending a winter in Kaldakinn?'

She laughed too, remembering the lack of privacy in the village. Everyone knew everyone's business.

He helped her down off her horse and protectively held his cloak in front of her while she expressed some of her milk.

'Damn, this is painful,' she said. 'Being a mother is not as simple as I thought. I have new appreciation for my Mama.'

Erik smiled. She was still a child in many ways – very innocent and naïve and he found it endearing.

They mounted their horses again and Isabel took a sip of the herbal mixture her mother had given her.

'Are you all right?' Struan asked concerned.

'I'm fine, let's get going,' she replied as she nudged her horse forward.

⌘

Cillian had not gone home after Elder Merek had taken the child. His conscience had gotten the better of him. Mackenzie Hamilton had become the better man and deep down he knew it. He had changed his life – picked up the broken pieces after everything had been stripped from his family and he had moved on. He had created a new destiny for himself. He had found a new vocation and purpose in his life. Cillian secretly admired his tenacity. He had tried to do the same by moving to a new village but his past deeds kept following him. He realized that simply moving was not enough. Making the right choices and facing the consequences is what brought freedom. He had never faced up to what he had done. Yes, he had found reasons why it was Mac and Imogene's fault that his life had been ruined, but he had never admitted that he had the ability to change his own world. It was time he did the right thing – no matter what the cost to his own life. He wanted to do the right thing now.

He followed the old priest to see where he was taking the child. He stopped at a small cottage in the village and spoke to a woman who opened the door. He passed her some coins and she took the child. He waited outside for a while before she opened the door and handed the infant back to him. Then he carried the child back to the inn.

Cillian assumed that she was a wet nurse and had fed the child for a fee. At least the babe was getting nourishment.

⌘

Gwendolyn looked out her carriage window as they passed through the countryside of Griswold. She had to get this business behind her and get back to Griswold castle as soon as possible. She had heard the Northmen had sailed upstream toward Cragshelm and so Griswold was safe for the time being. She did not want to be away long in case they came back and attacked. She had gone to enough trouble to ensure that Isabel could not steal her inheritance so she was not going to let those savages from the north steal it from under her nose and plunder her lands. She hoped to be at the old sanctuary by nightfall.

⌘

Isabel, Erik, Struan and Balfour rode into New Haven as the sun was starting to set. They searched for an inn – somewhere they could get some food and refreshment. Isabel groaned as she dismounted, her body protesting the long ride. She stumbled momentarily and Erik caught her against his strong chest.

'You need rest Isabel,' he said worried.

She did not argue. She was pale and every inch of her ached. He helped her inside and organized a room for her. Then he scooped her up in his arms and carried her up the stairs as she protested weakly. Struan tried to intervene on his niece's behalf but Balfour intercepted.

'She will be safe with him, don't worry.'

As they had agreed to keep Isabel and Erik's marriage a secret, he did not tell Struan. All he could do was reassure him that Isabel was in no danger. Struan had his own problems. He too was sore and uncomfortable. He was not used to riding so may hours with his new leg. He ordered a large tankard of ale and hoped it would help to dull the pain.

They had discussed their plan of action on their ride to New Haven.

'We need to find a wet nurse in the village. Whoever took Griffin will want him fed as he will be fretting,' Isabel had said.

They agreed that the inn would be the obvious place to start as most travellers stopped there first after a long journey. Balfour asked some questions, flirting outrageously with the tavern maids. He discovered that someone had indeed been asking about a wet nurse in the village.

⌘

Isabel lay on the bed as Erik prepared her a steaming hot bath. He poured some lavender oil into the hot water hoping it would help ease her aching muscles. Then he carried her over to the bath. She could hardly stand and he helped her to sit on the edge of the tub. She winced as she sat down.

'Who knew sitting could be so painful after giving birth,' she joked.

'Well, most women I know don't go horse-riding all day just a week or so after they've had a baby Isabel. No wonder you are in pain.'

He gently untied the leather belt holding up her trousers and they fell to the floor. He took them and set them aside. Then he lifted her tunic and pulled it over her head. She made noises of protest as she sat in her sheer undergarment.

'Don't argue with me Isabel – you need my help.'

Before she could say another word he pulled the undergarment over her head leaving her naked and vulnerable. Then he picked her up and lowered her into the steaming water.

She felt embarrassed that he had seen her naked but the steaming hot water felt so good and her body began to relax. She closed her eyes breathing in the lavender scent. He sat behind her and rubbed her neck with the sponge letting water drip over her shoulders as he gently washed her.

'I will leave a wrap here for when you are finished. Call me when you are ready to get out and I will help you,' he said leaving her to soak her aching muscles in the tub.

Her soft, curvaceous body had not gone unnoticed by him and he had to gather himself. She thought she was fat and unshapely after giving birth but to him she looked beautiful – womanly in all the right places.

Stop it Erik. She will never be yours. Her heart belongs to another. Don't make this harder on yourself.

CHAPTER 37

CHOICES

NEW HAVEN

SHE WOKE during the night, icy cold. Her nightshirt was soaked with milk. That was when it hit her that she had lost her child and may never see him again. She began to sob quietly into the linen until her sobs became louder and grief overwhelmed her.

She had let Phoenix down. He had told her in a dream that she still had a lot to accomplish and that she had to raise their son. She hadn't even managed to care for their baby for a week before failing miserably as a parent.

She felt his arms wrap around her as he sat on the bed beside her, making soft soothing noises as a parent would to a child. He rocked her gently and she closed her eyes again.

The sun streamed through the shutters declaring another day. She opened her eyes slowly. Her body still ached from the exertion of the previous days ride but she felt surprisingly rested. She lay still, realizing that she was still wrapped in Erik's strong arms. She could feel his breath on the back of her neck as he slept. She tried to wriggle out from under his arms, hoping not to disturb him.

'You going somewhere?' he murmured sleepily.

She laughed remembering how he always knew what she was doing even when his eyes were closed.

'I'm starving,' she said.

'Me too.'

⌘

Balfour knocked on the door of the home he had been directed to. A young woman opened the door.

'I am looking for the wet nurse,' he said.

'I don't see any child,' the woman said. 'Who is asking?'

Balfour pulled out his money pouch and shook it. Coins rattled.

'Come in,' the woman said.

⌘

CRAGSHELM

The Northmen anchored their long boats along the riverbank. It had been a few days since they had left Griswold and the men were anxious to get ashore and begin raiding. They still grumbled among themselves and Gunnar stirred up trouble amongst those who would listen. Secretly he had not forgiven Erik for humiliating him in front of the men and Isabel. It especially stung that the evnukk had defeated him. Any other man would not have been a problem but a young man who had never even been with a woman was a complete humiliation. The thought of Erik being his Earl one day made it even more unbearable. He would not allow that to happen. So, he whispered rumours in the men's ears hoping to curry favour and support from them, making them promises for the future.

They set up camp and scouted the area looking for the villages and sanctuaries that would yield the greatest treasures. Raiding season was finally about to begin.

⌘

New Haven

They sat in the tavern and ate their breakfast. Balfour shared what he had learned from the wet nurse.

'She said an elderly man brought a newborn child to be fed and paid her well. She did not know where he was going but she said that he was a spiritual man because of his robes and the insignia he wore. He told her that a mother in his congregation had died in childbirth and that he needed her to feed the babe so that he could take it to its new family.'

'That doesn't give us much to go on does it,' Isabel said frustrated.

'Then it's a good thing we have come to help,' a voice chimed in.

'Ziah,' Isabel squealed leaping to her feet and embracing him. 'How did you know we were here?'

'Really Isabel, you know we see everything,' he laughed. 'Actually your mother called for us. We will get Griffin back, I promise you.'

Erik watched on quietly.

Who were these strangers?

'Erik, this is Ziah the Great One's son. These other fine gentlemen are Aedan, Regent and Nuada.'

Ziah clapped Erik on the back like a long lost friend.

'Thank you for looking after Isabel so well,' he said. 'My father and I appreciate all you have done to keep her safe.'

Erik could not respond. He was surprised.

How do they know I have looked after Isabel all these months?

He was equally surprised that the Great One actually existed and that he had met his son face to face. He wished he had met Thor, Odin's son face to face; but the only time he had ever seen any evidence of his god was in the thunder and lightning that filled the skies.

Is this man really a god? He looks just like one of us.

⌘

Gwendolyn waited outside the sanctuary. It was quiet and the only activity was the odd villager coming to pray and the spiritual elders moving through the buildings. She did not wish to go inside – she was afraid of what her heart would reveal – more than anything she was afraid that her intentions would be exposed and somehow the heavens would descend on her in fury. So, she waited outside pacing up and down the dusty path willing Elder Merek to arrive.

He arrived carrying a bundle which she assumed was the child. He looked around as though he too was afraid of being seen.

'The child will need to be fed again soon,' he said handing her the bundle. Gwendolyn took the child who whimpered. She peered into the quilt seeing her grandson for the first time. She caught her breath – he looked just like Phoenix as a baby – the dark hair and eyes the same colour. She felt her heart pounding and it ached.

'Thank you Elder Merek. Here is the purse we agreed on – it should be enough to build your sanctuary. If anyone asks, we have never had this meeting – I was never here.'

'What meeting?' he said reaching for the purse.

Gwen climbed back into the carriage. She had a supply of milk and a medicine dropper to feed the child on her return. She felt conflicted, her mind in turmoil.

What am I going to do now?

⌘

Cillian waited outside the inn. He was unsure whether to go inside.

What if they do not believe me? No, I have to do the right thing now – I need to stop being a coward and face the music.

He pushed the door open and entered the tavern before his courage deserted him completely. He saw them at the table and crossed over to them, fear on his face.

'Cillian,' Ziah said. 'What brings you here?'

Isabel paled. She had never met this man but she certainly had heard what trouble he had caused her family. What did he want now?

'I know where the child is,' he said.

'If you have harmed my baby I will kill you,' Isabel said leaping to her feet, knocking her chair over. Erik grabbed her arm and held her as she struggled.

'Your baby is fine. I do not have him but I know who does.'

'Why are you helping us?' Ziah asked. 'What do you want in return?'

'I don't want anything Ziah, except the opportunity to do the right thing. I am tired of hatred and bitterness. This is my way of trying to make up for all the wrong I have done in the past.'

'Tell us what you know,' Aedan said.

⌘

They rode hard toward the sanctuary. Cillian had followed Elder Merek and seen the exchange between him and Gwendolyn. They just hoped they would get there in time. Isabel had bound her breasts with swaddling cloth to help stem the flow of milk. She was afraid that her milk would dry up before they found Griffin.

⌘

Gwendolyn looked at the sleeping child. The motion of the carriage had rocked him to sleep. She felt her heart stir. She had planned to kill him but now she could not bring herself to do it. He was so like Phoenix. She felt she had been given a second chance to raise a child – her years with Phoenix had been stolen by her grief and bitterness. Now she could recapture those years – she could be the mother she never was to Phoenix. She would have to bide her time though. Isabel would come looking for the baby, believing that she was behind his kidnapping. She must convince her that it was not so. In time she would arrange for Isabel to have a nasty accident – perhaps make it look as though the grieving mother had been overcome with sadness and ended her own life. In the meantime she would find someone to care for and nurse the baby till all suspicion passed. She would rule Griswold until the child was old enough and then she would have an heir to pass it on to. She could have the best of both worlds.

'Yes Phoenix,' she smiled at the baby, 'you and I will have a good life.'

CHAPTER 38

MUTINY

NEW HAVEN

ISABEL was distraught when she realized they were too late. Both Elder Merek and Gwendolyn had left the sanctuary.

'We will find him Isabel. Don't give up hope yet,' Erik said.

'Every minute could mean he runs the risk of sickness or hunger.'

'He will be fine Isabel. He has the strongest and bravest mother I know, and his father was a fighter. His odds are pretty good I would say.'

Her eyes thanked him. She knew he was trying to keep her spirits up.

'We can track Gwendolyn easily,' Balfour said. 'Her carriage has left tracks. It looks as though she is heading back toward Griswold.'

'What are we waiting for then?' Aedan said as they mounted their horses again.

⌘

CRAGSHELM

The raids had been successful and the men marvelled at their plunder. They loaded the long boats and readied themselves to set sail. Thorfinn felt anxious. Erik had not yet arrived at Cragshelm. He did not know how he would convince the men to wait a few more days.

Where are you Erik?

'We are ready to set sail Thorfinn,' Niels said.

'We are not sailing yet,' Thorfinn said.

'Why not?' Gunnar challenged.

'I agreed to meet Erik here and he has not arrived. We will wait another couple of days for him.'

The men looked at each other, disgust written on their faces.

'We are sailing now,' Gunnar said defiantly.

'You dare to challenge your Earl?' Thorfinn roared.

'That's the problem. It's time there was a new Earl in Kaldakinn,' he countered. 'None of us respect your judgement anymore Thorfinn – you allow your personal agenda to dictate your decisions.'

He was surrounded by men. Gunnar's whisperings had shifted their allegiance.

'You can come without a fight or you can die here in a foreign land.'

'Why don't we just kill him now,' another Northman said.

'We may still need him. We don't want to alert Erik to his death. We need to be rid of them both to take Kaldakinn. There will be an accident at sea on our return journey.'

'How do you know Erik will find us?' Niels asked.

'If he does then we have his father as a bargaining chip – if he doesn't then we leave him here in the south. No one will ever know.'

They tied Thorfinn up and threw him onto the deck. Then they cast off and headed back down the river toward Griswold.

⌘

GRISWOLD

Gwendolyn was relieved to be back at the castle. She had become completely delusional, believing that Phoenix had returned to her through the baby. She had found a wet nurse in one of the small villages of Griswold and had paid the woman handsomely to care for the child.

'If anyone asks about the infant you are to tell them that it is your sister's child and that she took ill with the plague.'

The woman promised to keep her secret when Gwen had produced the gold coins.

Then she had returned to the castle.

'Lady Gwendolyn, there is someone to see you,' Holgrimm said.

He ushered the Great One in. Gwen's heart skipped a beat but she smiled graciously at the old man.

'Great One, it's been a long time. What can I do for you?'

'You know why I am here Gwendolyn.'

'No I really don't,' she said keeping her smile in place. 'Why don't you enlighten me?'

'Isabel and Phoenix's child has been taken. I know you have the child and I want to give you the opportunity to do the right thing.'

'That is awful,' she exclaimed feigning shock. 'What can I do to help?'

'You can give me the child,' he said calmly.

'I have no idea why you think I have the child Great One. Yes, Aislinn and I have had our differences but I have nothing against Isabel and I certainly would not take her child.'

'Gwendolyn, I see everything. I am not here to punish you or threaten you. Everyone has potential to change, to do the right thing. I believe you can end this. I am simply here to remind you who you are and to give you the chance to change your destiny. Legion came to discover this and turned his life around. You can do the same if you choose.'

'That is very generous of you Great One, but there is nothing I need to fix. There is nothing I want to change about my life. I am content the way I am thank you. You are welcome to search the castle if you believe the child is here. I will get Holgrimm to accompany you.'

'That won't be necessary Gwen – I know he is not here. You do realize though that if you go down this path that whatever consequences come your way will be of your own choosing?'

'I am quite capable of taking care of myself thank you.'

'If you change your mind just let me know,' he said as he left the hall.

She was a stubborn woman and her delusion was so great that she was not willing to relent. Even knowing that he knew where the child was would not deter her. Yes, he could have removed the child himself, but he believed in giving people opportunity to make right, to win their own battles and conquer their demons. He would give her a little more time.

⌘

They arrived at Griswold castle as it was getting dark. Isabel drank the last of the herbal medicine her mother had given her. It had helped her but she still felt tender and sore. Erik lifted her down from her horse and they led the animals to the stables to be watered and fed. Balfour took them to the kitchens to get some food. They ate hungrily, thankful for the meal of soup and bread

'You will sleep in the stables tonight,' he said. 'My father oversees them and he will not tell Gwen about this.'

'Thank you Balfour. How are we going to know where Griffin is?' Isabel asked.

'I think it best that I ask around first before we make accusations,' Balfour said. 'Gwendolyn could not have brought a child here without someone noticing. She would need someone to feed the child. Let me talk to some of the servants and see what they know.'

They all agreed this was the best plan of action. They settled down in an empty stall in the stables, making beds out of the fresh hay. Erik spread his cloak out for Isabel and she gratefully sank into the soft bed. Ziah smiled at the gentle giant's actions. Isabel was oblivious to how much he loved her or she pretended not to notice. He was not sure which was the case.

⌘

The long boats sailed silently down the river to the mouth. Ebondeen passed on their left and the kingdom of Griswold spanned the hills to their right.

'I think we should stop at Griswold on our way out and take what we need for our journey home. We will need fresh food supplies before we sail,' Gunnar said.

'Did you see the size of that castle?' one of the Northmen said. 'I guarantee you there is prize plunder there.'

'Yes, but it is even better fortified than Ebondeen. There is no time to breach the walls. However we will raid the surrounding villages and get what we need for our journey home. Next summer we will breach the walls of Griswold and her treasures will be ours.'

Thorfinn listened to them plotting. The seer's words echoed through his mind, *'Don't be greedy or it will be your downfall.'*

⌘

Balfour enquired around the castle but no one had seen the child or heard anything about him. He finally did a quick search himself but came up empty handed.

Wherever Gwendolyn had hidden the babe, it wasn't at Griswold castle. He dreaded telling Isabel.

She withdrew when he told her that there was no sign of Griffin. She would not believe him- believing him would be as good as giving up hope. Staying at the castle however, was not an option. It would only put Balfour and his father at risk and neither Isabel nor the others wanted to do that. If Gwendolyn found out they were harbouring them they could be tried for treason. They decided to leave and set up camp within the forest.

'We will watch and wait,' Aedan said. 'If she has the child hidden somewhere then she would have to leave at some point and we can follow her.'

Gwendolyn did not leave.

Isabel felt frantic.

CHAPTER 39

CONFRONTATION

'WILL YOU help me Erik?' she asked desperation in her voice.

They had camped in the forest for three days and still Gwendolyn had not left the castle walls. Isabel outlined her plan.

'Are you sure you want to do this Isabel? It could be very risky.'

'I have to know for myself,' she said. 'I know Balfour did not find him but unless I search every inch of that castle I will not be able to rest.'

'Then I will help you, but we will have to go in when everyone is asleep.'

'I know a way in,' she said excited. She remembered her grandfather telling her the story of how they faced up to the Dark Lord. He had mentioned the secret passage they had used. If it was still there then they could get in at night without being seen.

Isabel could hardly wait till it was dark and the others went to sleep. She felt like a caged lion and she paced up and down.

'Isabel, sit down and relax,' Aedan teased. 'You are making us all anxious.'

She smiled and tried to sit around the fire, but her mind would not relax. She mentally ran through the layout of the castle from when she had been there training the men. They would not have much time.

Eventually the others settled down for the night and Erik agreed to take the midnight watch. He shook Isabel awake when everyone was snoring.

'Time to go,' he whispered.

They kept to the shadows of the trees till they got to the castle. Then they moved into the undergrowth that grew alongside the bridge and slipped into the tunnel. Erik lit a torch and the light bounced off the stony walls. They followed the damp passage to the underground well. Then they took the other passage that led them to the stairs leading up to the stables.

'This is it,' Erik said. 'Are you sure you want to do this?'

She nodded.

⌘

Gwendolyn could not sleep. She was desperate to see her baby Phoenix but she knew that it was still too risky. She was surprised that Isabel had not come to the castle and she expected the young woman to turn up at any time.

Perhaps the Great One had told her that the child was not here.

She had word from Balfour that the Northmen's long boats had been spotted sailing toward Griswold. She hoped they were simply passing by enroute to the open sea but just in case they had a scout watching. She had enough on her plate at the moment – the last thing she needed was to fend off the northern savages.

⌘

Erik and Isabel silently crept through the castle, searching every nook and cranny. It was deserted, except for the guards that manned the battlements searching for any threat from the Northmen. Their focus was outward – none of them suspected that there were intruders within the walls. They hid a couple of times when they thought they heard someone coming. It was simply the old castle echoing in the silent night.

Isabel was losing hope. They had found no sign of Griffin. Now she stood in Phoenix's chamber, sadness creeping up on her again. She lovingly touched his robe and the books on his desk. This was where she would have lived with him had their lives been different. She could feel him as though he had been here yesterday. She twisted his signet ring on her finger subconsciously. She did not want to leave - it would mean leaving him and acknowledging once again that he was truly gone and not coming back.

Erik could see her internal struggle.

'I'll wait outside Isabel,' he said giving her time to gather herself.

She sat on the bed then lay down where Phoenix would have slept every night.

'I'm sorry my love, I have let you down. I won't rest till I find him - I promise you.'

Griffin was the last connection she had to Phoenix – she could not lose him or she would lose them both.

She heard the scuffle that ensued outside the chamber. Her thoughts instantly left Phoenix, her concern for the great Northman overwhelming her.

Erik!

She was unsure what to do.

She waited, her hand on the door-latch, her heart hammering in her chest. Surely the whole of Griswold could hear it?

'Who are you?' a man's voice said.

I must do something, her mind raced.

Isabel threw the door of Phoenix's chamber open.

'What is the meaning of this?' she demanded in her most authoritative voice.

Three guards looked surprised to see her there.

'I am Lady Isabel. Phoenix and I were wed before he died. Let go of my servant,' she said icily.

Her heart felt like it would explode from sheer terror.

'He looks like a Northman,' one of the guards said suspiciously.

'Of course he's a Northman, you idiot,' she said coldly. 'He was taken captive at the last attack on Ebondeen. Now he's my servant.'

The men looked unsure. Erik kept silent, his hands in shackles.

'Let him go,' she said again more firmly.

Please let them believe me.

A door opened down the hall and Gwendolyn stepped out in her nightclothes.

'What is all the noise about?' she demanded.

Her eyes widened as she saw Isabel and the Northman in the stone corridor.

'Isabel, what are you doing here at this hour of the night?'

'Where is he?' she said moving toward Gwen with lightning speed. 'I will kill you if you have harmed him Gwendolyn.'

Isabel grabbed her around the throat, squeezing as hard as she could as Gwen tried to pry her hands loose. Her strength was surprising. The guards raced to their mistress, pulling a furious Isabel kicking and clawing from her. Gwen coughed and wheezed as she gulped in the air that had been denied her.

'Take them down to the dungeons,' she croaked. 'You saw what she did. She tried to kill me and that is treason. She must be punished for it.'

Isabel dropped her head, realizing what she had done. Her emotions had gotten the better of her when she had seen Gwen and now she had put herself and Erik's lives in jeopardy. She would never be able to save Griffin now.

Gwen smiled triumphantly as they were taken away. Isabel had just signed her own death warrant. What better way to end this. Now she and Phoenix could be together forever – without that witch to separate them.

⌘

Ziah woke as the sun started to come up. The fire had gone out and it was cold. He shivered and looked around. Erik had not woken him for his watch. It took him just seconds to realize that he and Isabel were gone.

What has she done?

⌘

'The Northmen are here,' Balfour said to Gwendolyn, 'and they have made camp on our shores.'

'Take me to them,' she said.

'That is extremely unwise Lady Gwendolyn. They have little respect for southern women.'

'They haven't met me then,' she replied. 'I think it is time we came to an agreement with these men. I have something they may want.'

Balfour rode with Gwen toward the river bank. He was alarmed to see Gunnar giving instructions to the men. The Northmen watched as they approached their hands ready on their swords. The guards pulled their swords in response. Gwendolyn raised her hand to let them know all was well.

'Where is Thorfinn?' Balfour asked.

'Thorfinn is no longer our Earl,' Gunnar replied. 'If you want to talk then I am your man.'

'I am Lady Gwendolyn of Griswold. I rule this kingdom and I am certain that we can come to a mutually beneficial agreement without there being war and bloodshed.'

Gunnar scoffed. 'I don't take orders from a woman.'

'Well that's a pity because I have many men in the tree-line with bows and arrows. They have been instructed to shoot fire arrows at your boats should anything happen to me. I may be a woman but I still have something you may be interested in.'

'What could you offer me that I couldn't just take?' Gunnar asked.

'I have your Northman, Erik, in my dungeon at Griswold castle. I am willing to release him to you if you do not attack our castle. I am also willing to give you enough food and grain to take back with you on your journey if you leave us alone as well as some coins.'

Gunnar laughed.

So Erik had gotten himself captured – how ironic and how perfect.

'That is a very generous offer but I don't actually want the Northman back. You see he is next in line as Earl and I would have to kill him anyway. You've just saved me the trouble. Perhaps you have something else I might like instead.'

Gwendolyn smiled – she and this greedy Northman had more in common than she thought.

'Perhaps we can solve one another's problems then. I too have someone who threatens my rulership. The Lady Isabel is also in my dungeon and I was planning to kill her but the thought of her being your slave is actually far more pleasurable than killing her. Would you consider her a suitable gift? She is truly beautiful, I assure you.'

Gunnar roared with laughter. This was too good to be true – Isabel would become his after all. The gods were looking on him with favour – this trip had not been a disaster after all.

Thank you Odin!

Balfour felt sick. When had Gwendolyn captured Erik and Isabel and why did he not know about this as head of the guard? If Gwendolyn gave Isabel to these brutes she might as well be dead. Without Thorfinn or Erik to protect her who knew what they would do to her. He had to get word to Ziah – he needed their help.

'I accept your offer,' Gunnar smiled.

⌘

'I'm sorry Erik,' Isabel said wiping his bloody nose with her sleeve.

'It's not your fault Isabel. I know how desperate you are to find your baby.'

'She has a reason to kill me now and no-one would bat an eyelid in Griswold.'

'That is not going to happen. I won't let her harm you.'

She hugged him.

'Do you think Odin could save us from this dilemma?'

'What about the Great One?' he teased. 'I thought you didn't believe in Odin.'

'I think we need the Great One and Odin to rescue us from this mess,' she sighed.

'Then they will,' he smiled.

CHAPTER 40

THE EXCHANGE

ZIAH listened as Balfour told of Isabel and Erik's capture. Isabel had played right into Gwendolyn's hands. It was history repeating itself all over again, only the players were different.

'What are we going to do?' Aedan asked.

'When is the exchange happening?' Ziah asked.

'I don't know. If Gwen knew that I was here she would have my head on a pike.'

'All right, go back to the castle and keep an eye on her. Let us know when she moves Isabel.'

Gwendolyn was well aware of Balfour's divided loyalty. She knew that he would find someone to help him. Now it was confirmed by the man she sent to trail him. All she had to do was send him on a wild goose chase.

⌘

Gunnar loaded up the bags of grain and the salted meat that Gwendolyn had promised them. He thought of Isabel and what it would be like to have her in his bed. She would definitely please him well.

Thorfinn grunted and asked for water. Niels gave him a sip.

'Don't let him do this,' he whispered to younger man.

Niels turned away leaving the old Earl without an answer.

⌘

'They are moving Isabel tonight,' Balfour told Ziah. 'She will be taken from the castle after dark. I think Gwendolyn suspects I might try something as she has me running an errand to Trenton tonight. You will have to keep watch and follow her.'

'You do exactly as she tells you,' Ziah said. 'We will watch for Isabel and rescue her.'

⌘

'Where are you taking me,' Isabel screamed as the guards pulled her away from Erik.

'Say your goodbyes Isabel. You won't be seeing your Northman again,' Gwen said. 'I have a surprise lined up for you. Another Northman has offered to take you off my hands. He seemed awfully keen to take you although he wasn't keen to have Erik back. I wonder why that is?' she taunted.

'Gunnar,' Erik growled. 'Where's my father?' he asked Gwendolyn.

'You must be referring to the old Earl,' she said sweetly. 'Well I haven't seen him but it seems he is no longer Earl as far as I can tell.'

'Erik, don't let Gunnar take me please.'

'I will find you Isabel, I promise.'

She was dragged away as Erik was punched in the stomach.

⌘

Ziah, Aedan, Regent and Nuada hid in the trees waiting for the group to emerge from the castle. Struan returned to Ebondeen due to his leg which had become inflamed. Eventually a wagon carrying a young girl jostled across the wooden bridge. They could see the girl was bound but her face was covered with the hood of her cloak. Four guards rode alongside her. The wagon also carried some supplies they assumed was part of the deal that Gwen had made with the Northmen.

'Let's go,' Ziah said. 'We don't attack until we are well away from the castle.'

They followed the wagon silently, waiting for an opportune moment to free Isabel.

Their opportunity came when one of the cart's wheels became wedged in a rut. The guards dismounted their horses and as they attempted to free the wheel Ziah and his men surrounded them. They went to draw their swords.

'I wouldn't do that if I were you,' Aedan said.

Regent hopped into the back of the cart and untied the woman's hands.

'You're going to be okay Isabel,' he said looking up into her hooded face.

A strange face stared back at him.

'It's not Isabel,' he shouted. 'Where is she?' He shook the young woman who started to cry.

'I don't know what you mean,' she said. 'I work at the castle and Lady Gwendolyn told me that if I wore this cloak and went on the cart with the guards that she would let my brother go. He stole a pig and was caught. Please, I was only trying to help my brother.'

'She played us,' Aedan said. 'We need to get to the river now.'

⌘

'It's about time you got here,' Gunnar said annoyed.

'I had to create a little diversion as we were being followed. I didn't want your prize possession being stolen before we made the exchange.

'What about Erik,' Gunnar asked.

'Oh he was very angry when he found out about our deal. He promised to rescue her,' she laughed.

'You have to kill him,' Gunnar said fear in his eyes. It was not lost on Gwendolyn.

'Don't worry about him – he won't bother you again.'

Isabel kicked and squirmed as the guards dragged her to where Gunnar stood waiting. He looked her up and down and smiled leeringly.

'Not so high and mighty now, are we?'

Isabel spat at him and she was rewarded with a hard slap to the cheek.

'You'll have to learn some manners little lady,' Gunnar said as he wiped his face.

'Put her in the boat with Thorfinn,' he instructed one of the men.

'It was a pleasure doing business with you Lady Gwendolyn.'

Isabel was afraid when she saw Thorfinn shackled. There was no one to help her now. She was thrown down beside him and shackles placed on her hands.

'Isabel,' Thorfinn said surprised. 'Where's Erik?'

'He's in the dungeons at Griswold castle. Gunnar did not want him as he is a threat to this little mutiny of his.'

'I'm sorry Isabel. This does not look good for you. Gunnar will want his revenge and he is known to be very cruel to women.'

'I know, but I will not go down without a fight.'

'Where is your baby?' Thorfinn asked tentatively. He did not want to upset the young woman but curiosity got the better of him.

'I don't know – Gwendolyn has taken him,' she said it so softly. He could hear the pain in her voice.

The gods will not be happy with this. Gunnar thinks he has it all but it will come back to haunt him.

'What will happen to you?' she asked.

'Gunnar will not take me home – it will cause division and war within Kaldakinn. Leif will never follow Gunnar and neither will some of the other men and women. The only way he will ever become Earl is if I am dead. He will throw me overboard once we are far from land.'

'This is my fault,' Isabel said. 'None of this would have happened if I hadn't stowed away. I made the gods angry, didn't I?'

'No Isabel, this is not your doing. This is Gunnar's greed. The seer warned me before we sailed that greed would bring disaster on us and it has.'

⌘

Ziah berated himself for being misled by Gwendolyn. He should have known better. They rode hard toward the river, hoping that Isabel would be all right and that they would find her. There was no sign of the long boats when they got to the riverbank. Ziah's heart sank.

We're too late.

'What do we do now,' Aedan asked seeing the disappointment on his face.

'We return to the castle and find out exactly where she was taken. There is no point going on a wild goose chase till we have definite information. We also need to find out where Erik is. They may be together but they may not. If all else fails we have to find Griffin. That is what Isabel would want above all else.'

They turned their horses toward Griswold castle and set off.

⌘

Gwendolyn descended the steps to the dark and cold dungeon. It was a depressing place and she hated coming down here.

She waited as the guard opened the door to Erik's cell.

'I thought you would want to know that Isabel is safely away with Gunnar. He looked very pleased with his plunder.'

'Why do you hate her so much?'

It was not the response she expected. She sighed.

'It isn't her I hate. I hardly know her. It's the whole family and especially her mother that I loathe. For years Aislinn took my family from me. She killed my brother and she stole my husband's heart and loyalty. It is time that she learned the pain of losing a child. Phoenix would not be dead now if he hadn't met Isabel. She bewitched him and he lost his reason. My son was a well-trained soldier. He would never have been distracted in battle. It was her that made him weak. He was probably protecting her when he was shot.'

'That is not true,' Erik said. 'Isabel was not even with him when he was shot with the arrow.'

'How do you know that?' Gwen asked.

Erik kept quiet, realizing he had said too much.

'You were there – it was because of your men that he was even at that battle. Did you kill him?' Her voice rose in anger.

'No I did not.'

'But you watched him fall. Isabel had to have been there because you took her back to the North. It was you she arrived with when her baby was due.'

Erik kept quiet.

'She loves you, doesn't she?'

'No,' he shook his head. 'Her heart still belongs with Phoenix.'

'I don't believe you. You will pay for what you did to my son and Isabel will know that I have taken not only her child but the man she loves. I will make sure she hears of it.'

'So you do have the child?'

'I do but she will never find him. Phoenix is safe and will eventually become the Lord of Griswold when he is old enough.'

'Phoenix is dead Lady Gwendolyn. The baby is named Griffin.'

Gwen looked at him blankly.

'You're wrong. Phoenix has come back to me, raised from the ashes and he lives. How dare you say otherwise.'

Fury rose up within her, uncontrollable, wild and overpowering; two decades of pent up emotion ready to erupt. She pulled her dagger from her belt and plunged it into Erik's chest, his flesh giving way under the deadly blade. He looked shocked and coughed as she pulled it out. Blood trickled down his right side as he slumped to the floor, the shackles clanging loudly as he fell.

'It would be too easy to kill you right now. I will leave you to suffer and bleed out – think about what you have done to my son and think about Isabel being beaten and raped every day of her life. I hope your last thoughts bring you incredible pain and suffering.'

She turned on her heel, storming out the cell. The door echoed as it shut behind her and she hurried up the stairs. Her hands shook uncontrollably – she had stabbed a man and he would surely die from his wound. Somehow this did not disgust her as she thought it would – instead it made her feel powerful, it made her feel surprisingly good.

⌘

The longboats headed further out to sea. The day was coming to an end and the sky turned orange and then slowly pink. Its beauty seemed crude considering their circumstances. Isabel felt hopeless. Once Thorfinn was thrown overboard she would be alone with Gunnar and the men. She did not need to use her imagination to know what would happen to her then. She thought of Griffin and prayed that he was safe and being cared for. She looked up into the sky which was turning dark blue. The stars were starting to shine and she watched as one streaked across the sky before fizzling out. Everything had to come to an end but she didn't want her life to end this way. She had too many dreams. She nodded off to sleep as the boat rocked. Her body was tired after days of travelling.

He was there, sitting on the long boat watching her.

'When did you get here?' she asked.

He smiled at her.

'I have been with you all the time Isabel.'

'What do you mean?'

'A part of me will always be in your heart and I love that – I love how much you loved me, so I will always be with you.'

'It's not enough though, Phoenix. I miss holding you, kissing you.'

'That is why you need to open your heart again Isabel – let yourself be loved.'

She could not reply – tears rolled down her cheeks and she shook her head.

'I want you to be happy Isabel; I want you to be loved and to be able to love in return. I give you permission to love another.'

'I don't know if I can,' she whispered.

'Yes you can, and you already do – you just won't admit it yet, but it will happen in time. Don't be scared Belle, you have your whole life ahead of you. Don't give up, fight for yourself – fight for our son.'

She woke with a start as hands grabbed her –rough hands. She gagged as she smelled the sour breath of Gunnar. He had been drinking.

'Let me go,' she growled as he tried to kiss her. She bit him and he punched her on the side of her head. She saw stars and little dots bounced before her eyes.

She felt him pulling at the belt that held her trousers up. She kicked her legs and he cursed at how difficult it was. Finally he had the belt undone and the trousers slid off easily, leaving her barely covered. He licked his lips and grinned at her.

'Finally,' he said as he launched himself upon her. Isabel punched and hit him with bound hands but it had no effect on him.

'Don't make this harder on yourself lass,' Gunnar said. She could feel his arousal and panicked. 'I'll show you what a real man is like Isabel.'

'Leave her be,' a deep voice growled. Thorfinn grabbed him round his neck, the chains from his shackles tightening across his windpipe. Gunnar wheezed and gasped for breath, his face turning red then purple. He gurgled as his arms flailed the air, to no avail. Thorfinn kept up the pressure grunting with exertion. Finally Gunnar's legs slumped and his body went limp. Thorfinn dropped him to the floor, out of breath after the scuffle. Incredibly the men still snored. There were some benefits of a good wine. Isabel pulled up her trousers and fastened her belt.

'Thank you,' she said gratefully.

'Find me an axe he said.

She moved slowly across the deck trying not to let her shackles rattle as she moved. She thanked the Great One that the men had had too much to drink. She found an axe and returned to Thorfinn. He placed Gunnar's cloak across the shackle and then hit it, deafening the blow with the thick fabric. Finally the chain gave way. Then he did the same on Isabel's chains.

'What now,' she whispered to him.

'We get rid of Gunnar.'

They picked him up and dropped him gently over the side of the boat. They watched as he sank like a stone. Isabel was not sad to see the last of the man who had tried to rape her on more than one occasion.

Thorfinn surveyed the sea. The other long boats seemed equally quiet.

Thorfinn found Niels and shook him awake.

'Wha...at,' he said sleepily rubbing his eyes. He seemed shocked to see the old Earl free of his chains.

'Shhh...' Thorfinn whispered. 'I am taking this boat back. Either you are with me Niels or you can join Gunnar at the bottom of the sea.'

'I never liked him anyway,' Niels smiled. 'Good to have you back Earl Thorfinn.'

One by one the men were woken and pledged their loyalty to their Earl once more. They were too fearful to do otherwise. Some believed that the gods had come during the night and taken Gunnar away as Thorfinn was destined to be Earl. Others said that the seer's words had come true – that Gunnar's greed to be Earl and to steal Erik's wife had caused his death. None of them wanted to cross the gods.

'We are going back to Griswold to get Erik,' Thorfinn said.

The men cheered – they had not seen much battle this raiding season and they loved a good fight. They would satisfy their lust for battle in Griswold.

CHAPTER 41

RESCUE

GRISWOLD

'WHERE is she Gwendolyn?' Ziah asked his face set. 'We will not leave here until you give us some answers.

'She is gone and you have no way to find her. The Northmen took her.'

'And Griffin? Where is he?'

'I don't know anyone called Griffin,' she said stubbornly.

'The baby,' Ziah said patiently.

'How would I know? Isabel took the child and left. Perhaps you should ask Aislinn and Drew Williams. They seem to have a way of making people disappear without incriminating themselves,' she said sarcastically.

Aedan was beginning to get impatient. Hid red hair glowed and his emerald eyes flashed.

'Enough of this Gwendolyn. We will not hesitate to let the entire realm of Lionsgate be unleashed on you if need be.'

'Do you think I really care?' she ranted. 'What more can I lose? I have lost everything important to me – you cannot take another thing from me – I am already dead inside.'

'It is never too late to do the right thing,' Ziah said. 'You know that from Legion's experience.'

'I'm nothing like Legion. My guards will escort you from the castle,' she said with finality.

⌘

Erik's chest felt like it was on fire. He felt weak and he lapsed in and out of consciousness. This was not the way he pictured dying.

Help me Odin.

He heard the eagle calling – Odin was watching him, calling him home. He wanted to follow it, to be free to soar on the wind currents and leave the pain in his chest behind. He closed his eyes and let himself go. Then he heard it – a roaring sound that was so deafening it alarmed him.

What was it?

It was nothing he had heard before. Then the creature came into view. He recognized it instantly – the strong body and full mane of hair. The jaws were strong and the eyes piercing. It was a lion – the creature he carved on Isabel's bow and Griffin's crib. What did it mean? He remembered Isabel telling him that a lion represented courage, strength and leadership. She also said they protected their young.

It was clear to him. Odin was calling him home, to give up the fight and let it all go, but the Great One was telling him to take courage and find the strength to fight and protect both Isabel and Griffin. He could die here or fight for the woman he loved. He made her a promise that he would find her – he would not let her down. He ripped his tunic and bound his wound, stemming the bleeding as best he could. This time he would follow the Great One.

⌘

The long boats sailed back to Griswold. Thorfinn hoped that Erik would be all right.

Isabel worried too that the huge Northman may have been killed. She prayed that he would be safe. She hoped they would not be too late. She breathed a sigh of relief when the river mouth came into view. It would not be long till the castle loomed on its steep hill.

⌘

The Great One knew where Griffin was being kept. He could easily have rescued the child but he always hoped that somehow Gwendolyn would step up to the plate and take responsibility for her own actions. It amazed him that mankind always seemed to expect him to make things right, to rescue them and solve all their problems. He wanted them to learn that they were the ones who could make a difference, bring peace and goodness to their kingdoms. They were the ones who had the power to bring change. They needed to have faith in themselves. For now the infant was being cared for and was safe – that was all that mattered. He knew that Isabel needed to rescue Griffin – she had lost her confidence. He would give her that that opportunity, to believe in herself again as a mother and woman. He would let her discover the power of true love.

⌘

The longboats pulled alongside the river bank. They could see the castle in the distance but had no wish to alert the watchmen of Griswold of their arrival. They would travel on foot to the castle.

They stayed within the forest as they made their way cautiously toward the dark castle that sat atop the hillside, dominating with its stone walls and turrets. Thorfinn thought of his promise to Erik not to raid Griswold. Now he had no choice if he was to save his son's life.

⌘

Erik coughed and the pain that shot through his chest almost rendered him unconscious. He gritted his teeth to keep from fainting. He was worried – his breathing was ragged and there was a sucking noise from the hole in his chest as he inhaled and exhaled. He knew that only a miracle could save him.

Keys rattled as the lock was opened.

Has she come back to finish me off or to gloat as I die?

Quick footsteps made their way down to Erik as he slumped against the wall.

'Erik, it's me Balfour. I've come to get you out of here. Help me,' he shouted to one of the soldiers.

'Lady Gwendolyn will have us killed for this Balfour. I can't help you,' the guard shook his head.

'She's not the rightful heir to Griswold. Here's the letter of proof written and signed by Phoenix himself. Lady Isabel is the true ruler. Gwendolyn is a usurper and if you aid her you could be tried for treason. Now are you going to help me or not?'

The soldier scanned the letter and the marriage documents. He nodded to Balfour as they helped Erik to his feet.

'Where are we going?'

'I am taking him to Ebondeen where I have Aislinn and Doctor Williams waiting for him.'

'Do you think he will make it?'

'I don't know, but we have to try.'

Balfour and the soldier carried Erik to the stables where his father had a horse drawn cart ready to leave. They lay him on the bed of straw and covered him with a blanket. Then they set off for Ebondeen.

They had just entered the forest when they came across Thorfinn and his men.

'Whoa,' Balfour said surprised to see the Earl alive and blocking their way.

'Thorfinn, what are you doing here? I thought you were dead? I have Erik but he's wounded. We're taking him to Ebondeen to be treated by Isabel's parents.'

'Erik,' Isabel called alarmed, hearing Balfour's admission as she ran to the cart. She climbed up beside him shocked at his grey pallor and erratic breathing.

Balfour seemed even more surprised to see Isabel, but smiled relieved that she was safe.

'We need to go now,' she shouted to him. He nodded.

'We cannot follow you on foot,' Thorfinn said. 'We will sail upstream to Ebondeen and meet you there.'

'I'm staying with Erik,' Isabel said.

Thorfinn nodded gratefully.

They set off again as fast as they safely could.

'Erik, its Isabel. I'm here and I won't leave you. Promise me you'll stay with me.'

Erik groaned his eyes flickering open momentarily. He saw her beautiful face. He must be dreaming.

'Belle,' he tried to whisper but the words would not come.

'Rest,' she said cradling his head in her lap.

She remembered her Mama and Papa helping someone who had been struck by a sword once. She remembered the horrible sound his chest had made as he breathed. Erik's chest was doing the same. How had they treated him?

Quickly she tore a strip of fabric from her shirt. Then she removed the binding Erik had made. She remembered her Papa saying that if the wound was completely covered that the air being expelled would become trapped in the chest and this would cause a build-up of air around the lungs. She quickly covered the wound on three sides leaving the fourth side open for the air to escape. Mentally she thanked the Great One that her parents were medical practitioners. She may not have wanted to follow in their footsteps but she had learned a thing or two from them over the years.

'Balfour, I need a reed from the river bed as soon as possible,' she said.

⌘

EBONDEEN

Aislinn and Drew waited anxiously for Balfour to arrive. He had sent them a message via a Monwing. They had been surprised to hear that Erik had been wounded by Gwendolyn. They had also been told that Isabel had been taken by the Northmen again. Aislinn felt sick to her stomach. She trusted Erik because Isabel did, but without him to protect her, what would they do to her daughter? Gwendolyn's hatred for their family was evident to her now. She wanted revenge for Daemon's death and this was how she was going to get it. When would this all end?

⌘

Balfour snapped off a couple of reeds and ran back to the cart where Isabel waited. The Northman did not look good.

'Here,' he said handing her the reeds.

'Can you break it so that it is about so long,' she said indicating the length with her hands.

Balfour snapped it again.

'Give me a knife,' Isabel said.

She took the tip of the knife and began to hollow out the inside of the reed till she had a hollow tube. She worked quickly aware that time was not on their side.

'Do you know what you are doing?' he asked.

'I hope so,' she said as she took the tube and slipped it under the open side of the cloth and into the wound, leaving the one end protruding. Then she covered the wound around the tube. They could hear the air that had built up being expelled each time he breathed.

'It's working. Let's get going,' she said.

CHAPTER 42

THE OTHER SIDE

EBONDEEN

THE CART rolled across the bridge toward the castle. Usually Isabel always felt emotional whenever she came to this place. This was the last time she had held Phoenix in her arms – the place where her love was ripped away from her, but today she did not have time to think of that. Erik was deteriorating rapidly and she was desperately afraid for him.

Her parents met her in the courtyard and helped Balfour to carry the wounded Northman into the castle.

'Can you help him Papa?' Isabel asked worried.

'We'll do our best Isabel, but a long journey in a wagon will have caused great damage. He would have to be very strong to survive this.'

'Please Papa, you have to save him. Don't let him die. He's my husband.'

Drew and Aislinn looked at one another speechless. When had this happened and why hadn't she told them before?

'We'll do our best Isabel, I promise,' her mother said.

'Did you cover the wound and put the reed in?' her father asked surprised.

'Yes, I hope that didn't cause more damage?'

'You may just have saved his life Isabel. How did you know to do that?'

'I remember you and mother helping someone with a chest wound when I was much younger.'

'You remember that?' Aislinn said. 'You did well Isabel. Now we need to operate and close this wound. He's lost a lot of blood Drew.'

'I know and I'm concerned that unless we transfer blood to him he may not make it.'

'Has that ever been done before?' Aislinn sounded concerned.

Drew sterilized the wound and began to close up the hole, stitching carefully as he did so. Erik groaned and Aislinn gave him opium to ease the pain.

'It has been attempted by a man called Francis Potter on chickens without success but both he and another physician, Johannes Colle believe that it is possible.'

'I think it's a huge risk Drew.'

'I agree Aislinn, but we may have no choice if Erik deteriorates further. Let's get set up for it just in case. We will need some tubing and two goose quills to act as a type of needle. They need to be well sterilized,'

Balfour and Struan went to find the quills and something that could be used as tubing. This would not be an easy task.

Drew finished stitching the wound and then sterilized it before covering it with his bandages. Isabel wiped Erik's forehead with a cold cloth and held his hand.

'I will stay with him,' she said to her parents. 'You go and help Balfour and Struan get what you need.'

She sat with him, worried at how pale he looked.

'Don't leave me Erik, I need you,' she whispered.

⌘

It was no easy task finding tubing and Drew was getting frustrated.

'What about a pig's bladder?' he asked Struan. 'Have you slaughtered a pig recently?'

'Yes, one was slaughtered two days ago and has been salted. 'I'm not sure where the innards have been sent though.'

'Find out, we need that bladder.'

Struan managed to locate the innards in a barrel to be taken to the end of the lands to be dumped. It was a most unpleasant task digging through the smelly body parts of the pig but he persevered till he had found what he was looking for. The bladder was washed and sterilised, then stretched over a long stick while Drew meticulously stitched the sides so that it would not leak.

They were ready to start the procedure when Thorfinn arrived at the castle. He looked concerned and was taken to see his son.

'He does not look good,' he said and Isabel shook her head, her eyes filling with tears.

'There is one more thing we can try,' Drew said to Thorfinn but we cannot guarantee its success. It will also require your help.'

'I will do anything to save my son. I can see he is dying. I know that look - I've seen it many times in battle.'

Drew explained the procedure to Thorfinn and what they planned to do.

'I believe that by using your blood we stand a better chance of success as you are his father. You will have to stand and hold your arm above him so that the blood flows down to him.'

Thorfinn nodded.

Drew carefully sterilized his arm and then took the sharp goose quill he had prepared and pushed it into the vein in his arm. They strapped the quill tightly into place and Drew quickly did the same to Erik. Thorfinn's blood began to run down the tube towards Erik and into his arm.

'Balfour you need to hold Thorfinn up as he may become lightheaded from this and we cannot have him crashing to the floor.'

'Do you know how much blood he can give?' Aislinn asked concerned.

'Not exactly but I have an idea – this is all guesswork I'm afraid.'

Erik began to arch his back as though he were having a seizure. His eyes opened briefly before they glazed over and went blank.

'We're losing him,' Aislinn shouted.

⌘

Erik was floating, weightless, free of pain and serene. He could see people below, his father and Isabel – thank the gods she was safe.

Why does she look so sad?

The picture changed to a beautiful village and the peace he felt overwhelmed him.

Where am I? Is this where Odin lives? Is this Valhalla?

Then he saw him – the Great One with his son Ziah waiting for him.

'Erik, you have come to us. Welcome.'

'Where am I?'

'You are in Lionsgate.'

'Why am I here and not in Valhalla with Odin?'

'Because this is where those who pass on come to. Valhalla, Lionsgate, Heaven, The Life Hereafter – it is all the same place Erik – people just like to call it by a different name just as they like to call me by different names. I don't mind what they call me – they are all connected to me no matter what name they use.'

'So you are Odin then?'

'I am Odin if that is what you want me to be Erik. It is not the name that is important but what you believe that determines your reality. If you trust in something wholeheartedly then that belief can come to pass.'

'So I am dead then?'

'Look down there at Ebondeen and you tell me Erik if that is what you believe.'

Erik looked in the Mirror of Time at the room in Ebondeen where his body lay, where the people he loved stood over him, working on his lifeless form.

⌘

EBONDEEN

'It's no good,' Drew said removing the quill from Erik's arm. 'He's gone, we can do no more.'

'Nooo...' Isabel wailed rushing over to his still body, throwing herself over him, her face to his chest. Her mother moved to pull her away but Drew shook his head.

'Let her say goodbye Aislinn.'

They moved to the back of the room as Isabel sobbed uncontrollably on the big Northman's chest.

'You can't leave me,' she sobbed. 'I need you Erik. I love you,' she said broken. 'I don't want to live without you and now you'll never know how much I love you – how much I've loved you all this time.'

Her tears ran down his side as she sobbed. This place had taken both the men she loved. How could the Great One be so cruel to her – why was he punishing her?

⌘

LIONSGATE

'Do you hear that Erik? She loves you'

'Why is life so cruel?' he said angrily. 'I would do anything to be with her but it seems the gods have ordained otherwise.'

'Do you believe that Erik, or do you believe that love can overcome anything – even the pain of death?'

'What do you mean?'

'Love is a powerful thing – it has the ability to heal, to let go when necessary, to create new life and bring change. What do you want to do Erik? You can stay here with us or you can be with Isabel if you choose. I am giving you the chance to create your destiny, to explore what you believe.'

Erik had to admit that this place felt so beautiful and peaceful that he knew he would be happy staying here but then he looked at Isabel, her beautiful face streaked with tears and pain and he wanted more than anything to be with her – to live the life he had dreamed of, having children with her and knowing his love was returned wholeheartedly.

⌘

EBONDEEN

Thorfinn gently lifted Isabel off Erik's body and hugged her tight.

'He knew you loved him Isabel.'

'Yes, but he thought I loved him as a friend,' she sniffled.

'And he was content with that,' he reassured her.

Aislinn moved over to Isabel and hugged her daughter.

'I'm sorry Issie that we could not save him.'

'It's not your fault Mama. I am going to kill Gwendolyn with my bare hands. She won't get away with this. She won't take everything precious from me.'

'Forget Gwen right now Isabel. We will get Griffin back, I promise.'

Isabel dissolved into tears again.

'That's what Erik said to me.'

'And he was right. None of us will let her get away with this,' Thorfinn growled.

They barely heard it, their grief masking it - a sound like a whisper.

'Belle?'

She spun around, shocked to see Erik's eyes open.

'Erik,' she cried flinging her arms around his neck, kissing him all over his face.

'Slowly, I'm still sore Belle.'

'How is this possible?' Aislinn asked Drew who looked astounded.

'I don't know,' he stammered. 'He was definitely dead – for once my science fails me.'

Aislinn laughed, 'All things are possible for those who believe. Someone must have believed. Who was it?'

'It was me,' Erik said. 'I was with the Great One, Belle. He told me that if I believed in love that I could overcome anything. He gave me a choice.'

'Thank you Great One,' Isabel whispered.

Thorfinn was confused. He had never heard of this Great One. Why hadn't Erik seen Odin? He would have to ask him about it when he was well enough.

CHAPTER 43

MOMENT OF TRUTH

IT WAS two days since the miracle had occurred and Erik was up and about. The Great One had given him healing oil in Lionsgate and although he still had the scar from Gwendolyn's wound he was well again.

He and Isabel walked through the gardens of the castle.

'Can we go to the place Phoenix was killed?' she asked him.

Erik was surprised and his heart sank. They had not discussed her declarations of love and as far as she knew he was unaware of them. He hoped she was not going to deny her feelings out of loyalty to Phoenix.

'Are you sure?' he asked.

'Yes.'

He nodded and they headed to the edge of the forest surrounding the stone walls of Ebondeen castle. Isabel carried some wild flowers in her arms. She stood quietly on the spot where she had held Phoenix as he bled out then she bent down and placed the flowers on the ground. Erik could not read her expression and a knot of tension settled in his gut.

She's not ready, he thought.

'Isabel?' There was a measure of fear in his voice.

'Don't say anything Erik, let me speak please.' She faced him and held his hands.

'This place is where I lost someone I loved more than life itself, but it's also the place where I found something beautiful. I met someone who has protected me more than once; someone who has opened their heart to me and kept me safe and loved me even when I pushed them away. I may have lost Phoenix here, but it wasn't until I almost lost you that I realized that my heart is ready to love again and that I love you as much as I ever loved Phoenix. I want to be with you and to be your wife in the true sense of the word, to make new memories together. You are my best friend in the whole world and I don't want to ever be without you.'

Erik gazed into her deep grey eyes and saw the love there. There was no more fear or sorrow, only peace and happiness as she smiled at him.

'Belle, I can't tell you how long I have waited to hear you say that. I love you beautiful woman.'

He bent his head and claimed her lips – soft, sweet lips that melted under his touch as he pulled her close. She responded to his caresses and his heart leapt with joy.

'I want you so much,' she whispered.

'I want you too Belle, but you have just had a baby a few weeks ago – your body needs time to recover.'

She was touched by his thoughtfulness.

'Promise you won't make me wait too long,' she smiled.

'I guarantee you,' he laughed kissing her again.

⌘

They packed their saddlebags ready for the ride. Thorfinn and his men were already heading downstream back to Griswold in their long boats. Ziah, Nuada, Aedan and Regent had joined Balfour, Isabel and Erik in their quest to get Griffin back and Gwendolyn out of the castle. They mounted their horses and made their way toward Griswold. Now they would get back what was rightfully theirs.

They made good time reaching Trenton within the day. Drew had drafted a letter for the local doctor asking him to assist Isabel in their inquiries. He was only too willing to help, writing down all the names of women who were wet nurses in Griswold.

'One of them must be caring for Griffin,' Ziah said to Isabel.

They made their way to the villages asking at each as they went. Isabel was beginning to despair when they came to an isolated cottage set deep in the foothills of Griswold.

She could hear the sound of a crying baby in the cottage. She leapt off her horse and ran to the door, pounding on it furiously.

'Isabel,' calm down,' Erik said. 'It may not be him.'

'I may not have had him long Erik but I know my baby's cry.'

She banged again on the door and the child wailed louder.

The door was pulled open and an angry woman glared at Isabel.

'What the blazes are you doing?' she snapped.

'Where's my baby?' Isabel demanded pushing her aside.

'You can't just barge in here,' the woman shouted angrily.

Isabel picked up the crying child and held it close. Instantly the infant stopped crying.

'I'm here Griffin,' she whispered to the child. 'No one will ever hurt you again.'

'Give me the baby,' the woman said trying to pull the child from Isabel's arms. 'This baby is my sister's child.'

Aedan stepped between the two angry women, sensing a battle was about to ensue.

'This child is Lady Isabel's baby taken by Lady Gwendolyn of Griswold. How much did she pay you? We will pay you double to give us the child,' he said.

The woman looked afraid.

'I don't know what you are talking about. I told you this child is my sister's and I am looking after it until she is well again.'

'You fear her don't you?' Isabel asked. 'I don't blame you - she is evil to the core. Look, I am Lady Isabel the true heir to Griswold.' Isabel held out her hand with Phoenix's signet ring. 'Balfour can show you some letters that were written by my husband before he was killed to prove it. You don't have to fear her. She will not be ruler of Griswold for much longer. We will pay you double to keep the child here until I return. That way she will not know that we have found the child and your life will be safe. When we return you will not have anything to fear as she will no longer be in power.'

The woman looked at the letters Balfour produced and paled.

'I'm sorry Lady Isabel,' she stammered. 'I did not know. I've taken good care of him I promise.'

'I know you have and thank you,' Isabel said handing her a heavy purse of gold coins. 'Keep him safe till we return.'

The woman nodded as Isabel hugged her baby and kissed his cheek before handing him back to the wet nurse.

'Be a good boy Griffin. I love you,' she said as she turned.

'You don't have to come with us Isabel,' Erik said. 'We can handle this without you.'

'Not a chance! That witch is going to look me in the eyes when she answers for everything she's done.'

Isabel pulled herself into the saddle. 'Let's finish this,' she said kicking her horse into motion.

⌘

Griswold Castle

Gwendolyn paced up and down the battlements. She could see the long boats in the distance on the river.

Why are they back? What is Gunnar up to?

She would personally kill him if he had become greedy and had come back for more.

She had enough problems on her plate. Balfour had betrayed her and released the Northman from the dungeons. Her only consolation was in knowing he could not possibly have survived the wound she had inflicted. Perhaps that was why the long boats were back. Balfour might be giving them his body to return to the North. Still they would have to be on their guard.

Gwendolyn made her way up to Skull Hill. She wanted to tell the men in her life that she didn't need any of them – that she and baby Phoenix would rule Griswold fine without any of them. She stood over her father's grave and scoffed.

'You thought you could have it all at our expense father, but thanks to Daemon your evil was stopped in its tracks.'

Then she moved to Legion's grave.

'I did love you once but when you chose to protect Aislinn and Drew Williams over me, that love died. You became weak Legion and I will make sure I never make that mistake as ruler of Griswold.'

She looked across at Daemon's grave and a tear rolled down her cheek. His was the most painful betrayal of all.

'For years I lost my life grieving for you brother and it turns out it was all for nothing. I never really knew you, did I?'

Finally she stopped at Phoenix's grave.

'I know you are not in there my son. You have done just what your name says – you have risen from the ashes and come back to me in that baby and now together we get to start over – to rule Griswold together. I finally get to be your mother.'

She turned back to the castle, stopping dead in her tracks. Isabel faced her, pity written all over her face. It was not possible. She held a bow and arrow in her hands. Behind her was the Northman.

Am I hallucinating? He's dead and she is on Gunnar's boat – a prisoner.

'I see you are surprised to see us Gwen. No you are not dreaming, your evil plans have been thwarted. You need to come without a fight. You are surrounded.'

Gwen noticed the other men closing in around her.

'I won't become your prisoner Isabel,' she said looking for a path of escape.

'You can't get away Gwendolyn.'

'You will never find your baby if you don't let me go,' she threatened.

'I already know where my child is Gwen. I don't need your help.'

'You're lying.'

'He's with a wet nurse a few miles from here at a little isolated cottage at the foot of the Silver Hills.'

Gwen paled. They had found her boy. She would not live out her days in the dirty damp dungeon of Griswold. She reached into her cloak and pulled out her dagger. She would not let the Williams family win.

'You can't beat us with that,' Isabel said. 'Put the dagger down Gwen. Phoenix would not want this for you.'

'Phoenix would not care Isabel. He chose you over me, just like his father chose your mother over me. Even my brother chose her over me. The men in my life were weak fools.' She laughed hollow and empty.

She lifted her arm and in one fluid motion she slit her throat. She fell to the ground, her blood running into the earth to join her ancestors.

Isabel gasped, shocked at the sudden turn of events. She hated what Gwen had done to her family and to Phoenix, but she had not believed she would kill herself. Erik pulled her close to his chest so she would not have to see her mother-in-law's bloody body.

CHAPTER 44

REKINDLED

IT HAD BEEN a week since Gwendolyn had taken her life. She was finally at rest alongside her family on Skull Hill. Isabel had asked Thorfinn to delay his departure to Kaldakinn as there was something she wanted to do. Time was running out and summer was coming to an end – the Northmen would need to leave soon before the cold weather descended on them.

Now, she sat with Nuada in the gardens. They truly were beautiful – Legion had done a good job keeping them maintained. It was a pity that they had not helped Gwen to heal but they certainly made Griswold Castle more attractive. Isabel resolved to plant a tree in honour of Gwendolyn as her way of making peace with the woman who hated her so much. She had Gwen to thank for her short time with Phoenix and her beautiful son. If Gwen had not had Phoenix her entire life would have been different – she would honour the woman for that at least.

'Nuada, we need to talk about this castle. I know that it was originally in your family line before Legion usurped it. I believe that you should be the rightful heir. I can go back to Kaldakinn with Erik and Griffin.'

'No Isabel, I don't want Griswold Castle. I appreciate your offer but I have no family and I love living and working with the Great One. This castle is yours – it is what Phoenix would have wanted. Besides, what better way to unite the North and South by having you and Erik here?'

'I'm not sure Erik will want to stay.'

'Well then this castle is yours to do with as you wish.'

'Thank you Nuada. You do know that you have chambers here whenever you wish.'

'Now, I will take you up on that,' he smiled.

⌘

Isabel looked into Erik's eyes and smiled. He was a giant of a man and some would find him intimidating and terrifying but she knew the heart of the man behind the outward appearance. He was the kindest man she had ever met and she loved him fiercely. It was a relief to finally acknowledge her feelings, to be rid of the guilt that she was betraying Phoenix with another. She had only had one more dream of him since she had declared her love for Erik. He had come to her and although he had said nothing he smiled at her. She knew it was his way of saying goodbye. She did not feel sad anymore – just really grateful that she had the opportunity to love him – even for such a little while. Now she had a new future to look forward to.

'Erik would you do me the honour of re-pledging our vows in front of our family and friends, without the blood and animal sacrifice this time?'

Erik laughed remembering her horror and shock on their wedding day.

'I will Isabel, on one condition.'

'What's that?' she said narrowing her eyes suspiciously.

'Only if we can keep the bridal run,' he teased.

'Oh definitely,' she smiled, 'and this time expect to be thoroughly beaten.'

⌘

They pledged their love a few days later before their family and friends. Then they feasted late into the night. It was good to finally be in Griswold castle without fear and trepidation, the skeletons and ghosts of the past chased from the walls by their joy and hope for the future. It was the beginning of a new era, one they looked forward to.

Isabel could wait no longer. She looked at the man beside her, her stomach fluttering with desire. She wanted to know him as more than a friend, to give herself completely to him.

'Take me to our chambers, Erik,' she whispered when the celebration was in full swing.

'Now?' he smiled.

She nodded. He whisked her off her feet and carried her out the Great Hall as all the Northmen cheered.

Once alone he set her on her feet and poured her a goblet of wine. They had chosen new chambers – neither of them wanted to live in Phoenix or Gwen's old chambers – they wanted a fresh start together.

'What are the chances that your son will want to be fed?' Erik asked.

She laughed.

'Don't you mean our son?' Her expression became serious. 'I want you to be his father Erik – to raise him and love him as your own.'

'Isabel, I would be honoured but I assumed that you would want him to remember his father.'

'Phoenix was born into an evil family and although he was nothing like his parents his history is tainted. I want Griffin to grow up knowing that he is loved and comes from a family who are good and kind. Of course I will tell him about his father, but I want him to look to you to learn about love and kindness and bravery and strength and....'

He silenced her with a kiss drawing her close and running his fingers through her thick hair. Then he unlaced her dress allowing it to fall in waves of silk at her feet. He scooped her up and carried her to the bed.

He kissed her again, savouring her sweet taste as she pulled off his shirt. She ran her hands down his chest touching the scar that was a reminder of how she almost lost him. She kissed it gently and he moaned.

'Isabel, you don't know what you do to me,' he murmured.

She claimed his mouth once more moving her hands across his back, feeling his strength.

'Make me yours,' she begged.

He pulled back momentarily, hesitant.

'Erik?' she said gently, encouraging him.

He looked apologetic, slightly embarrassed.

'Isabel, I've never wanted a woman more than I want you right now, but I've never been with a woman before. I've seen men rape women like animals in our culture and it has disgusted me. I am not sure what to do and the last thing I ever want to do is hurt you.'

She smiled, remembering how scared she had been the first time she had been with Phoenix. She had never seen him so vulnerable and his lack of confidence was endearing. It was why she loved him so much. He was so strong and masculine, yet he was also the kindest, gentlest man she had ever met.

'Don't worry my love, you could never hurt me. I will show you what to do.'

She kissed him tenderly, becoming more passionate as he pulled her to himself. It felt good to feel their bodies against one another – their hearts beating in anticipation of the love they would share – a love that had grown over the icy winter months in Kaldakinn. She knew when he was ready, his body responding to her touch and she slipped off her undergarments revealing her perfect skin. He followed her lead, removing his trousers as she admired his strong limbs before she pulled him back toward herself wrapping her legs around his waist. Erik groaned as they moved together becoming one finally.

'Belle, my beautiful Belle,' he whispered tenderly.

⌘

They lay side by side and Erik smiled up at the ceiling.

'I could never have imagined it to be so good,' he said.

'Mmm,' she said sleepily curling her body against his like a cat. 'Do you regret waiting so long then?' she teased. 'Just think of all the maidens you could have conquered in Kaldakinn.'

He laughed loudly.

'I have to confess, I am terrified of some of those shield maidens.'

Isabel giggled at his admission. 'So you should be – I experienced their welcome firsthand,' she said remembering the bruises they gave her.

'I have no regrets Isabel. I am glad I waited for you – my one true love,' he said kissing her again. 'I love you woman. I think I have loved you from the moment you shot me with that arrow.'

She gently traced her finger along the fading scar on his face. She smiled thinking about both the men she had given her heart to – she had met them both while aiming her arrow at them.

'And I love you,' she said rising on her elbow, her hair tumbling over her bare shoulder.

'Now show me how much you love me again,' she said pulling him close.

EPILOGUE

GRISWOLD AUTUMN 1651

ISABEL looked at the sweet infant sleeping in her arms as her two year old son raced noisily around her.

'Give your mother some peace Griffin,' Erik said scooping the squirming toddler into his arms. He kissed his wife on the cheek and took the active child outdoors to play.

It had been a good summer. Erik's parents and some of the Northmen had travelled to Griswold during the warm months but there was no longer any raiding that took place. The seer had been correct when he prophesied that the North and South would be brought together through love and that it would change their worlds. Isabel and Erik had made their home at Griswold. Now the men came and learned about farming and crops and took their produce back with them for the winter. In return they brought furs to the Southerners. It had become a mutually beneficial agreement for both clans.

Siobhan made the trip with Thorfinn to see her son and her new grandchildren. She had been delighted to finally meet Griffin and the new addition to their family. Their beautiful daughter had been born half way through the summer and because it had been such a good year they had named her in honour of it.

'Summer Rose, you are so beautiful,' Isabel said to the sleeping child. She kissed her on the nose then placed her in the crib. She lovingly ran her hand over the beautiful crib that Erik had made for Griffin. Although Griffin had never used it, his parents had brought it to Griswold on their trip so that Summer could use it. Isabel smiled remembering how he had carved the lion onto it. She adored the tall Northman and he had been all that she had dreamed as a father and husband.

It was amazing how life turned out. She had feared him and his people and yet now they were her family too. She still thought about Phoenix often, but that suffocating sadness and pain was gone. Instead she just felt gratitude. She had been given the chance to know great love not once, but twice in her life.

She watched Erik rolling on the lawn with Griffin who gleefully jumped on him as he groaned in mock pain. The Great One was right, love did change the world. They had risen from the ashes of pain and a beautiful future awaited them.

⌘

LIONSGATE

The Great One watched them in his Mirror of Time. Phoenix stood beside him and the old man patted him on his shoulder.

'She looks happy,' Phoenix said.

'She is, and it's all thanks to you.'

'What do you mean?' he asked.

'You gave her permission to love again and to be happy. You set her free.'

The young man smiled at the Great One.

'Isn't that what love is about - doing what is best for the people you love the most even when it hurts?' he asked.

The Great One nodded at the young man as they walked back to the Great Hall. Legion was waiting for them and embraced his son. They were together and nothing would ever separate them again. One day they would all be reunited but till then Phoenix felt peace that Isabel would be loved and protected, that Griffin would have a father.

Father and son walked out into the beautiful garden to where she stood waiting for them. She smiled at their approach – they were finally a family now – it had taken years to get to this point and she had learned that the Great One truly did love all – he had not shut her out of Lionsgate because of her evil deeds.

'Why did you give me another chance?' she had asked him.

'It has nothing to do with who you are Gwen, but has everything to do with who I am.'

She had not fully understood what he meant but she was grateful to him. She had the opportunity to make things right with Legion and Phoenix – to get to know them both. One day she hoped to be able to look Aislinn Williams in the eye and apologize to her for all she had put them through. They had gone through some difficult times and had made some tough choices but they had become stronger and more importantly they had learned one thing:

LOVE ALWAYS WINS.

⌘

ALSO BY CAROLINE HEMINGWAY

⌘

THE AWAKENING

BOOK 1 OF THE DESTINY CHRONICLES

One Family, One Tyrant, One Truth...

Mackenzie Hamilton and his wife Imogene always did what was expected of them. Leaving their homeland to fulfil the prophecies spoken over them by the Elders of the Clan, they journey to Griswold with their four children. There they encounter a power hungry tyrant who rules his people with fear and manipulation. When tragedy strikes and all is stripped away, tearing their family apart, they have to dig deep to find courage within to take back what is theirs and to discover who they really are. Will the mistakes of their past be their undoing or will their faith in the Great One be enough to conquer an evil that threatens to consume them?

A novel where tragedy confronts belief and victory depends upon it.

THE RECKONING

BOOK 2 OF THE DESTINY CHRONICLES

One woman,Two men, Many secrets ....

Four years have passed since the Hamilton family escaped the clutches of the Dark Lord to make a new life for themselves. Aislinn Hamilton, now a young woman, is on the brink of following her dreams with a desire to change the world. As she embarks on this new journey she meets someone who will change her life, challenge her values and beliefs and will capture her heart. Love takes her on a road back to the awful past she has tried so hard to forget – a past she does not want to relive.

Aislinn will discover shocking truths about herself, her beliefs and the relationships she has developed.

A novel where love and trust are challenged to their limits.

About the Author

Caroline Hemingway lives in Melbourne Australia with her husband Hamilton and their four children. The Destiny Chronicles were birthed when she undertook putting pen to paper as a therapeutic exercise, discovering in the process a love of writing. This was followed by short stories and children's books she hopes yet to publish. She and her family are Foster Carers to children who are at risk in the community and she is passionate about human rights. She is also an enthusiastic blogger and loves all things creative.

THE RISING is Book 3 of the Destiny Chronicles. Other Titles in this series are THE AWAKENING Book 1 and THE RECKONING, Book 2.

To follow Caroline's blog visit her website at http://carolinehemingway.wix.com/carolinehemingway